Dark Towers

by

Colin Campbell

COLIN CAMPBELL

DARKWATER

TOWERS

Blackie & Co Publishers Ltd

A BLACKIE & CO PUBLISHERS LTD
PAPERBACK
© Copyright 2000
Colin Campbell

The right of Colin Campbell to be identified as the author of this work has been asserted by him in accordance with the Copyright, Designs and Patents Act 1988

All Rights Reserved

No reproduction, copy or transmission of this publication may be made without written permission.
No paragraph of this publication may be reproduced, copied or transmitted save with the written permission or in accordance with the provisions of the Copyright Act 1956 (as amended).

Any person who does any unauthorised act in relation to this publication may be liable to criminal prosecution and civil claims for damage.

A CIP catalogue record for this title is available from the British Library
ISBN 1 903138 02 7

First Published in 2000

Blackie & Co Publishers Ltd
107-111 Fleet Street LONDON   EC4A 2AB
www.blackiepublishers.com
Cover designed and produced by
Creative Identity –
creativeidentity@compuserve.com
Printed and bound by
PROPRINT
Riverside Cottages, Old Great North Road, Stibbington, Cambs, PE8 6LR

Printed and Bound in Great Britain

FOREWORD

Snow swirling around the cold night sky. A concrete monolith on the edge of Armageddon. Gutted apartments. Empty corridors. A stone dead lift shaft. Fire and ice and bloody carnage.

It is Christmas Eve in Darkwater Towers and Someone dark, dangerous and sinister stalks the cold grey corridors and descends to the rust hued boiler room, cleaning its larder of human waste, and, as Christmas Eve creeps into Christmas Day, Theo must put his past to the sword.

I would like to dedicate this book to

Mr Cox, the first teacher to make me feel special . . .

and to Mr Radler who let me write during Religious Instruction . . .

And to my wife, Karen, who showed no interest whatsoever, but who loves me all the same.

Colin Campbell

-----------oOoOoOoOoOoOoOoOo-----------

PART ONE

LAND OF THE BLIND

The soul's dark cottage, batter'd and decay'd

Lets in new light through chinks that Time has made;

Stronger by weakness, wiser men become,

As they draw nearer to their eternal home.

Leaving the old, both worlds at once they view,

That stand upon the threshold of the new.

- Edmund Wallace

CHAPTER 1

The cold wind cut like a scalpel as Theo reached up into the darkness for the balcony rail. Seven floors down, night blanked out the swathe of industrial wasteland, a black carpet of tangled metal and dusty masonry. Only the gaily-coloured light of Carl Stensel's barbershop sign showed in the distance.

Everything else. Nothingness. He could be looking out across a hole cut in the fabric of the universe, only the stars above and the red and green "Gents Hairdresser" sign below shedding any light on the world. Nothing else existed.

Except the balcony rail.

A crash came from inside the flat as the bookcase was thrown free. No time. Theo stood on the rickety pigeon-loft in the corner of the veranda and thrust upwards. His ageing joints complained. Pain flared in his left arm and fresh blood began to flow. The ten-storey block of flats seemed to be a mile high. Bing Crosby crooned about a White Christmas on The Major's new CD player in the flat, then that too was sent crashing as a twisted shadow lurched towards the balcony.

The pigeon-loft shifted under Theo's weight as the shattering of a coffee table sounded inside. The shadow made a beeline for the veranda door. Theo's good hand reached up as dried wood splintered underfoot, the pigeons fluttering restlessly.

Balcony rail. Where's the bloody balcony rail?

The door trembled with his approach.

Got it. Theo grasped tight on the cold hard metal and shoved off with his foot. The pigeon-loft leaned over, its sides splitting with a crack; then Theo lunged out into the clear blackness of the night. He hung for a second, and then grabbed with his other hand, ignoring the pain, swinging up with the momentum from the loft.

Pigeons exploded into the cramped space of the veranda.

Theo's legs hooked over the next balcony's floor and he pulled himself up. Sweat broke out on his face despite the cold wind. "Aaargh..." He banged his arm as he landed on the disused veranda. Below him the door burst open.

No thought, just action. Theo was up and moving before the pigeons cleared the pigeon-loft. The door in front of him was frosted with starlight. He twisted the handle but his hand had lost all its strength.

He tried again.
Locked.
There were curses from below, then the pigeon-loft was kicked aside.

The bloody doors don't lock, Theo chided himself. *Wrong way.* He quickly turned the handle the other way and pulled the door open. Then he was inside, away from the bitter wind, and into the eighth floor apartment. Outside, there was a scrabbling noise as eager hands tried to follow suit, then more curses when they couldn't reach without the pigeon-loft. Now banging sounded inside the flat indicating a new course through the carnage towards the landing.

And the stairs.

Blood soaked through Theo's sleeve. He felt faint. The empty flat, like the rest of the top three floors, was dusty and cold, but not as cold as outside, and nowhere near as cold as Theo's heart. Shock was beginning to set in. Not just from the arm, but from...

...everything else.

Where to hide? That was the immediate problem. *Where to hide and get his bearings? Regroup and make some sense of all this.*

If ever there was a time that Theobald Wolff had wished he'd planned his retirement better it was now. The exertion of climbing over the balcony was beginning to tell on his sixty-nine year old muscles. His hands were shaking.

Not here. Can't afford to wait here. With an effort he forced himself up and through the living room door into the equally blank kitchen. Another door - into the hallway - and another.

Too late he realised he'd boxed himself in. This was one of the two-bedroomed flats, and instead of heading out onto the landing near the lift, he'd come into the second bedroom. *No time. There never seemed to be any time.* Up until now he'd had nothing but. Not any more...

Heavy footsteps came from outside. Shuffling footsteps. They were on the stairs. *No escape. Not at his age. No good trying to run for it, he hadn't run anywhere in fifteen years.* He stared round the gloom, panic shortening his breath. That pretty blue frosted light reminded him this was Christmas Eve. Bing Crosby had given way to Nat King Cole and "The Little Boy Who Santa Claus Forgot." The music drifted up the stairwell.

Pain. Cold and pain.

The footsteps were outside the door now.

Only one place left. In the corner of the room was the airing cupboard, long since stripped of its boiler. Mick McCracken - the caretaker - had seen to that. Once he'd realised the flats were never going to be filled, he'd sold off anything that wasn't nailed down and painted, and some things that were. What had they said when he was in the Army? "If it moves, salute it. If it doesn't, paint it."

Theo yanked the cupboard door open, and shuffled in. With his knees drawn up to his chest he just had enough room. He gently pulled the door shut behind him, and waited.

It seemed like an age before the footsteps retreated but in fact it was only twenty minutes. Theo's legs began to cramp. No, didn't begin to cramp, cramped solid right there and then. He could hardly move them. He nudged the cupboard door open with his shoulder and swung his legs out as best he could. His best wasn't very good. They swivelled round like a rusty dockside crane, but they felt better once out of the confines of the cupboard. A little better.

Theo waited for the circulation to return, and with it pain slammed into his thighs and calves. Body shaking pain at first, then that tingly pain that's almost pleasant. He felt that if he put his feet to the ground they would bounce right back up again. Pins and needles. Much underrated.

Light flooded the empty bedroom. After the total blackout of the airing cupboard, the stars shone through the window like a thousand tiny beacons, their frosty blue light picking out every knot in the floorboards, and every grain of dust and plaster. Theo got as far as the window before his legs decided they'd had enough. He sat unceremoniously on the floor, and leaned against the wall under the starlight.

Images flooded through his tired brain. Questions. *Where were they? All the others. What had happened to them? What had driven Mick McCracken - because he was certain that's who was stalking him now - over the edge? Was it the rat in the basement?*

What had he done to the others? Uriah Lovelycolors he knew about, poor old Uriah. Theo tightened the old man's home-knitted scarf around his wounded arm. *But what of Charlie Brewer and the other residents?*

And Delia?

Theo felt a pain that was nothing to do with the cramps or the wounded left arm. A pain he hadn't felt since his wife died. His heart ached. *What of Delia?*

His head couldn't hold onto the thought. His mind seemed to be slowing down and the faces, which drifted before him, began to fade. Even the pain began to fade.

It's getting brighter in here, he thought. *Not dawn already is it? Not Christmas Day already?*

He shuffled round the wall on his bottom so he faced the window. The stars were indeed brighter. They threatened to whiteout the night sky. Then Theo realised it wasn't the stars. It was everything. Everything was getting brighter. It was like turning the brightness up on his old Phillips TV. The picture was still there, but less distinct. Merging with all around it.

"Jingle Bells" sounded gaily from afar. A man was hiding under the covers of a huge four-poster bed, his head poking out to see who was knocking on the door. The man was Alistair Sim, Theo was sure it was. *What's he doing in my dream?* But it was all blending together. The light made it difficult to tell what was happening.

Rattling chains. Theo heard them, plain as day. *Of course. Jacob Marley's ghost. Or was it?* He wasn't sure. Alistair Sim's Scrooge wasn't sitting up in bed any more, it was Theobald Wolff. Only he wasn't hiding in a Victorian four-poster bed, he was hiding in a dusty apartment on Christmas Eve. Swirling. Spinning.

The pain had gone. The empty flat on the eighth floor of Darkwater Towers had gone. Theo knew he was passing out, and he tried to fight it, but it was no use. His head swam dreamily as he canted to one side against the wall. Nothing mattered any more. Not the pain. Not the questions. Not anything.

Then the Ghost of Christmas past visited through the light, its hearty laugh booming inside Theo's head. It took him back to the day of the letter. The day the bottom fell out of Theo's world.

A world already devoid of any hope, or happiness, or peace.

CHAPTER 2

It was two weeks to Christmas when Theobald Wolff learned he was going to die. More accurately, when it was confirmed he was going to die, because deep inside he already knew. At sixty-nine you tend to accept that you've got less to come than you've had, but you expect a good bit more than five months.

"Well, old girl," he said to his wife Melinda, squaring his shoulders and expanding his chest in that old army way she so liked. They were broad shoulders, and it was an impressive chest. Not as impressive as hers he used to say. He looked her in the eye. "Looks like the monster's come for me as well. The big "C". John Wayne didn't beat it. Doesn't look like I will either."

Theo suddenly felt tired. Tired and empty. He slumped down in the easy chair next to the radio, and looked round the flat. The fifth floor apartment in Darkwater Towers was dusty but tidy. The grandfather clock he'd rescued from Melinda's parents after they'd died ticked contentedly. The well-stocked bookcase stared stolidly back. An old Phillips colour television, that could only get three channels, gathered dust next to the coal effect gas fire. Theo knew Melinda wouldn't approve of the dust, but dusting had never been his strong suit. He reckoned it made a place look lived in.

Melinda said nothing.

Her photograph on the dark wood dresser seemed vaguely admonishing.
As if she didn't approve of the self-pity Theo was sinking into. It was funny how, depending on the circumstances, that photograph could convey his dead wife's feelings. Even now she could share in his happiness, or disapprove of his sadness. Her eyes seemed to follow him round the room, like one of those clever paintings where the eyes are staring directly out of the canvas.

She stared at him now. The piece of card he'd wedged into the corner of the frame, after the monster had taken her, was stained yellow and curled at the edges. The message, in his firm hand, reinforced her stare.
WE WILL NOT DIE, UNLESS WE ARE FORGOTTEN...
No, she wasn't forgotten. Never would be. But she had died. More of a realist than his wife, Theo understood that, but in his heart he always felt she was still with him. When he slept - which was infrequent in this rat-hole of a block of flats - she sometimes came to him, as young and beautiful as she'd always been, in his eyes, and they'd dally together, passing the wee small hours until wakefulness took her away from him again.

Sixty-nine. It would have tickled her - had it not been so serious - that that was the age he would reach. From their courting days, right through their married years, he'd joked about sixty-nine being his favourite number, a lascivious grin usually following the statement. His sexual appetites had been stronger than hers, but even she could raise a smile at the thought of the position he complained they didn't use enough. Towards the end she'd wished she had. After all, how can you be embarrassed with the one you love? Especially when that love is as strong as theirs was.

The letter hung limply from his hand. The results of his hospital tests. He didn't need to read it again, the doctor had all but told him to prepare for the worst. One word stuck in his mind. CANCER...

That old monster had been stalking him ever since it had taken Melinda. He wished he could wrestle it to the ground, take it on and beat it, avenge his lost love, but this monster was a sly one. It slunk around unseen, invading your body by inches, until it had a foothold. Even then it didn't announce itself. A few extra aches and pains. *What were they once you were in your sixties? Only to be expected, right?*

Wrong. Why should you have to put up with more pain simply because you were old? Why the hell should you?
Another line.
AT THE MOST, FIVE MONTHS...

Five months? That sounded ominously precise. How about a ball-park six months? Or somewhere between three and nine months? But no. A bald statement. Five months. At the most. Could be less, but look on the bright side. Five months.

Bright side? Theo 'grumphed' at the thought. Since when had there been a bright side at this happy retirement home for the sick, lame, and lazy? At best Darkwater Towers was tolerable, at worst it was Hell in ten stories. Theo was the youngest, and most able bodied, of a sorry bunch. He stood six foot three - when his back permitted - with a square jaw and fiery brown eyes. His hair was grey and thinning though, showing his age, and soon the rest of his body would follow suit. They were life's cast offs. If any of them had any money they'd have moved away in a shot. If they'd had any relatives who gave a damn they'd have likely done the same, but with neither one nor the other you were sunk. Stuck here in God's waiting room. At the mercy of Mick McCracken, the caretaker. *Caretaker that was a laugh. Liberty-taker more like.*

Theo looked into his wife's eyes. *Maybe it was a blessing you didn't have to put up with this place for very long,* he thought. But in the end, he would have given anything to have had her with him a while longer. *Selfish isn't it?*

He screwed up the letter in one strong hand, and lobbed it expertly into the waste bin next to the door. He sighed deeply, then stood up. The chest went out and the shoulders stretched. No more self pity. He'd spent most of his working life as a prison warder, and had seen the damage self pity could do. Worse than any punishment inflicted by the courts, self-pity was a slippery road that led only one way. Down.

Besides, he had his chores to do. Not cleaning the flat, that could wait. No. Today was shopping day, and as the self-appointed, Darkwater Towers deliveryman he had his customers to think about.

Since he was the only resident who could make it to the end of the street without a seizure, Theo had taken it upon himself to go out twice a week for the little luxuries the WRVS didn't provide. Or if they did provide them, that Mick McCracken took out before they reached the apartments. It sometimes struck Theo that they were in a prison camp, with the Red Cross parcels being rifled by the guards before they reached you. He saw himself as the scrounger, who conjured up little treats to help pass the war.

For Uriah Lovelycolors it was fresh balls of wool for his interminable knitting. For Charlie Brewer it was the latest "Boxing Weekly" and forty Benson and Hedges - smoking wasn't banned but it was discouraged. Metal polish and cleaning rags for Newton Wimer, who had been a Major in the Royal Armoured Corps and always kept his brasses and collected firearms spotless.

And for Delia Circelli it was Cadbury's Drinking Chocolate, and Galaxy Fruit and Nut chocolate bars.

Aahhh... Delia.

Theo glanced guiltily at Melinda's photograph. On her deathbed she'd made Theo promise to look for someone else after she'd gone. After much cajoling, and not a little weeping, he'd agreed.

"No, don't agree," she'd said. "Promise."

So he had, but it was a promise he hadn't expected to fulfil. And he hadn't. Not looked for someone else anyway. Delia Circelli had just been there. Had been there since Theo and Melinda had moved in. He'd just not noticed her for a long time. Now he considered her to be more than just a friend, and that embarrassed him somewhat.

Anyway, it was time to take his shopping list and stretch his legs. Time to escape the oppressive atmosphere of Darkwater Towers, if only for a short while. He took his heavy winter coat from the back of the two-seater settee - another thing Melinda would have disapproved of - and shrugged into it. One elbow was patched, and the cuffs were frayed, but that couldn't be helped. There was no money for a new one. He saw the dirty breakfast dishes on the kitchen table but made no effort to go clean them. They could wait.

He crammed a Russian fur hat from Help-the-Aged on his head and turned to the door. The waste bin winked up at him, and he thought of the letter again. *Five months. Not even another summer.* He checked his pocket for the keys, and then opened the door. Behind him, the letter uncurled a touch in the bin.

Five months.

No, not long at all, but the letter was wrong.

The lift went down one floor then shuddered to a stop. A high pitched groan hummed through the cable above, echoing in the hollow blackness of the lift shaft, and the doors struggled open. To Theo it always seemed like it would be the last time they would. A pause halfway, then they slid all the way open.

"Now then you old rascal," he called through the doors, and Charlie Brewer shuffled into the lift, eager eyes darting from corner to corner as if he was afraid of missing something.

Charlie was seventy-nine, just ten years older than Theo, but the years hadn't been kind to him. He was a short wiry man, an ex-boxer who had taken one too many blows to the head. Back in his fighting days his frame had been lean and muscly. Now it wasn't even lean, it was skeletal. His shiny baldhead dodged from side to side, not evading an invisible punch but dithering with age. The nose was amazingly straight for a one-time middleweight contender - not broken once in over a hundred and fifty fights - but his once-strong hands were curled into claws, his shoulders hunched and broken.

In short, his body was giving up the fight, but his mind was sharp as a razor. "Due out today," he said as the lift doors struggled shut, enclosing them in a grey metal tomb.

"What? Come up for parole have you?" Theo joked.

"Nooo." Charlie's face wrinkled into a mischievous grin. "Boxing Weekly. Once a week. Every Tuesday."

"Yes, I haven't forgotten." The lift jerked, then began to descend, bringing a groan of complaint from the cable. "Will forty B and H be enough 'til the weekend?"

Charlie's head stopped quivering, and Theo thought he saw a look of sadness in the old boxer's eyes. "Tell you a secret," Charlie said. He paused for effect, drawing Theo in. "Don't smoke 'em. Haven't for over a year."

A knot tightened in Theo's stomach. *Cancer.* The word drifted into his head like a puff of smoke from one of Charlie's Benson and Hedges. The gaunt features, the too thin hands, the yellowing skin. They all stamped the word onto Theo's mind. Instead of asking, he said, "Must have a fair few packets stashed by now then. Maybe I should give it a miss today?"

"No, no," Charlie rejoined. Again that look of sadness. Or was it Theo's imagination? "I can't bring myself to stop getting them. Been buying them for as long as I can remember. Got to be a bit of a habit. I'd miss not getting them."

Theo's heart went out for the old codger. *Old? He's going to outlive me,* he thought. Sometimes the little rituals we live by are hard to give up, but still the question wouldn't come. It was a very private thing after all. He was finding that himself now. Had found it to be so when Melinda had been diagnosed as well.

Charlie's face suddenly lit up. A cheeky chappy grin twisted his mouth, and a twinkle danced in his eyes. "Getting in training for my next fight," he confided. "Got to get up to fighting weight by the New Year." He laughed, well, cackled and spluttered, and thumped Theo's arm. The fist was surprisingly solid.

Theo brightened up. "And who's your next opponent? Tyson? Holyfield?"

"What? A jailbird and a one-eared man?" Charlie's head resumed its dithering. "Naw. Dynamite McCracken. Tricky Micky."

This time Theo laughed first. The Draconian caretaker could do with being taken down a peg or two, but he thought the age gap might be too much of an advantage at this stage. Even for Theo, who had handled tougher men than him in his time.

Charlie was suddenly serious. "Better watch out for him Theo. I don't think he likes you. Don't think he appreciates you getting extra supplies for us wrinklies."

"He wouldn't appreciate a good shit if he was constipated," Theo answered, and with that they both burst out laughing. A sound all but banished from Darkwater Towers. The lift reached the ground floor with a thump and a groan. After a moment's thought the doors decided to open, and Theo stepped out. Charlie stayed put.

"Coming out?" Theo asked.

"Naw," the old boxer replied. "Can't walk too far these days, so I'll let the lift do the work for me." He wheezed a tired laugh. "Two or three trips up and down, and I'll have clocked up my daily mile."

The doors closed, and Theo was sorry to see Charlie go. In the claustrophobic atmosphere of his apartment it was easy to believe you were alone in the world. Like spending too long in solitary. Could drive you mad. Any human contact was welcome, and should be treasured.

He turned away from the dull grey lift doors - amazingly graffiti free, the old fogies of Darkwater Towers had passed that stage long ago and no youngsters ventured into this neck of the woods - and surveyed the duller and greyer concrete walls of the entrance hall. It was only twelve feet square, fronted by a pair of double doors with wire-reinforced glass. The glass was stained and cracked. To his left were the stairs - which hardly anyone here could manage - and to his right, the door to the cellar. Next to that was the caretaker's flat. A place to be avoided.

Apart from the creaks and groans from the departing elevator the building was silent. Theo took one step towards the front doors, then heard a distinctive click from his right.

"Hello there, Wolfy," a sly voice taunted, and Mick McCracken stepped out of his flat.

Theo hated being called Wolfy, but he tried not to show it. He didn't think he'd ever succeeded. If there was one thing Melinda had both liked and disliked about him, it was the fact that whatever he felt, it went straight to his face. She had liked it on the one hand because there was no falseness about him. No two-facedness. He was as straight as a die and twice as honest. On the other hand, it had been the source of much embarrassment whenever her mother had dropped in unannounced. There was no hiding his displeasure at being interrupted by a flying visit from the Gruppen Führer, and Melinda used to spend hours smoothing out an atmosphere that was spikier than a bedside chart.

Now his irritation climbed up his throat and threatened to spread over his face. The heavy-set caretaker, his ample stomach straining the buttons of his crumpled shirt and overhanging his jeans, took two paces towards Theo. "And where's Wolfy going today?" He teased.

"Catch some fresh air," Theo muttered. "And top up on a few things."

"What's that?" The caretaker cupped a hand to his ear.

"Have to speak up. Loud and clear, that's the way to do it. Don't want to be losing your voice as well as your faculties."

Theo bit back his annoyance. Apart from not wanting to show this playground bully that he had hit the mark, there was something else. Something Theo didn't want to admit, even to himself. He was afraid of him, and that embarrassed him. After twelve years as a munitions expert in the Royal Army Ordnance Corps, and twenty-five years in the prison service, fear was a new animal that had sneaked in under the fence with the onset of old age. Not only fear of the physical harm the burly caretaker could wreak on Theo's brittle bones, but the fear of being humiliated. Belittled. Made to feel small and worthless, and unwanted.

Those last things were the hardest to swallow. Like all the other residents of this God forsaken retirement home - this funeral home in waiting - he was poor, ailing, and unloved. Nobody got any visitors here, because nobody cared enough to come a-calling. If anyone had cared, they'd never have allowed their kith and kin to end up in such a miserable place. Theo remembered a sign, which had been tacked over the holding cell door, back in better times.

ABANDON HOPE, ALL YE WHO ENTER HERE...

More prophetic words could not have been spoken to anyone moving into an apartment at Darkwater Towers, and Mick McCracken was living proof that there was no hope.

"I didn't hear you, Wolfy," McCracken growled.

"I said I was going for a walk," Theo answered. He tried hard to keep the quiver out of his voice, but was afraid he hadn't. There was that word, afraid, again. How he hated that feeling.

"Well don't forget to wrap up. Wouldn't want to have to call out the emergency doctor because you caught yourself a cold." McCracken appeared to grow bored at baiting Theo, and walked over to the stained door in the corner of the lobby. White lettering flaked off the sign on the doorjamb. CELLAR - STAFF ONLY KEEP OUT

He turned the handle, and then threw one last barb. "And don't forget your way back Wolfy. No search parties round here after dark." Then he opened the door and went down the stairs to the boiler room.

Theo breathed a sigh of relief and headed for the front doors. He was embarrassed to feel his hands shaking, and it wasn't with the cold. He pulled out a battered pair of woollen gloves all the same and stepped out into the clear bright air.

Freedom, he thought. *At least for a little while.* He marshalled his thoughts, checked the shopping list in his pocket, and went down the three steps to the pavement. Behind him, the frightening bulk of Darkwater Towers glowered down at him, but he didn't care. Not for now. Now he was out, and that felt good.

CHAPTER 3

Darkwater Towers was a relic of the fifties development boom. It was one of three blocks of flats built on the grave of Waterford Hospital, which had been razed to the ground by the Luftwaffe during the war. There had been Clearwater Towers, Deepwater Towers and Darkwater Towers.

Now, Darkwater Towers was the only one still standing.

Some said it had the luck of the Devil, but most said it under their breath, if they voiced it at all. Clearwater and Deepwater went up in flames in 1976, the result of a chemical spillage at Tibbet and Archibald Dye Works. A fireball the size of a small nuclear explosion had engulfed the factory across the road, killing twenty-three people. The explosion weakened the foundations of the two nearest blocks of flats, and the wind took sheets of flame into the first three floors. The flames should have been fanned towards Darkwater Towers but a freak eddy held them at bay.

Forty-two people burned to death as the flats became twin infernos. There would have been more had it happened two hours later, when the rest had returned from work. The flats were demolished six weeks later, deemed too far gone for repair, and too dangerous to leave standing. All Darkwater Towers received was a few cracked windows and some scorched paintwork.

The other two blocks were never rebuilt.

In the early eighties a Boeing 727 had a near miss when its radar went down in the fog. Its approach to North Ridly Field was way off and, as it forged through the pea-souper at a hundred feet, the curtains of mist had suddenly drawn back. Amidst miles of low-slung factories and the sprawling railroad goods yard a solitary black finger jutted into the night sky. The pilot had almost filled his pants, and banked to port just in time. After that a flashing red beacon was added to the tangle of aerials on the flat roof. It looked like the Devil's finger, pointing its glowing tip to the heavens. Giving God the bird.

Now, the factories were gone. Victims of the recession. Most had been flattened as part of the Government's inner city regeneration plan, and the rest had simply sagged and died. The railway sidings and goods yards, empty of rolling stock, were now crumbled and decaying, the bright silver slashes of the railway lines, hundreds of acres of them, now dirty brown scars on a barren landscape.

All that remained was a hellish monolith in the Devil's backyard. Darkwater Towers. The last residence left standing, and the last place on God's earth you'd want to live.

The Council had sold it to private enterprise in eighty-five, the year Boris Becker was conquering Wimbledon with Teutonic bluster. While he was laying waste to the gathered tennis players of the world on a patch of grass in London, further north, Darkwater Towers was defying the conquering hordes of the property developers. Holding them at bay.

A survey of the area had shown a fault line running through the railroad yards in a southwest to northeast line. It passed beneath the ten-story block of flats and put the lid on any idea of redeveloping the site. The new owners conveniently overlooked this, and turned the building into a low profit residential home for the elderly. The 'arse end' of the Old Folks Homes scale, and the last place most of the residents would ever live. This was a place where you shoved your unwanted relatives, or where the great unwashed and down-on-their-luck wrinklies could wait for the call to the Great Hereafter.

If aliens came down and wanted to feast on human flesh, this was a ready stocked larder where nobody would notice if the pantry was stripped bare.

In fact, the likes of Mick McCracken would probably thank them. Less old fogies like Theobald Wolff to worry about. And he did worry, not about how to care for them, but how to exploit them to their full advantage. It wasn't something he would care about for much longer though, as he went down the cellar steps to the boiler room.

As with all bullies, Mick McCracken was a coward at heart. He would deny it of course, if questioned but he couldn't hide it from himself as he descended the bare stone steps to the cellar. The grey concrete of the entrance hall gave way to a dirty brown cavern down here. Decades of moisture had turned the walls and ceiling into a rust-smeared paint box, all smudged ochres and browns. The floor itself was a tapestry of coal dust and fuel oil stains.

On top of that it was dark. Not pitch black; that might have almost been better, but just dark. The kind of dark that came from inadequate lighting and dirty walls. The kind of dark that encouraged shadows, and the kind of dark that shifted and moved like an oily sea when the dangling bulbs shifted in the breeze of his passing.

Mick McCracken was afraid of the dark.

"Godawful, shitwanking, bastard boilers," he muttered as he carefully took one step at a time. The treads were worn in the middle and the risers crumbling, making the simple task of coming down the stairs a risky proposition. He'd almost come a cropper more than once, and the last thing he wanted was to be laid low among the creeping shadows of the boiler room. "Why the fuck they can't get a gas-fired system fitted I don't know," he continued. The sound of his voice gave him courage, making him feel less alone.

He paused on the bottom step, glancing over at the twin boilers on the right. The viewing window in each door glowed malevolently, staring him down. The flames of their stare flickered across the dusty floor, and licked at the shovel leaning against the coal-bunker. Its shaft moved restlessly, sending a shiver up McCracken's spine. *Ain't nothing moving,* he told himself. *Just the light.*

He wasn't convinced, and came down the last step warily. Feeding the boilers was the worst part of looking after the old relics upstairs. *If it were not for the perks, like sifting through the food parcels and creaming off the best for himself, he'd tell the owners where they could shove their job.* Or so he told himself. It made him feel better that he believed that. Made him feel in control. When he was down here, every bit of support helped.

The shovel stopped moving, and Mick moved quickly towards it. The boilers glared at him as he passed, and he gave them a wide berth. To the right of the boilers was the fuse panel, a six-foot high Bakelite board, dotted with dials and six-inch solid bore fuses. A pair of fuses - one main and one backup - and a large brass circuit breaker, controlled each circuit of the ten-story block of flats. They shone dully in the light from the swinging bulbs, one near the stairs and one in front of the coalbunker. Orange tongues of light from the boilers licked the circuit breakers like sensuous lovers, sparking off the shiny metal of the connectors.

Mick barely gave the circuit board a glance, making a beeline instead for the coalbunker. He picked up the shovel before it could start slithering again. "About time they put a fucking light in there as well," he grumbled, standing in front of the black hole of the coalbunker doorway.

A noise from behind made him spin round. *What was that?* Sweat broke out on his brow. It didn't take much. At his weight he was a sweat machine anyway. The cellar seemed darker, the bulbs struggling to hold the shadows at bay. The stairs in the far corner cringed away from him, and the boilers leaned forward, trying to reach him.

Stop it. Stop trying to scare yourself you silly fat bastard. Then he heard it again. A scurrying noise. Where was it coming from? A whisper of smoke rose from the crack in the floor. The crack had been there as long as Mick McCracken had worked here. It was a legacy of the chemical explosion, which had destroyed the other two blocks of flats. It ran across the floor and part way up the back wall, but he couldn't remember seeing smoke coming from it before.

He looked closer, but didn't move. The coward in him rose again, and he stayed put. The smoke thinned then disappeared. The crack was just a gap in the concrete again. After a second Mick plucked up courage, and took a step towards the hole in the floor.

Darkwater Towers wasn't the only building clinging onto life amongst the ruins. There was the local Eight-til-Eight, a stack-it-high-and-sell-it-cheap general grocery store run by Bob Harris, and Carl Stensel's barber shop on the corner of Roundwood Avenue and Brewer Street. As a wintry sun struggled through the thin covering of cloud, the barber's was Theobald Wolff's first port of call.

Carl Stensel looked up as he came through the door. To Theo's trained eye he looked more subdued than usual. The sixty-one-year-old Polish barber was working a cutthroat razor up and down a leather strap. The blade flashed expertly, first this way then that, always trailing the blade as it became honed to a fine edge.

"Welcome, welcome," he chimed, sheathing the razor after closing the blade. "Thank goodness for my regular customer, or where would I be?"

The little barbershop was a brick built afterthought, the size of an outhouse. It had once stood against the side wall of Grimley and Company Tannery but now stood alone. The side wall - and come to think of it Grimley and Co.'s entire premises - had long been demolished, and Carl's wall skimmed with cement to smooth over the scars of its rending separation.

The shop window and the door took up the whole shop front, the bottom half of both boarded and panelled in dark wood. A two-line neon sign hung in the window between yellowing lace curtains, which had been drawn back and tied. GENTS HAIRDRESSER the sign announced in green and red. The top line was green and the bottom red, and it licked the curtains with an eerie combination. Outside, the traditional barber's pole jutted out from the wall, its red and white candy stripe twirling slowly. That pole had been one of Carl Stensel's little extravagancies, a defiant gesture against the local council who had issued an ordinance banning barber's poles as dangerous intrusions onto the public streets. Just how tall they thought the public were baffled the old hairdresser, because you would have to be over seven feet tall to stand a chance of banging your head on it.

Inside, the pump action chair stood alone in front of the mirror, its black leather upholstery cracked and worn. Behind it, against the wall beside the door, three wooden chairs waited in vain for the rush of customers that would never come again. A Calor-gas stove in the corner filled the room with friendly warmth, and an old-fashioned hand-tuned wireless - Carl hadn't got round to calling them radios - soothed with the Jimmy Young Show.

"And what will it be today?" Carl said, beckoning Theo towards the chair.

"Thick and curly please," Theo answered, shrugging out of his coat. He hung it on the coat rack next to the door and topped it off with his hat.

"Ah, in your dreams I think," Carl chuckled.

This was something of a ritual between the two men. It was plain to see that Theo's thinning grey hair was never going to be thick and curly again. Hadn't been thick and curly in the first place. In fact, since the two weeks when he'd last been here his hair had hardly grown at all, but it was one of life's rituals that Theo liked to observe, and in any case, the warm friendly atmosphere was far more enticing than the cold stark confines of Darkwater Towers.

Theo climbed into the chair, and Carl draped a faded green cloth round his neck and shoulders. Two presses of the chrome barred foot pump to lift the chair to optimum height, and Carl was ready. He sprayed water from an atomiser over Theo's pate, and combed the hair straight.

Scissors in hand he prepared for the first cut. "How's that fat lump of lard, Mick McCracken treating you?" he asked, and began to snip away.

The fat lump of lard wasn't thinking about how he treated the old bastards upstairs. Instead, he was thinking how he'd like to be upstairs with them right now. "There's something in that hole," he muttered to himself. "So why the fuck am I going nearer?" He argued. The answer to that was, he didn't know.

He was almost standing over the crack when a tiny puff of dust blew out of the black void. A scream climbed into his throat but wouldn't come out. He jerked back a step and raised the shovel in two hands. Sweat made the handle slippery. It ran down his face and stung his bulging eyes. His breath came in little sighs.

Another puff of dust, this time slightly bigger. Mick grasped the handle tighter, not wanting it to slip if he needed to swing the club. He braced his legs. Coward or no coward, he edged closer to the hole.

He stared so hard his eyeballs felt like they'd pop right out of his head.

His muscles ached with the grip on the shovel.
The gaping black hole...
Flaming orange furnace light licked the edges.
Black and impenetrable...
Every grain of dust seemed the size of a boulder.
Deep...
Mick's eyes focussed, his arms preparing to swing.

Then movement. From somewhere inside the fissure two pinpricks of light blinked at him. Another puff of dust, then the eyes came closer to the surface. Every inch closer, they grew in intensity. They reflected the flames of the furnace doors in their black heartless ink-drop eyes.

Mick stood transfixed.

Not just eyes now. Teeth, as well. Jagged saw tooth jaws worked hungrily. They neared the surface and appeared to grin. Mick felt himself losing his grip on the shovel. He felt light-headed, dizzy. He swayed gently. The black eyes bore into him. He shook his head to clear it...

...then the rat came out of the hole like a shot.

Mick swung the shovel in a haymaker blow. Sparks leapt from the concrete as it connected, but he missed the rat by a good two feet. He swung again, but the rat darted between his legs and scurried into the coalbunker.

"Fuckin' little black bastard," he yelled. Adrenalin dumped into his system and bolstered his courage. A rat. That's all it was. A stupid verminous fuckin' rat. The fear evaporated. Now he knew what he was dealing with, the playground bully returned. "Come on you furry little fuck," he challenged bravely. "Come see what I've got for you."

Even as he advanced on the coalbunker, something nagged at the back of his mind. Something about the way the rat had looked, but he was in full flow. Brave as you like now he wasn't dealing with the unknown, and he wasn't going to let anything stop him.

Theo watched Carl in the mirror as he expertly trimmed round his ears. On the shelf to the left, half a dozen bottles of Vitalis waited to be bought. They'd waited in vain for over fifteen years it looked like. Theo thought they must surely have exceeded their sell-by date by a good decade. The liquid was a dull yellow, not at all what he remembered from the last time he'd used any, back when Melinda was alive.

On the next shelf down were a dozen tubs of Brylcreem; their familiar red lids dusty and unused, and hanging from a card on the wall were a range of Styptic Pencils. Black and brown combs hung below the red-tipped plastic tubes but it wasn't those that Theo's eyes were always drawn to.

It was the shrunken head standing by the sink under the mirror.

Black, pickled, eyes stared back at him as the barber worked his way round the back of Theo's head.

"You can't get any of the others to come out for a trim can you?" Carl said, snipping expertly between his fingers.

"I couldn't get any of the others to come downstairs, never mind all the way out here," Theo replied, his eyes still glued to the shrunken head.

Snip, snip, brush. Carl beavered away. "You know, I think that place is a bad kingdom. You, my friend, do not belong there."

The shrunken head nodded its agreement. Theo kept quiet.

"It should have been pulled down twenty years ago. When the others were." Snip, snip. "I have a theory about that. Do you want to hear it?" Snip, snip.

Theo would have nodded, but he didn't want to lose an ear. The shrunken head seemed to have stolen his voice. Carl carried on regardless. "That place survived the explosion when it really shouldn't have. Then there was the air crash that nearly was. I think it is all to do with the power."

"The electric?" Theo found his voice.

"No." Snip, snip. "The power from below. You know the fault line runs beneath The Towers don't you? Well, I think there is a connection... you know... with below. I think He is protecting it."

"Now why would Old Nick want to do that? Planning on sending his old lady there?"

"Do not scoff, my friend." The scissors were silent. "I have seen many things before I came here." Carl nodded at the shrunken head. "He probably laughed at the thought of having his head shrunk." Snip, snip. The scissors started up again.

"If you take any more off, my head will likely be as small," Theo chided, good-naturedly. He was certain the amount Carl took off depended on the length of the tale he was telling you at the time.

"Ah, the Land of the Blind," Carl sighed. "They are so blind they cannot see." He came round to Theo's left ear. Snip, snip. "You really must open your eyes my friend. If only a little bit. Because in the Land of the Blind, the One-eyed Man is King." As he said that, his hand slipped for a second. The flashing blades bit flesh, and blood seeped from the top of Theo's ear.

"Oh, I'm so sorry." Carl was distraught. He pulled a tissue from the box next to the sink, and dabbed at the ear. Blood ran down the side of Theo's neck.

"What do you say about the One-Eared Man?" Theo quipped, trying to take the sting out of the situation.

"I am a clumsy old fool." Carl looked a picture of misery. "Please forgive me."

Theo was about to, when a darkness settled over his heart. A black depression that rivalled how he felt when he'd received the letter this morning. A certainty that something bad was going to happen. Something worse than having his ear nicked by the barber. Then the moment passed as quickly as it had come, and he told Carl Stensel not to worry, he'd had worse cuts shaving. The blood was beginning to slow down anyway and a patch of tissue would soon put a stop to it.

Blackness was settling over Mick McCracken as well, but it wasn't the portent of imminent doom, it was the darkness of the coalbunker. His courage was back now he knew he was picking on something smaller than himself, so it was business as usual for the playground bully. He approached the doorway to the bunker, shovel raised, and prepared to squash him some rat.

"Come out, come out, wherever you are," he called sweetly.

The twin eyes of the boilers followed his progress, flames twinkling in their irises. A dull throbbing roar murmured gently, like a big cat purring before the kill. Steam hissed intermittently from the pipes. The dials quivered in anticipation. The two bulbs on their twists of cord stopped swaying.

Everything waited with bated breath for...

McCracken neared the blackness of the door, and paused. Momentarily the fear came back. And that uneasy thought about the rat. What had looked so strange about it?

The dark beckoned. It gestured for him to come into its arms. The caretaker weighed up the pros and cons. The size of the rat versus the splat factor of the shovel. He thought briefly about the possibility of disease, or the chance of a nasty bite. Then he discarded the ideas as ludicrous. He reassured himself. *He was an eighteen stone, shit kicking, bad ass motherfucker after all. What did he have to fear from a scrawny little rat?*

Scrawny. That's what had caught his attention. Scrawny and under-nourished, and ailing. That's right, the little bugger looked sick as a two-week-old Big Mac. But its eyes had said something else. Something else? What the fuck am I thinking about?

He stepped to one side, and let what little light the bulb behind him could muster drift through the door. It picked out a section of the floor and the edge of the coal heap, but nothing more. He squinted into the gloom, waiting for his eyes to adjust. Conquering his fear of the dark might be a hell of a struggle, but his fear of looking foolish, even to himself, was proving just as tough.

Good job for him there was no one around to witness his dithering.

He'd just about made up his mind to go in after the rat, when it clambered down the pile of coal and sat on the bare concrete floor. Its feet left tiny footprints in the coal dust, and its tail swished a clear patch as it curled around its backside for balance. The rat sat on its hind legs and folded its front paws across its chest. It looked like a squirrel rubbing its hands together while it waited for a nut or an acorn.

It stared at the caretaker with indifference. A calm self-confidence that belied the situation it was in. The rat did indeed look sick, but not your average ratty sickness. Its fur had split in great rending stretch marks, but there was no blood. It just looked like a balloon, which had been over-inflated, then let down a touch. The flesh sagged off its bones and its eyes were bloodshot. Bloodshot, but knowing. As if it knew it would soon be out of its misery, but wasn't worried about it.

Mick McCracken felt the fight draining out of him. He felt a dreamlike sense of well-being replace it. The eyes bore into his, and he began to lower the shovel. As he did, the rat came back down onto all fours, and crawled towards him. It limped badly.

The boilers began to pant. Flames pulsed behind the doors, throwing yellow light across the floor.

The rat got closer, and the caretaker didn't move.

Electricity flashed across the circuit breakers in sparkling arcs. The atmosphere was heavy, like before a big storm. A huge dark presence had entered the cellar of Darkwater Towers, and it was taking over. It exuded from the shrivelled frame of the rat and spread out like stains from an oil spill. The shadows grew deeper, swallowing the walls and stairs of the cellar, drawing the light and focussing it on one spot.

The spot where Mick McCracken, the overbearing schoolyard bully, stood transfixed. His fear of the dark had evaporated. His need to bully and belittle his charges dried up.

All that was important was here and now, and here and now meant the rat. It reached his feet, then sat back on its haunches again. The shrunken head tilted up to meet the caretaker's eyes...

...then it opened its mouth. The jaws opened wide, and then just kept opening. Wider than it was possible for them to go. Wider than...

White smoke spewed out of its mouth. A steady stream of wispy ghostlike tendrils shot upwards, hitting Mick McCracken full in the face. It bombarded him, buffeting his head and neck, forcing its way into his nostrils and ears. Then his mouth opened and the spew of smoke rushed in. His fingers jerked out, rigid as the shaft of the shovel, which he dropped on the floor.

His head disappeared in a swirling white cloud, then it was all inside him. Filling him to bursting point. Threatening to stretch his skin and pop his eyes out of his head, and the last thought to go through that saggy, slack-jawed brain, was that he really didn't mind the cellar any more.

CHAPTER 4

By the time Theo picked his way through the bombed out streets back to Darkwater Towers the sun had set, and only its dying breath painted the sky a murky red. The thin veil of cloud which had held the sun at bay for most of the day was replaced by threatening black ghosts, spread across the darkening sky like so many witches' capes dripping blood.

Theo was deep in thought. It seemed today was a day for bad news. Not a red-letter day, but a black-letter day. A, "commiserations-on-your-loss" kind of day.

Not only had he been told that his time was short, but Carl Stensel had nearly separated him from his ear and now he learned that Bob Harris was going to close the Eight-til-Eight in the New Year. Theo had been stunned at the news as he'd worked through the shopping list.

"There simply isn't the custom around here any more," Bob had explained sadly. The stoop shouldered shopkeeper - bald as a badger at forty-five - looked even more depressed than usual and that was some achievement since he could moan for England. This was more than just a good moan though, this was terminal.

Theo looked around the shelves of the general store, and noticed for the first time the number of empty spaces. The packets of Kellogg's Corn Flakes were pulled to the front of the shelf, hiding their lack of strength in numbers by standing at parade rest in single file. Cans of Heinz soup once famous for their Fifty Seven Varieties were now only able to muster seven, or so it seemed from the meagre selection on offer next to the vegetable rack, and the vegetable rack itself hardly bristled with fresh greens. Not much iron to be gleaned from there.

The National Lottery terminal had been taken out six weeks ago - the gamblers among Bob's customers having to make do with the scratch cards at a pound a time - and the cigarette counter only marshalled its troops four deep, pipe tobacco being almost non-existent.

Yes, it was a sorry sight and one which struck Theo cold in his heart. He picked a copy of Boxing Weekly from the news-stand, and laid it on the counter. Working from the list, which he almost knew by heart, he slowly amassed a substantial pile. *Forty Benson and Hedges to go with the magazine for Charlie Brewer. Six rolls of Dove Grey heavy-duty wool - the type adorned with the British Wool Mark - for Uriah Lovelycolors. A new tin of Brasso and a smaller tin of Duraglit for Newton Wimer - The Major must have more brass than a Chelsea streetwalker,* Theo thought.

Then there was the family size packet of Cadbury's Drinking Chocolate. Theo reached gingerly for the packet on the top shelf next to the door. He was tall, but even he had to stretch. Lord only knew how some of Bob's shorter customers managed. The shopkeeper saw the familiar blue and purple packet come off the shelf, and it gave him the chance to change the subject.

"How is Delia?" he asked, a knowing smile pushing the usual gloom off his face. "I haven't seen her since they closed the Roxy."

"Not too good," Theo said, placing the drinking chocolate with the rest of the shopping. "The arthritis is getting to her knees a bit now."

"She won't be cutting a rug at the Christmas bash then?" Bob said, trying to make light of a situation that could only be tolerated with a brave face.

"Christmas bash? It is Darkwater Towers you're talking about isn't it?" Theo scoffed then paused, his eyes turning inward as if deep in thought. "I'm sure her legs got worse once we couldn't go dancing any more," he said, more to himself than to Bob.

Bob picked on the remark though. "Yes," he agreed. "I sometimes think it's a case of use 'em or lose 'em."

"A bit like the shop then," Theo offered soberly.

"Yes, a bit like the shop." Bob began to ring the sales into the till. "Since Garbutt's Foundry on Station Road closed, there aren't any buildings left standing between here and The Towers. Except Carl's hairdressers that is."

Theo helped load the canvas shopping bag he felt embarrassed about carrying - though he drew the line at those bags with the little wheels and the pulling handle. "Carl only stays open to get himself out of the house," he said. "I think Mary must be giving him hell at home."

"Well, there are all sorts of reasons for staying in business and that's probably as good a one as any." Bob brought the bag round the counter, and rang up the subtotal. "Twenty-nine fifty-five," he said, but didn't ring in the final total.

Theo glanced at the list, but he didn't really need to. He knew what he'd missed, just as well as Bob. He nodded towards the confectionary stand. "Yes, you're right," he acknowledged Bob's unspoken prompt. "A large Galaxy Fruit and Nut please."

"Thirty-two straight." The till rang its joy at another sale, snapping the money away like a greedy moneylender as Theo tucked the chocolate into the top of his bag. He thought about the chocolate as he rounded the corner of Brewer Street. It cheered him slightly. Seeing Delia's face when he brought her supplies was about the only thing that did these days.

He passed the barbershop, which was now closed, the red and green neon sign turning the little shack into Sweeney Todd's. The red dripped blood from the curtains and the green conjured up corruption and gangrene. The colours mingled and spilled onto the street. The thought of Carl's slip of the scissors made Theo touch his ear, an unconscious gesture that said much about where his mind was.

It was all over the place in fact. Absently surfing the waves of his subconscious. He thought of the letter and its stark message. He thought of Mick McCracken, probably lying in wait to have another dig at him when he came in. And he thought of Bob Harris finally giving up the struggle to keep his business running.

The only light on his horizon was a drink and a chat with Delia Circelli, and he looked forward to that with all his heart.

The final corner, then it was down the home straight. Along the left hand side of the road mounds of bricks and concrete bulked around the rusting tracks of the railroad yards, twisted girders pointing skywards in jagged crosses, like tank traps on the Normandy beaches. It was a depressing scene. A sight that could dampen the brightest of spirits.

As Theo followed the lengthening shadows down the street, another, darker sight met his eyes. As colour slowly bled out of the darkening sky, the sightless monolith of Darkwater Waters jutted black and horrible out of the desolation. It stood alone, like a sentinel of the night, and the witches' capes gathered around it. Night was coming, and it formed the clouds into a new shape. A new inkblot in the twilight. A grinning skull stared down at him, and with a downward glance at his feet, he mounted the steps to the front doors.

Theo's heart might have ached as he pushed open the door to the front lobby, but for Delia Circelli the pain was much more immediate, and much more severe. The arthritis she had suffered since she was fifty had not only sunk into her knees, it had bitten deep into every joint of her body. It ravaged her five foot two inch frame during every waking moment, and flared into a cruel agony whenever she moved. It made walking difficult, and dancing impossible.

So, no, she wouldn't be cutting a rug this Christmas, or any other time.

Not ever again. She was more philosophical about it than Theo though, more accepting of it, and because of that, she was more able to cope with the pain, and get on with life as it was lived in Darkwater Towers.

Her flat was on the sixth floor, one floor up from Theo's. It was neat and tidy in a fussy, old lady's way, the walls decorated with fine patterned wallpaper of pink roses. The motif was echoed on the print covers of the three-piece Cottage Suite, and was counter-pointed by the plain pink velour of the full-length curtains. The plush fabric was now faded and worn, but they were spotlessly clean, the ragged tears which had appeared in the corners over the years hidden in the folds.

The faintest hint of Glade peach blossom lingered in the air, covering the smell of the salad dressing she'd had with her tea. She had always been proud of her salads and dressings, mixed from fresh vegetables and tossed in olive oil, and attributed her good health to a lifetime of eating it, but now her hands wouldn't allow her to shred the lettuce or slice the tomatoes. Her fingers couldn't even hold a cucumber let alone skin and chop it. So, now it was Paul Newman's dressing out of a bottle mixed with prepared salad from the supermarket.

She still enjoyed it though. Even in the depths of winter Delia would live off salads. A slice of pepper ham, a boiled egg, a dozen chips and the salad dressing. Top that off with two slices of wholemeal bread and she was set. To vary the feast she would change the ham for beef or pork, and occasionally a brace of chicken drumsticks, but always with salad.

Delia stacked the last of the dishes in the drainer, her hands protesting at the exercise, and closed the kitchen door as she went to the living room mirror. She wasn't a vain woman, and Lord knows she didn't have much cause to spruce herself up but she was proud. She wouldn't let Theo see her looking anything less than clean and tidy. It was the least she could do. It reminded her that she wasn't completely spent, even at her age.

Seventy-three. A grand old age. An age when you would expect to be enjoying a peaceful retirement. Don't I wish, Delia thought, as she tidied her collar-length dark hair, hair whose colour had more in common with a bottle of Belle Colour than her natural genes. It was cut short and curled under at the neck, and it was at odds with the fragile paleness of her skin. Sun tanning was a thing of the past for her, and she didn't hold with painting herself bright orange just for the sake of a bit of colour. What you see is what you get with Delia, and in that she was very similar to Theo.

That, and the fact that circumstances had laid them both low and left them scraping a living in the only place they could afford. That retirement home from Hell. Darkwater Towers.

Delia Circelli had become an actress in 1947, just after the war. She had enjoyed moderate success on the northern stage, and had appeared in several small-budget films, usually in a supporting role. The spotlight of fame had never shone on her, but she had made a reasonable living. A blissfully shortened marriage - to the stage manager of the local repertory theatre - hadn't soured her, although it did turn her into a lifelong spinster. She could claim to be a spinster - instead of a divorcee - because nobody knew her. Her family had been killed in the war, mother and father in a direct hit during an air raid and her elder brother on the beaches of Normandy, and Bert had long since moved on to fresh fields. That left her free to indulge herself, and wipe away the memory of a period in her life she could well do without.

Unfortunately, a life in the arts does not prepare you for a secure future. Short of funds, and shaken by a string of bad investments, the yellow brick road had eventually led her here. The only consolation she had was her friendship with

Theo. A friendship that had sprung out of his grief at losing his wife to cancer, and his money to the taxman.

She glanced around the room, checking that the gas fire was on low and that the radio was switched off. There was no television; she preferred the erudite voices of Radio Four and the Book at Bedtime. Soon Theo would call by with her shopping, and she would make them both a mug of hot chocolate. It was something she looked forward to every Wednesday and Saturday. It would have caused quite a scandal if anyone could be bothered.

"Are you sure it wasn't just something he knocked over?" Theo asked.

"Course I'm not sure," Charlie answered. "I weren't there was I?" The old boxer took the proffered cigarettes, and with a shaky hand put them on the fireplace. He waited eagerly for the Boxing Weekly.

Theo tried to forget about the burly caretaker, pulling Charlie's magazine from the shopping bag instead. He handed it over, but his mind came back to the ex boxer's comment. "It could have been the furnace door slamming," he said.

"Could have been." Charlie leafed through the pages. "But why would he scream out?"

"Trapped his finger?"

"If he did, it couldn't have happened to a nicer fella." Charlie had lost interest in the remark he'd made when Theo had come in, and frankly he was beginning to wish he'd never said it. After all he'd only said he thought Mick McCracken had come a cropper in the cellar judging by the noise he'd made.

Theo on the other hand, was coming to the limit of his oxygen in the pugilist's flat. Theo might not have been over zealous with the duster, but Charlie didn't appear to have been introduced to one at all. Not a duster, nor a Hoover, nor anything to do with cleaning. The apartment was a mess. Not only a mess, but a smelly mess. Stale sweat attacked Theo's nostrils, and the acrid scent of dried urine joined it.

In short, it was a flat to be visited briefly, and infrequently. Twice a week at the most, and that was just what Theo did. Apart from the twice-weekly shopping runs he didn't spend too much time in Charlie Brewer's flat, his nose simply wouldn't take it, but there was something he had to ask.

"Did you go down and check?"

"In the cellar?" Charlie's head stopped shaking for a moment. "Theo, I need the lift to go anywhere."

"Well, did you call to him?"

"No. But I heard him moving around after."

Theo felt a little better at that. "Can't have been fatal then," he said, pushing aside the thought that he might have to go down there and check on the caretaker. The snide bastard didn't deserve any consideration but Theo wouldn't have been able to just leave him there if he'd had an accident. At least if Charlie heard him moving about afterwards it couldn't have been too serious. Now Theo wouldn't feel guilty leaving it at that.

"Don't read it all at once," he said, retreating to the escape hatch of the door. He tried not to touch the frame, which was stained yellow and sticky, and flicked the door open in one deft movement. With a quick wave he was out on the landing, and took a deep lungful of unpolluted air.

Only another two calls then it would be time for a drink. That thought cheered him, and he headed for the lift.

Half an hour later he was standing outside Delia's apartment door. The sixth floor landing was as bleak and forbidding as all the rest, but two dried flower arrangements hanging on the wall either side of flat twenty-one's door lifted the gloom. Grey concrete and peeling paintwork were held at bay by a pretty spray in pink and beige, dried grasses and artificial flowers woven into a wicker half-basket, and tacked at shoulder height. It was a very pleasing effect, and typical of the woman Theo had come to visit.

It would be a visit in stark contrast to his previous two deliveries. The debilitating senility of Uriah Lovelycolors was bad enough, but the black depression, which had gripped him in The Major's flat, had almost been too much to bear.

Theo pushed the thought out of his mind, and pressed the doorbell. A faint ding-dong sounded from inside. *Avon calling*, he thought, echoing the old cosmetic firm's advert. It worked every time. Melinda had spent several years being an Avon home-call rep, and the TV advert always amused him. *Ding-dong, Avon calling.'* His mind just couldn't help it. He supposed he was as programmed as Pavlov's dog.

The security chain rattled inside, and the bolt was drawn. Theo slid the shopping bag behind his legs - it still embarrassed him to think of a grown man carrying a shopping bag. A sexist thought if ever there was one! He braced himself, a little flutter of butterflies in his stomach, and waited for the door to open. It surprised him that he still felt like a schoolboy on his first date whenever he called on Delia, but after thirty years of marriage to Melinda this was tantamount to the first faltering steps on the road to romance. A road into the unknown he hadn't travelled for a long time.

The handle turned and the door swung inwards. A flush spread up Theo's neck, and Delia's warm smile greeted him.

Steam spiralled up from the mugs of Cadbury's Drinking Chocolate on the coffee table. One of Delia's dainty antique saucers lay between them, half a dozen blocks of Galaxy Fruit and Nut spread across it. The fire threw out just enough heat to take the chill out of the air, and Radio Two serenaded them with soft music. With Christmas just around the corner it was Val Doonican's rendition of "Oh Little Town of Bethlehem". Delia put a battered cardboard box down in the corner of the living room.

"Are you sure you don't mind?" She asked, straightening up.

"Of course not," Theo answered, noticing the involuntary wince of pain as she straightened her back. He watched her walk gingerly to the chair and slowly lower herself into it. He almost let out a sigh of relief once he saw she was settled. It upset him to think of the pain she must be in practically all the time, and he felt a little guilty that he had escaped the clutches of arthritis, that old man's disease that could lay you so low. *Escaped the arthritis, but not the cancer,* a voice prompted. He ignored it. Now wasn't the time.

"Well, if it's not inconvenient, that would be splendid," she said.

"Cost you another drink afterwards though."

"I think I can stretch to that." She reached a shaky hand for her cup.

Theo smiled, and took a sip of his drink. It was still too hot, so he put it back down. This little dance had become something of an annual ritual. The, "would you like a hand with the trimmings?" offer, which he had made several years ago, was now as much a part of the festive season as carol singers and Christmas crackers, and with each passing year it became more imperative. The cruel curl of her hands made it impossible for Delia to put the decorations up herself. Theo argued that she needn't bother putting any up at all, after all it was mainly for the benefit of children but she insisted that Christmas simply wasn't Christmas without the decorations. Lord only knew they needed something to brighten up the gloom at Darkwater Towers.

Christmas Day was definitely a day to look forward to in her book. She would cook a full Christmas Dinner for herself and Theo - even though their digestive systems complained like crazy afterwards - and settle down to at least one day in the year when she could forget the cards Fate had dealt her, and that she was eking out her final days in a rat infested hovel on ten floors. Rat infested not necessarily meaning the four-legged variety either. Mick McCracken more than qualified on that score.

Val Doonican gave way to Paul McCartney, one of the new breed in Delia's eyes, and she blew gently across the top of her cup. Steam whispered away then steadied. "Have you completed your deliveries?" She asked, knowing full well that Theo always saved her shopping until last.

Theo burned his throat, taking too big a drink. He nodded, waiting for his voice to return. "Yes. All done," he said finally. He thought about the knitting fool, one floor down. Poor old kid didn't know what day it was, but he knitted like there was no tomorrow. If he'd had any inkling that Christmas was coming, they'd all be wearing oversized jumpers and scarves on Boxing Day.

Theo felt sorry for Uriah, but in a way he thought he was probably the lucky one amongst the residents of Darkwater Towers. After all, he didn't know what an awful place he was living in and he didn't realise what an evil man the caretaker was.

At eighty-five, Uriah was the oldest resident of The Towers. He was tall and lean and bald as a cue ball, making Bob Harris look positively hirsute, but his fingers were surprisingly nimble, not a hint of the arthritis which blighted so many of the others, Delia included. His flat was sparsely furnished and tidy, his bureau stocked to overflowing with left over wool and knitting patterns.

When Theo had delivered the six balls of Dove Grey, Uriah had pointed to the small brown envelope on the fireplace, and told Theo to keep the change. The envelope contained three crisp five-pound notes, more than enough for the wool, but Theo didn't argue. When he began the shopping trips he'd tried to give the old man his change but it had always been refused. After a while Theo had given up, storing it instead in a coffee jar until it built up. His intention was to buy Uriah something for the flat, but he hadn't figured out just what he needed yet. The jar had over forty pounds now, and Theo was still no nearer to knowing what to do with it.

The drinking chocolate was cooler now, and Theo gulped two mouthfuls down, and stood up. The warmth from the fire slayed the demon cold, which had settled in his bones, and the hot drink laid it to rest. Now it was time to get started on the trimmings. He brought the box and plopped it in his chair, folding the flaps open. Sparkles of gold and silver twinkled at him, the feather boa strands of tinsel catching the light. He began to lay the tree ornaments on the settee, golden parcels in miniature, plaster Santas, tiny ornate wreaths with a smiling face in the middle, and a long plastic star, which had bent with age. The silver plating had peeled in places, and two of the points had broken off, giving the star a lopsided look. As Theo picked it up it nuzzled in his hand like a futuristic pistol: the long shaft the barrel; the remaining points the handle.

He shivered involuntarily. The pistol seemed all too real as Newton Wimer's voice urged caution. Theo felt himself flush at being caught out with his thoughts, and he was suddenly back in the Major's flat, contemplating...

By the time Theo reached the seventh floor apartment of Newton Wimer, his bonhomie at the prospect of hot chocolate with Delia had faded. The days' events weighed on him like a heavy load, and try as he might it was beginning to get him down. The letter, the feeling of dread at Carl Stensel's barbershop, and the imminent closing of the Eight-til-Eight, they all wormed their way into his guts and twisted.

The Major's flat was the only one occupied on this floor, the landing bleak and empty except for the ghosts of past tenants. Two bulbs were out, and the further you got from the lift doors, the darker it got. Cold grey concrete and dirty green paint added to the gloom, and the whole effect was capped off with the banshee wail of the wind. It screamed like the devil and pricked a rash of gooseflesh on the back of Theo's neck.

    The seventh floor was the outpost of a bleak frontier. No apartments were occupied above here, and the top three stories were ghostly shells of bygone days. Theo imagined it would be like walking the decks of the Titanic, long since devoid of life yet holding the essence of those who had gone before. The twelve flats up there had been empty for almost five years, becoming a no go area for the residents - not that many of them could make it up there if they tried. Theo had a feeling that Mick McCracken had long since stripped them of any valuables, and would probably strip the occupied flats as well as each resident pegged out. He was glad he didn't have any gold teeth or they would more than likely go as well.

    The Major's door was pristine. After the split wood and peeling paintwork of the rest of the floor it was a revelation. If there was one thing you could say about Newton Wimer, it was that he was a stickler for details. The door had been stripped and painted every six months for the last ten years. Theo felt that if he sat down long enough once inside he'd likely get a coat of paint as well. The old military adage, "if it moves salute it, if it doesn't, paint it" certainly applied here.

    Theo knocked smartly, startling the dust to attention. The door opened almost immediately. The Major must have a sixth sense for when I'm coming round, Theo thought, and saluted smartly. Newton smiled knowingly, and nodded for Theo to come in. "Stand easy," he said, tucking an imaginary pacing stick under his arm. He about faced and marched into the living room. Theo followed, closing the door behind him.

    "Brasso and Duraglit at the ready," Theo said, rummaging in the shopping bag.

"A little spit and polish never hurt anyone," Newton said, standing in front of the fireplace like an old colonial in his hunting lodge. The only thing missing was the tiger's head on the wall, not that there was any room, because the walls were adorned with wave upon wave of military insignia, medals, brasses and firearms of every conceivable type. The Major might not have any money apart from a paltry pension, but he had collected a wealth of weaponry and military paraphernalia.

The walls of the apartment were painted neutral beige, the carpets and curtains different shades of grey, the carpet light and the curtains dark. A pair of plush leather chairs dominated the room, arranged either side of a low heavily carved coffee table. It was only when you looked closely that the cracks in the leather became visible, neat patches welded to the creases and polished into an almost seamless finish. The table had been repaired twice, once on the far leg and once on the surface itself, but unless you looked carefully it was impossible to tell.

Spread out on a cloth across the coffee table was a methodically stripped Browning 9mm semi-automatic pistol. Gun oil stung Theo's nose. Newton Wimer stood over it like a proud father. "It is very good of you to drop by." He spoke as if Theo's visit was a casual house call, and not part of the twice-weekly shopping expeditions. "I will be able to give my collection a thorough clean before Christmas."

Theo held out the tins, noticing the Major's stiff gait as he came round the table to collect them. The injury, which kept Newton housebound, and caused him considerable pain in the winter, wasn't some old war wound or a memento from one of his military campaigns.

In one of his more sombre moods he had explained to Theo how he used to go out to "take the air" as he put it. This was before Theo and Melinda had moved in. He had slipped on a patch of ice on the front steps as he'd escaped for the day, and the hungry maw of Darkwater Towers had swallowed him ever since. A compound fracture of the right shin and a bad dislocation of the hip had sealed his fate, and the block of flats had seemed to smile down at him darkly. When the Major slipped into one of his melancholy moods he could be quite creative, and it was possible to believe the ugly monolith held its residents captive out of spite or some malevolent self-interest. Anyway, the bottom line was, Newton Wimer was as much a prisoner here as the other seventeen tenants, and only death or a sudden windfall would release him.

"I would like to show you my latest renovation," Newton said.

"You haven't painted the toilet seat again have you?" Theo joked, but the humour fell flat even in his own ears. Things were beginning to catch up with him, and they were slowly dragging him down like quicksand in a marsh.

"No, no. Nothing so trivial, although I do believe it is overdue a coat of varnish." Newton limped over to the Welsh dresser against the far wall, setting the tins down on the worktop. He reached up and plucked a dark grey egg from its stand on the top shelf.

"What's that?" Theo asked (rather unnecessarily), "I sincerely hope that it's not armed."

"That is a nineteen forty-seven, mark two British Army hand grenade," Newton beamed. He held the chunk of metal out reverently in his upturned palms. The curved edges gleamed dully, light catching the square pineapple segments. The trigger lever curved sensuously down one side, and Theo was glad to see the shiny circle of the safety pin. The whole thing, like everything else in the flat, was squeaky clean.

"Don't worry," Newton reassured. "It won't bite you. Not while it's on its leash." He waggled the safety pin, and Theo flinched.

"Has it been disarmed then, Major?"

"Of course not," Newton blustered. "That would be like neutering your prize bull. I have spent seven weeks stripping and cleaning every part, and I can assure you it most certainly isn't neutered." He turned and placed it carefully on its stand amid the silver trophies of a career spanning three decades. "My next project is on the table there."

Theo glanced at the stripped down pistol. A pulse was beginning to beat in his temples.

"A Browning 9 mm," Newton said proudly. "A gentleman's weapon."

The pulse grew into a steady throb. He heard himself speak, but his voice sounded distant. "Where do you get them all?"

Cancer... The word invaded his mind.

"Oh, I still have quite a selection of..." The Major's voice droned on, but Theo didn't hear it.

Cancer... Again the word. The monster which had eaten Melinda inch by inch. The monster that had its own malevolent self-interest. Which acted with spite, and greed, and cruelty. The day was not only catching up with Theo it was overtaking him. Swamping him. The closing of the 'Eight-til-Eight.' The sense of foreboding in the barbershop, that feeling that something bad was going to happen. They all gathered round him like dark spectres in the night. Harrying him. Bullying him.

And the letter,

Cancer...

which had dropped through his letter-box so innocently this morning. The letter which warned that the monster was unleashed again, only this time it was stalking him.

Five months...

Not only stalking him now, but had been stalking him for months, maybe years. It had slipped in under cover of night, as it had done with Melinda and set up its base camps.

Its troops had spread unseen through his body, eating their way in, until it was too late.

Cancer...

He hadn't seen it coming with Melinda, and he had been just as lax himself. He tried to shut out the memory of the pain she had suffered towards the end. The inability to move, or control her bodily functions. The shame in her eyes, and the unutterable sadness. The pleas she had rained on him to end it for her. To release her from the monster's jaws. The final agonising request he had been unable to grant.

"Kill me. For God's kill me."

A tear formed in Theo's eye.

"If you love me, then please make it stop."

"I do love you," he'd said. "But I can't." In the end, her final agony had been short lived. Death took her after two endless days and nights, and Theo could never forgive himself for not granting her that final wish.

"I do love you." He blinked to the present. Had he said that aloud? He glanced round the apartment, wiping the tear from his eye. Newton Wimer had gone into the bedroom; Theo could hear the rustle of paper and cardboard.

On the table, the Browning grabbed his attention.

If I'd had you when Melinda was dying I could have... Theo cut the thought short. *Could he really have done it? Even if he'd had a gun, and bullets, and the time. Could he have shot his wife? Killed her with love, in order to save her further suffering?*

The Browning stared emptily, its innards spread out like a gutted fish. The question was pointless, the time for that action long gone, but what about now? What about the pain that was to follow when the disease strangled the life out of him? When the monster used its teeth to tear the heart out of him and show him for what he was, a weak, selfish, bag of bones and flesh.

The Browning posed an impotent threat. Or offered an empty solution. Its magazine lay beside it, stripped and empty. No bullets. Even if Theo could remember how to clean and rebuild it - there wouldn't be the time. Anyway it might not have any bullets.

The Major would soon find whatever he was searching for and come back in. The Browning would be no help at all. Just as Theo had been no help to Melinda.

But the Enfield .38. Theo saw the revolver on the wall above the fire. It was clean and dark and...

...loaded?

He thought about the hand grenade, stripped and cleaned and rebuilt.

"That would be like neutering..." the Major had blustered. Had the Enfield been neutered? Was the variation on the Webley Mk IV loaded and ready to go?

Theo walked round the coffee table and approached the fireplace. Heat from the fire warmed his legs, but his heart was cold as ice. He saw his hands reach up for the revolver, but it wasn't him controlling them. Someone else had taken over. A desperate, lonely, empty person. A man full of despair, and fear, and a complete lack of hope. That person lifted the Enfield from its rack, hefting it in one hand. It felt heavy. Full. Loaded. He squeezed the catch and the barrel broke forward. Light glinted off five golden orbs and one empty chamber. The bullet tips sparkled with promise. A promise to put him out of his misery, if he only had the courage to put the barrel in his mouth and pull the trigger.

The stranger's hand folded comfortably around the walnut grip while the other snapped the barrel shut. The hammer levered back with a double click. The black dot of the muzzle turned towards him. It lifted and looked him in the eye. One dark soulless eye staring at two dark hopeless ones. The black hole drew him in. The barrel grew larger as it closed on his face. It pressed, cold and hard, against his forehead.

The black heart of Darkwater Towers urged him on. It was like a solid presence cheering him home. It reminded him of how empty his life was. How bleak and depressing this place was. How dark and painful his future would be. *Go on, pull the trigger*, a deep and terrible voice whispered. It smiled darkly, waiting for the explosion. Waiting for the splintered bone and spew of blood to wash over it. His finger tightened on the trigger.

WE WILL NOT DIE, UNLESS WE ARE FORGOTTEN...

Melinda's face materialised through the fog of his mind. She looked vaguely admonishing, as she had this morning when he'd surveyed the dust in his apartment. Their apartment. His hand relaxed.

"Forgotten? How can I forget you? How can I live without you?" The hand re-affirmed its grip. The finger tensed, and squeezed gently. The barrel pressed into the flesh of his forehead.

"I'm sorry did you say something?"

Newton Wimer's voice snapped Theo back to life. Had he spoken those last thoughts aloud? Theo lowered the gun, thankful that he had his back to the bedroom door. "Just talking to myself," he mumbled, clearing his throat.

"You must be careful with that," Newton said. "As I have said, these are all fully functional, and should not be toyed with.

Theo felt himself flush at being caught out with his thoughts. He carefully replaced the Enfield in its rack. The moment had passed. The dark depression that had settled over him drew back, and The Towers didn't like it, that deep voice whispering its discontent as it withdrew into the walls. He turned to see what ancient weapon the Major had brought out to show him, while in the back of his mind those five little bullets glittered festively.

Despite the warmth from the fire, Theo shivered. He pinned the final decorations - a cluster of golden baubles - in position above the fireplace, and stepped back. Delia surveyed his handiwork from her chair.

"That looks very nice indeed," she said. "I don't know how I would manage without you."

"Well, if I wasn't coming round for Christmas dinner, you probably wouldn't need these up in the first place," Theo suggested.

"Nonsense," Delia smiled. "Christmas wouldn't be Christmas without them. And it wouldn't be Christmas without a friend for dinner."

"You sound like Hannibal Lekter."

"Who?"

"You know. Hannibal The Cannibal, from Silence of the Lambs."

"Oh, is that one of those dreadful horror books you read?" Delia feigned disgust.

"Seems like the thing to read in this place. Darkwater Towers is every bit as evil as Hill House, and look what Shirley Jackson made of that."

"No, no," Delia argued. "I haven't sunk to Mills and Boon, but I am afraid that sort of thing leaves me cold. I much prefer a good Freddy Forsythe or John LeCarre." She struggled to her feet, pain etched on her face before she masked it with a smile. "For your reward, I do believe I have a fresh bar of Fruit and Nut, and you most definitely deserve an extra piece with your drink. Theo watched her go carefully into the kitchen, then packed the rest of the trimmings in the box. When he looked up he was surprised to see Delia still standing in the kitchen doorway, watching him with a thoughtful expression.

"Is it bad news Theo?"

He noted the determined set of her jaw, and the serious look in her eyes. The playful, flirtatious girl was gone, replaced by a concerned friend. He considered lying; making some excuse, but one look at her told him she'd see right through that. Instead he said nothing.

"Theobald Wolff, how long have I known you?" She walked back into the room and sat on the two-seater settee. She gestured for him to join her.

"Long time."

"Christmas is a hard time for you without Melinda isn't it?"

Theo swallowed hard before answering. "It is. Sometimes it feels like she's only gone out for a while. Like she's just..." He tried to put into words the unutterable emptiness of the apartment without her. He couldn't, so he lapsed into silence. There was something else he couldn't express. A feeling of closeness to Delia, which he didn't want to spoil. It was a feeling so delicate, like fine lace glasswork, he thought a wrong word might shatter it beyond repair. A feeling of... love?

No. That was too strong a word for it, but it was something very close. Indecision furrowed his brow, and Delia misread it.

"Do I ask too much at this time of year? Would you rather be left with your memories? I will understand if that's the case."

"No. It's nothing like that." He reached for her hands, so fragile, and enclosed them in his. The intimate touch seemed completely natural. Despite their advancing ages, this felt right and proper. "I sometimes feel... like I let her down at the end." This was difficult to get out. "When she couldn't get around any more, when she couldn't... you know, control herself, her body and such, she asked me..."

"If you love me, make it stop..."

"...to put an end to it. She wanted me to..." The words dried up.

50

Delia looked sadly into his eyes. "It would have been a mercy killing, but an appalling decision to make."

"She wanted me to promise, but I couldn't do it. Not even knowing the pain she was in, or how much worse it would get. I couldn't help her."

The gas fire popped with a tiny backfire, then settled back into its rhythm. The heat was calming, almost hypnotic. Light glinted off the golden baubles he'd fastened over the fireplace.

...five little bullets...

"You cannot blame yourself. Theo, you can only do what you feel to be right." The words were meant to console him, but they didn't.

"The right thing to do would have been to finish it for her. Take the pain away. But I was too weak." His head didn't sag, but an invisible weight settled on his shoulders.

"Then perhaps you will be stronger next time." She was staring deep into his eyes now, her senses questing. "I would hope you could do it for me if the circumstances dictated. As a friend. A very close friend. I will do it for you when the time comes."

There was the kicker. Theo's body went cold. *She knows, he thought. Somehow she knows.* He met her gaze, and their souls touched in a deep and intimate way. It was more sensual than making love. More meaningful. In that moment he could have asked her to marry him, or to run off with him, or anything. He remembered the other promise Melinda had forced him to make, to look for someone else after she had gone, and he had promised, without any intention of fulfilling it.

Well, here was that someone else. That special person he could realistically spend the rest of his life with,

...which was at the most - five months.

except the rest of his life didn't amount to very long. He saw understanding dawn in her eyes.

"Is it the same thing?"

"Yes. Cancer. I got the letter this morning."

"And how long do they give you?"

"Five months." He thought he saw her flinch, but she hid it well.

The fire hiccupped again then the silence, apart from soft Christmassy music, stretched uncomfortably. There really wasn't much more to say. Delia struggled to her feet, and went towards the kitchen again. This time she didn't pause in the doorway, but went straight in. He thought he saw the glint of a tear in her eye but couldn't be sure.

Oddly enough he felt better now it was out in the open. The strain of keeping the secret had been eating at him almost as much as the cancer itself.

He decided he would enjoy the drink with Delia before returning to his apartment, and try to put a bit of festive spirit into the day.

A niggling thought crept into the back of his mind. He pushed it away, but it wouldn't stay pushed. For a moment he cursed Charlie Brewer for mentioning it at all, but he knew he couldn't ignore it, any more than he could let Delia put up her own decorations.

He resigned himself to the fact that before he returned to his flat he would have to check on Mick McCracken, like him or not, but not before his second mug of hot chocolate.

CHAPTER 5

"Oh for God's sake, what now?" The lift shuddered to a halt with a dull clunk, and from somewhere beneath Theo's feet there came a screech of metal and a loud clatter. Heavy chunks tumbled down the black hole of the shaft, making him acutely aware of the void beneath the elevator floor, clanking and rattling into the bottom of the shaft. The black finger of the floor indicator hovered just above the G.

"God damn your eyes." This might not be the season for cursing God, but in view of his immediate prospects he felt he could be forgiven a slight lapse. He pressed the doors open button twice with no response. All around him the inner dark of The Towers groaned its approval. It would throw any obstacle in your path it could, and be damned pleased about it. Or so it sometimes seemed to Theo.

He had left Delia's flat with the intention of going back to his own apartment to leave the shopping bag. Before calling the lift, which often took an age to come, he'd dropped her bin bag down the garbage shoot along the hall. When the doors finally opened, that feeling of dread crept over him again. He thought about the trip to the hairdressers, and that heavy darkness which had settled on him, and then he thought about Charlie Brewer telling him that Mick McCracken must have come a cropper in the cellar. The two things twisted together like a knot of fuse wire.

His finger went to press the fifth floor button, then stopped. He didn't like Mick McCracken, and in fact he heartily detested the man, but a worm of disquiet squirmed in his stomach, making him feel uncomfortable.

Then he pressed for the ground floor, and the doors shut. His stomach lifted with a lurch as the elevator dropped, and part of him wanted to leave the caretaker to look after himself. Part of him felt afraid, but he wasn't sure if it was fear that something bad had happened or fear that the overweight bully would poke fun at him. Either way it didn't do much for his self-esteem, and he was pondering that when the lift had shuddered to a halt.

He pressed the doors open button again, and this time the steely grey doors juddered open on their tracks.

Six inches.

A foot.

Eighteen inches.

They stopped at two-and-a-half feet, and began to close again. Through the gap Theo could see the cold grey concrete of the lobby walls, but the floor was two feet down. The doors groaned and inched shut. He put his shoulder in the gap to halt them, and then stepped out onto the ground floor. His back twitched at the large step and his foot hit the ground with a thud that vibrated through his body. The doors sighed shut but before they did, Theo caught a glimpse of the twisted metal track that had come loose and collapsed across the shaft. The lift didn't come down any further, and judging by the state of the track it was never going to reach the lobby properly ever again.

That worm of doubt persisted, twisting his stomach into a knot. He looked across the lobby at the caretaker's flat, and hoped McCracken would answer his knock. He wasn't sure what he would say if he did, but somehow he didn't think he'd have to worry about that. As he approached the door he wished he didn't have so much Good Samaritan in him.

The knock sounded loud in the silence of the lobby, echoing off the bare concrete walls like a rifle shot. It faded into the shadowy corners, and the night outside fastened itself against the glass of the front doors. The gentle breeze of the afternoon became a banshee's howl, forcing its way in through cracks in the structure, sniffing curiously under the cellar door.

Theo tried to ignore it, but couldn't. Goosebumps crawled up his spine; the short hairs at the back of his neck lifting like a million tiny erections. There was no sound from inside the flat. All around him the oppressive darkness crowded in, sucking the meagre light from the wire framed bulbs, leaving him alone in an oasis of dirty yellow light.

He knocked again.

No reply. The door marked CELLAR - STAFF ONLY KEEP OUT drew his eyes like a magnet drawing iron filings. It pointed him to his own magnetic north. He raised his fist to knock again, then paused. A sharp scraping noise sounded above the wind. It ripped into him like fingernails on a blackboard. His eyes glued to the cellar door, ears pricked like a gun dog on the hunt.

The scraping noise came again, longer this time, more frightening, and Theo lowered his hand. The noise was coming from the boiler room.

It was the heat that hit him first, then the subtle change of colour. After the cold grey of the lobby and stairwells, the cellar's warm browns and rusts were almost beautiful, in a darkly compelling way. The chill wind, which wandered the lobby like a hungry spectre, was put to the sword by a steamy, swamp-like heat, which both heartened him and scared him at the same time.

Standing at the top of the worn stairs, Theo felt like he'd stepped into Dante's Inferno, the twin furnaces spewing out heat, their eyes glinting redly. Orange and yellow fire twinkled in their irises, as they watched him come down the steps. Steam hissed at him to stay away.

In that moment, Theo felt the same fear of the dark that had beset the schoolyard bully McCracken, and for an instant he contemplated the same choices. To stay or go. Mick McCracken had forced himself to stay. So did Theobald Wolff. He carefully negotiated each worn concrete step until he stood squarely on the cellar floor. He glanced around, taking in the pressure gauges which now hovered ten points beneath the red markers; the angry eyes of the furnace windows; the rusty metal panel of the elevator shaft maintenance hatch; and the gaping black mouth of the coal bunker.

His eyes took all these things in, but his ears couldn't find what they'd been listening for. The sinister scraping noise which had drawn him here. Or was it the noise? Had he heard something, or was he being led into The Tower's hungry belly by some darker force? Every brick in the dingy cellar watched him. The yellow glow of the pair of bulbs pulsed like a beating heart, and the fiery eyes of the furnaces bade him enter.

He took a step into the room, scuffing coal dust into the crack in the floor. It blew back up in a tiny puff, as if a sigh of rancid breath had exhaled from the dragon's lair. The furnaces roared and the gauges hissed, like tigers and snakes in this concrete jungle. Sweat beaded on Theo's forehead, and his palms grew sticky. He stepped over the crack in the floor, not even noticing its existence, and walked haltingly towards the coalbunker. The cloying blackness sucked him in, drawing him on step by step.

The door grew closer as the gap diminished.
Ten feet...
It was just an average door.
Eight feet...
Now the size of a barn door.
Six feet...
The hole began to dwarf him.
Four feet...

It towered above him like a marauding grizzly. Theo stopped, halted by the unspoken threat of the unknown. The darkness blocked out his peripheral vision, drawing his gaze into its impenetrable blackness. Whatever walked in there, walked alone, and it was waiting for Theo.

Four feet...

Theo's feet wouldn't move. He tried to think why he was going there in the first place. The noise hadn't sounded from in there. The noise hadn't sounded at all since he'd come into the boiler room. Perhaps the noise hadn't sounded at all anyway. Only in his head.

No. I heard it. Stop playing mind games with yourself. You're not that old that your mind's gone silly. Theo looked around the cellar for confirmation of what he already knew. There was nowhere else the noise could have come from apart from here and the elevator maintenance hatch, and that was closed. Logic dictated this was the place.

But why does it have to be so dark?

God almighty, don't be such a pussy, another voice argued. A voice of reason which dated right back to his days as head warder at Scardale Prison. The voice of the man he used to be, not the one who had grown old and was afraid of the dark.

Theo squared his shoulders and expanded his chest in that old army way Melinda had liked so much. He took one more look into the darkness, letting his eyes adjust to the gloom, then stepped forward.

A dark figure swung out of the dark to meet him. Shock dumped adrenalin into his system, and the sweat turned cold on his body. He stifled a cry and froze to the spot...

As the ghost of Tim Ransom hung lifeless from his noose.

"What're you doing 'ere?" McCracken asked.

Theo couldn't speak. His voice wouldn't come out of hiding even as he realised that the long dead "Tiny" Tim wasn't hanging from the rafters before him. Tiny by name but not by stature, Theo's former charge had stood well over six feet five, and been built like a brick shit house. His sheer size had been memorable enough, but the manner of his death was more so.

It was size that played through Theo's shocked mind now, because Mick McCracken loomed over him in a way he couldn't remember before. The heavy-set caretaker had always been big, shifting a stomach the size of a dray every time he moved, but not so overwhelmingly huge as he seemed now. Theo stepped back and blinked away the shock.

"I said, what're you doing 'ere?"

Theo swallowed hard. Even though the caretaker stood intimidatingly close, the words held no threat. The eyes, squinting menacingly, held no menace. It was if the lights were on but no one was at home. Having said that however, the bulk of the man was menacing enough.

"I thought I heard a bang," he managed. "So I came to see if you were alright." The words sounded so inadequate. Fancy asking this hulking monster if he was alright? He waited for the scathing comment. To his surprise it didn't come.

"Been stoking coal." From nowhere McCracken produced a battered shovel. "Had to splat a rat first though." He smiled meaningfully, bringing a touch of the old McCracken back to the doughy face. The schoolyard bully who would enjoy pulling the legs off a jenny spinner.

"Oh." That was all he could think of to say. There was something unsettling about being this close to the terror of The Towers. More than usual, because at the best of times Theo wouldn't want to stand this close to him. Stale sweat and bad breath washed over him and he took another step backwards. He turned to go, tensing himself for the bully's parting shove. Like the snide remark, it didn't come.

Theo got all the way to the stairs before he allowed himself a glance back. McCracken was still standing in the coalbunker's doorway, the shovel hanging limply from one hand, watching Theo's progress with lifeless eyes. The eyes were the main things that bothered him. They stared intently, but with a vague disinterest. It was like they were torch beams in the night, spotlighting what they fell on, but not taking it in. They bulged horribly, as if he was squeezing out a hard one without the help of a laxative.

The eyes, and the oddly bristling bulk, were what stuck in is mind as he climbed the steps out of the cellar, so he didn't even notice the shovel. The shovel which had been used to "splat a rat", but which was curiously free of blood and gore.

Taking the steps two at a time, he reached the shallow landing, and without another backward glance went through the door into the lobby.

That night the dream came for the first time since Melinda died. It sucked him in cold and tired, and spat him out hot and sweaty.

"Tiny" Tim Ransom swung from his cell door, the noose biting deep into his neck. His feet dragged on the floor, the enormous weight of him having stretched his neck to almost twelve inches long. The ligature bit into his flesh like a cheese wire through a ball of Edam. The head all but fell off when Theo opened the cell.

In his dream the prison was in darkness, only moonlight through the barred window spotlighting the hanging corpse. Tim twisted and spun gently as the door was pushed wide, then his eyes opened and he stared at Theo from up close. Yellowing teeth bared as he spoke in a dry whisper. "Why didn't you help ...?"

Then blood gushed out of the mouth, splattering Theo's uniform, and he awoke screaming silently. Wind whistled round the windows of his fifth floor apartment, and Darkwater Towers welcomed him back into its dark embrace. The bedroom was cold and cheerless, and utterly black.

From a long way off, perhaps somewhere in his dream, a long plaintive cry built up gradually into a piercing scream. Theo tried to force himself awake before he realised he was awake already. The scream faded, mingling with the wailing wind.

It was a long time before sleep took him again, and while he waited for its welcome embrace, he couldn't decide if the scream had come from inside his tortured soul, or a deeper, darker place...

...somewhere in Darkwater Towers.

CHAPTER 6

In the eighth floor apartment, cold wind brought Theo round. Pain lanced through his arm, and his neck was stiff. He tried to work out how long he'd been unconscious, but when he glanced down at his watch he remembered it was broken, the hands frozen at nine fifteen. The best he could do was see how far the moon had travelled. The muscles in his neck wouldn't let him turn, so he looked at the shadow of the window instead. When he'd settled against the wall, the vertical opener had pointed towards the door. Now it angled across the dusty floor, pointing accusingly at the airing cupboard.

An hour at least.

What to do next? That was the question. As he shuffled upright the answer came in a bolt of bright red pain. His arm was on fire, and the slightest movement opened the wound. It's only a flesh wound; bullet's gone straight through. How many times had he heard that in one corny war film or another? The legacy of too many afternoons watching daytime television, avoiding those women's chat shows like the plague.

A flesh wound? In Theo's experience there was no such thing. In his army days he'd seen more than his fair share of bullet wounds, and if there was one thing he was certain of it was that if a metal projectile hit you anywhere at a hundred and fifty miles an hour, flesh wound or not you bloody well knew about it. The shock alone could kill you, but the loss of blood was more likely to finish the job, and Theo's left arm was bleeding badly. The sleeve of his jacket was a sticky black mess, a morass of dried blood painted over with a seeping red topcoat. The blood appeared black in the darkened room.

Theo knew if he didn't stop the bleeding and get something for the pain he was going to be no use to anybody.

If there was anybody left to help. He pushed the thought aside, concentrating on the more immediate problem, where to get bandages and disinfectant.

A shudder vibrated through the floor, and a faraway hum sounded through the walls. The elevator was on the move again. Subconsciously he had noted it going down to the lower floors, but now he felt its lumbering presence as it climbed the lift shaft again. His ears pricked up like a dog on the scent, listening for the sound of it grinding to a halt. Wondering where it would stop.

Fifth floor?

Sixth floor?

The hum grew louder. He could feel it through his backside.

Seventh?

Eighth?

He held his breath, waiting for the sound of the lift doors opening and the terrible shuffling steps, which would signal that he was being stalked again. The lift didn't stop. It ground on, ever upwards.

Ninth floor.

Tenth.

The lift stopped, and Theo imagined he heard odious footsteps on the top floor landing. He couldn't of course, but his senses were so geared up that he almost could. *What's he doing on the top floor?* Theo wondered, then dismissed the thought as he realised this was his chance. He couldn't wander the corridors of The Towers in case he bumped into McCracken, but now McCracken was on the top floor.

Bandages? Painkillers?

Apart from whatever supplies the residents might have in their flats, there was only one sure-fire bet for the things he needed.

The medical room.

Got it in one. The medical room was a small cubicle on the ground floor. It was round the corner from the caretaker's flat, between the lift and the rear stairwell. Back in the days when Darkwater Towers had been a viable old persons residence, many moons ago, a district nurse had been on call for any tenant who needed routine maintenance. It was stocked with all manner of supplies, including field dressings, gauze padding, ointments and tablets. For emergencies there was even a stock of stronger painkillers and syringes to administer them.

The only problem was, those days were long gone, and if Mick McCracken had anything to do with it, so would most of the supplies, but it was his best chance. Theo struggled to his feet, swaying dizzily as he got up too fast. Or was it the loss of blood? The arm sent fire through his nerves. Fresh blood dripped in tiny mortar bursts in the dust. He undid the top buttons of his jacket and carefully pushed his hand into the opening, making a temporary sling, and stopping the blood splatters. There was no point leaving McCracken a trail a blind man could follow.

"In the Land of the Blind, the One-Eyed man is King."

Carl Stensel's words played across his mind. They raised a painful smile on Theo's lips. He listened for the lift, but there was no further movement. He stretched his neck and hunched his shoulders, bones cracking loudly in the ghostly bedroom, and then he made his way to the door. Along the corridor and he was out on the landing. The lift doors stood firmly closed, their cold grey countenance inscrutable.

Next to the lift and opposite the flat door was the main staircase. It zigzagged back and forth, wending its way either up or down. If you looked over the balcony you could see all the way to the bottom, and if you looked up you could see...

Theo didn't want to look up. More importantly he didn't want Mick McCracken to look down and see the wounded pensioner struggling down the stairs. He turned right and walked along the landing to the junction of the next two flats. At the far end was the door to the service stairs. This narrower staircase was at the back of the tower block, and came out near the rear door. That door led out into the car park.

For now, that wasn't the door Theo was interested in. To get to the one he wanted he would have to go down the corridor towards the front of the building and head for the medical room.

With that in mind, Theo pushed open the narrow door, waiting for the giveaway creak with bated breath. It didn't come. The door opened silently, if not altogether smoothly. Theo set off down eight floors of hard concrete steps.

When he reached the bottom he felt dizzy and out of breath. His back ached, and his calf and thigh muscles screamed their complaint. He might be the fittest resident at The Towers, but to be fair the competition wasn't all that strong.

He paused to get his breath back. The downward journey had taken twenty minutes, Theo fighting the urge to take two steps at a time. That might have been all right for the first two or three flights, but after that his co-ordination would be shot. Better to come down steadily in single steps than tumble the rest of the way, head over heels. There was also the inadequate lighting to consider. If the rest of The Towers' corridors and landings were dimly lit, then the service stairs were subterranean. A single bulb in a protective wire frame illuminated each half landing, but almost half of those bulbs were out. Theo had negotiated three full floors with no light at all, working on autopilot the whole time, and most of the others were only lit on every other landing.

Now, as he sucked in a great lungful of stale night air, the ground floor bulb flickered ominously, and then steadied. Theo straightened up, the bones in his spine cracking loudly. A fresh burst of pain shot through his arm. His head swam and he felt nauseous. With an effort of will he steadied himself, then reached for the door handle.

It was locked.

The stairwell drew in around him like a tomb, its cold grey dampness as harsh and unyielding as the sides of a grave. The light flickered again. Theo felt his lungs deflate, his shoulders sagging resignedly. He tried the handle again. It turned but the door wouldn't budge.

He remembered the veranda door on the eighth floor, how he'd turned it the wrong way before realising the balconies didn't lock. He turned the handle the other way.

The door still wouldn't open.

A door banged somewhere in the dark emptiness above him. Wind sighed eerily through the upper landings. Theo's heart sank. Through this door, only twenty feet along the corridor, was the means of dulling the pain and stopping the bleeding. Just twenty bloody feet. He felt like sitting on the bottom step and giving up.

You will do no such thing. Melinda's picture drifted through his head, her eyes boring into him with such determination that he could not resist her. Those eyes always followed him around the flat, and they always expressed her satisfaction or otherwise with the way he was conducting his affairs. They stared at him now, burning into him from their position in his deep memory, and the look on her face said, you will do no such thing.

Theo puffed out his chest in acknowledgement and turned towards the stairs. *Okay* he told himself, *if the door won't open, then I'll have to go to the nearest one that will.* That meant the first floor landing. He tried to recall if he'd heard any movement from the elevator, and decided he hadn't, and then the light flickered one last time and went out, plunging the stairwell into darkness. Panic clawed at his throat and he struggled to control it. He took a deep, calming breath, his eyes adjusting to the darkness, and then climbed the first step towards the dingy light of the first floor landing.

At last Theo reached the corridor to the medical room. It was a narrow hallway leading from the lobby to the back of the building with three doors set along its length; the medical room halfway along on the right; the external door to the car park a bit further on the left, and the door to the service stairs blocking off the very end of the corridor. That was the door that had caused the dangerous diversion.

Theo walked along the corridor, the smudged grey walls sucking in behind him. Of the two bulbs spaced out along its length, only one was working. It threw a dim yellow circle on the floor at the far end, tinting the concrete a putrid green. Before going to the medical room he tried the door to the car park, realising that he was bottling himself in if he was caught in this dead end hallway. There was still no sign of movement from the elevator, so he felt safe for the moment, but it was best to be prepared.

The car park door. Theo didn't need to turn the handle to know it was locked. Of course it was. Why should he expect any different. The way today was going it was only to be expected. He tried it anyway. Locked. At the end of the corridor the service stairs door hugged the shadows, but something caught Theo's eye. He approached the door, picking out the hinges on one side and the handle on the other. Another shape jutted from the door just below the handle.

No wonder I couldn't get through. He looked down at the circle of metal protruding from the gloom. The key. For the first time that night he breathed a sigh of relief. *Maybe my luck's changing*, he thought, and plucked the key from its hole then turned back along the corridor towards the medical room.

His shadow preceded him like a great hunched giant, blocking out the meagre light from the bulb. It swallowed the door as he approached it, then swept past when he stood before it. The palm of his good hand felt sweaty, and a pulse thudded in his temple. After a brief pause he reached for the handle, and encountered his second stroke of luck of the night.

The door wasn't locked. He opened it and stepped into the cool blackness of the room.

The light switch was on the left, but it took Theo a few moments groping along the wall to find it. He flicked the switch, and a low humming noise came from the ceiling, followed by two or three stuttering flashes of antiseptic light. After a full minute the fluorescent came on.

Theo blinked at the brightness after the total blackout, taking a few moments to take in the little room that had last been used when old Mrs Dorda had tumbled down the stairs. That had been over two years ago. The dressing that was applied then was the last treatment she had received; she died of a heart attack the following year. The medical room hadn't been used since, any illness or injury being treated at St Luke's Hospital across town, after a short ride in the local ambulance.

The six-foot by eight-foot room welcomed him, begging him to sit in the single wooden chair next to the examination table. Theo obliged, grateful to take the weight off his feet. The room smelled musty, tinged with the coffee smell of old leather. Unlike the corridors and landings, the medical room wasn't grey; it was pale blue with the walls half tiled in white ceramic. At one end was a narrow desk, not much wider than your average school desk, with a single drawer across the top of the leg space. A two-shelf bookcase with glass doors stood on the desk against the wall, and an official looking six-foot cabinet, painted white with a red cross on it, filled the space beside it.

The desk and the cabinet took up the width of the room, but the leather topped examination table took up the bulk of the space. Copper fixing studs ran along the side holding the leather in place, and a neatly folded blanket lay in the middle. The chair Theo was sitting on was at the head of the table, conveniently placed for the obligatory bedside manner. He looked across at the desk. A pink blotter covered the centre, and a row of pencils stood to attention in a desktop organiser. A green mug with a teaspoon sticking out of it kept station next to the blotter. The effect was disquieting. Theo felt like he'd walked into the medical officer's room on the Titanic after abandon ship had been sounded. The teaspoon glinted in the light from the fluorescent tube as if waiting for its owner to return. A small sink clung to the wall behind the door. Everything was coated in a thick layer of dust which made Theo's apartment look sparkling by comparison.

His eyes fastened on the cabinet. As strength crept back into his legs, the pain throbbed more insistently in his arm. The Red Cross encouraged him, taking him back to his army days, when the sight of it on the battlefield signalled welcome relief. He got up and went to the cabinet, emboldened by the apparently untouched nature of the room. It looked like Mick McCracken might have left this room alone, on the off chance that it could be needed in an emergency. Slack as the powers that be were, they wouldn't want to be criticised if anything went wrong. Theo hoped the medicine cabinet had been similarly spared. He opened the left hand door.

The dust hadn't encroached in here, giving the shelves a pristine, antiseptic appearance. Rows of packets and bottles filled the shelves. Tubes of ointment and pull out trays of syringes and needles ranged across the middle shelf, while large cardboard boxes with the familiar Red Cross embossed on the front took up the space at the bottom. Theo scanned the treasure trove, trying to recall some of his medical training. Itemizing what he would need.

Bandages.

Bottom shelf in the boxes. Theo pulled a handful out.

Gauze padding.

Same shelf. One roll should do.

Germolene antiseptic ointment, and TCP.

Top left hand corner. Theo took a tube down, and reached for a bottle of TCP. He started to look for the best sell-by date, and then decided not to. Old stock or not, he was still going to have to use it, so why bother? He just hoped they had retained some of their strength even if it had been diluted with age.

The syringes and needles winked at him from the pullout tray. A spread of suture needles lay next to them. Theo wondered about stitches, whether he would be able to administer them even if they were needed. A sharp pain shot through his arm in protest. Rambo might be able to stitch up his own wounds but Theobald Wolff didn't think he was going to follow suit. The pain from the gunshot wound was bad enough without aggravating it with a probing needle and thread. Sod that for a game of soldiers.

He withdrew his left hand from his jacket. In the glare of the neon it looked sickeningly red but Theo knew it wouldn't look so bad once it was cleaned. He went to the sink and ran the hot tap. Murky water spurted out, dried up, then spat twice before running normally. The colour cleared, and the water began to warm slowly. *Thank goodness for the boilers in the cellar*, he thought.

He carefully took his jacket off, then rolled up his sleeve. With a wedge of gauze padding he dabbed away the blood, wetting it under the tap then rinsing away the gore, until the entry wound was clearly visible. A hole the size of a shirt button, all puckered around the edges, winked painfully. Theo checked the other side of his arm. A slightly larger hole, ragged and fleshy, hid under his armpit. Thankfully the bullet had missed bone, travelling cleanly through the soft meat of his upper arm. The exit wound was nowhere near as big as he'd feared, and was easily plugged with a wedge of gauze padding.

Pain exploded through the arm as Theo pressed a germolene-coated pad over the wound. It burned bright and angry while he bound the padding to the arm, wrapping it tight to hold them in place. Painful thoughts nipped at his mind, impishly provoking memories he'd been trying to avoid. *Where are they all? What has he done with them? Delia?*

He gasped as he tied the bandage and knotted it. Pain, physical pain, was preferable to the dark thoughts which plagued him, but even that pain was becoming too much. The scurrying noises in the upper floors he had ignored for too long, replayed in his head. The muffled cries he had attributed to his dreams, assailed his ears.

No. Not now. Theo forced the demons away. Instead he returned to the medical cabinet, his eyes scouring the shelves for...

There they were. Two brown bottles with faded type on their labels. DF 118's. Dehydrocodeine tablets. The strongest painkillers the duty nurse would have been allowed to stock. Theo remembered them well. The pain Melinda had suffered towards the end had been dulled for a time by those little white pills. Her face squeezed into his mind, and he felt guilty pushing it aside. He simply couldn't cope with the thought of her pain right now. Instead, he reached for a bottle and unscrewed the childproof lid with some difficulty. Two tablets popped into the palm of his hand as he tilted the bottle, then he added a third. He put all three in his mouth and rinsed them down with a handful of water, putting the tablet bottle in his pocket.

Then he waited for the pain to dull. All around him, isolated settling noises clanged in the upper reaches of The

Towers. Theo listened carefully for the first signs that the lift was active, but heard nothing. Soon, the settling noises changed into dreadful whispers, warnings emanating from the very walls that protected him.

"I'm coming to get you..."
"I'm coming to get you..."

The whispers grew strident, becoming bolder and more insistent.

"Coming for yoouuu..."
"For yooouuu..."

Theo's head began to spin. He sat heavily on the chair and nearly missed. The DF's narcotic properties were taking effect. The Heroin substitute drew him on an unwanted journey, a trip many addicts relished, even craved. The pain faded and vanished altogether, replaced by a feeling of well being.

He had the presence of mind to reach over and snick the lock, almost toppling off the chair, before unconsciousness swallowed him. His head lolled over onto the dusty blanket on the examination table, and he smelled coffee as fresh as if it was straight out of the grinder. The room swayed then tilted like the medical officer's room on the Titanic. The ship's going down, he thought. Too much ice in that last drink.

The ship settled at the bow, and water gushed up the companionways. Not enough lifeboats. Damn. I'm going down with the ship. The pale blue of the walls grew paler. The white tiles spilled over everything, and the room became lighter. Whiter. Ebenezer Scrooge poked his head above the examination table blanket and, as before, Alistair Sim morphed into Theobald Wolff. Theo watched the locked door bulge with malicious intent, feeling detached and far away. He recognized that he was passing out, but wasn't worried about it. Hell, he wasn't worried about anything. Those three little tablets had done more than take the pain away, they had taken everything away.

The door pulsed inwards, stretching like the walls of a balloon, in a vaguely familiar human shape. Theo's mind jarred awake, but his body slid into a deep, dark sleep.

   The Ghost of Christmas Present entered the glittering white medical room, his hearty laugh thudding through Theo's brain as he took the wounded ex-prison warder back. Back to the beginning of the day. Back to the hallway, and the blood, and the start of his last day at Darkwater Towers.

CHAPTER 7

The breakfast dishes peeked guiltily through the kitchen door at Theo, fragments of Kellogg's Corn Flakes clinging to the cereal bowl, and half a bacon sandwich standing on the plate. His appetite had deserted him this morning, and as he adjusted the threadbare cuffs of his Marks and Spencer shirt he looked into the understanding eyes of his dead wife.

"Two weeks down, eighteen to go," he said to Melinda's photograph. There was no reply. Even in life she had been notoriously taciturn, often not replying when Theo started to run off at the mouth. He remembered one occasion when she had been particularly infuriating. It had been towards the end of his service at the prison and at the end of a gruelling shift on "E" Block. He had come back to their semi-detached home in a foul mood, washing off the smell of the prison with hot water that burned his face. After dumping the towel in a heap over the banister rail, Melinda had calmly straightened it out so it draped neatly, allowing it to dry.

"What the blazes do you do that for?" He'd snapped. "Everywhere I go you follow like a council dump truck. If I leave the lid off the toothpaste you snap it back on before I've finished my molars. You whip my cup away in mid-swig..." He snatched the towel off the banister and screwed it up, wedging it between the twin newel posts at the top of the stairs. "...and you shag about with the fucking towel before the steam's even gone off my face."

Theo shocked himself to silence. In twenty-five years of marriage he had never sworn at her. Now he felt ashamed, but he was still too angry to apologise. Instead he lapsed into an uneasy, heavy, silence.

Melinda slowly straightened the towel, shook out the creases, and hung it over the banister rail. That simple act of defiance reinforced her strength. No histrionics. No smart backchat or lengthy argument. She knew just when to keep quiet and let the storm blow over. It was maddening and deeply caring. It reminded him just how much he loved her.

Later, when he had calmed down, he came up behind her in the kitchen, slipping his arms round her waist, one hand running up her body to cup her right breast. "I'm sorry," he whispered in her ear. "I feel a right tit." He squeezed it gently until the nipple hardened, pressing into the palm of his hand.

Melinda had swivelled in his arms to face him, putting her arms around his neck. "Bad day?"

Theo nodded. As they held each other tight in front of the sink he told her about Tim Ransom's suicide, about his part in it, and about his decision to take early retirement. "I've seen enough misery. It's time to live the way God intended."

Melinda's photograph stared questioningly from above the handwritten message.
WE WILL NOT DIE, UNLESS WE ARE FORGOTTEN...

No, she wasn't forgotten, never would be, but those eyes sensed the pain behind his expression. Sensed the turmoil behind his own eyes. They pleaded with him to explain.

"Eighteen weeks. Do you think that's enough time to enjoy someone's company?" The question was rhetorical. It required no answer and got none. Melinda waited patiently for him to elaborate. "I've been thinking about Delia. I know she's older than me, but... I thought it might be nice to spend what time I've got left with her. If she'll have me. If you don't mind."

The eyes answered. They reinforced what Melinda had said on her deathbed. What she had made him promise. "...look for someone else after I've gone."

He felt better, and a little guilty. Not at the prospect of courting Delia Circelli, but at what he had left out. The other things that were worrying him. The noises in the night, and the growing stillness within Darkwater Towers.

Theo straightened himself, squaring his shoulders and expanding his chest in that old army way she liked so much. He shrugged into his coat, hiding the worn cuffs as best he could, and crammed the Russian hat on his head.

He was going to break his routine today and call on Delia before going to the barber's. His fingers checked that the shopping list, unchanged in over two years, was in his coat pocket, then he turned to the door, a warm feeling spreading through his chest.

* * * * *

Delia felt a flutter of excitement when she heard the knock on the door. Despite the growing unease she felt at the oppressive atmosphere around The Towers, the sound of Theobald Wolff's distinctive knock brought a touch of much needed warmth on a cold winter's day. *He's early*, she thought, not caring a jot.

As she'd pottered about the apartment, preparing the meat and vegetables for tomorrow's Christmas dinner, she'd had the strangest feeling in the pit of her stomach. Not the tightening sensation she had been experiencing over the last few days as the noises in the night were countered by the increasing silence of the day, but a warm friendly glow of anticipation. A sense of well being, which spread up from her stomach and into her heart. She had chided herself that the heart was only a pump for the lifeblood which flowed through her veins, but couldn't deny that her heart was full, and the reason for that was Theobald Wolff.

A momentous decision was about to be made. She knew it.

The knock again. Delia removed her pinny and folded it neatly over the kitchen chair, patted her hair in place, then went to the door. Without looking through the little glass spy hole she slid the chain off, drew the top bolt, and turned the key. Her aching knuckles grasped the door handle and turned.

Theo smiled down at her as the door swung open, making her heart loop the loop and tying a hitch in her throat. For a moment she was a schoolgirl on her first date again, unable to speak. Teddy Bowlighter had come to pick her up on April tenth 1941. She was fifteen to his sixteen. He had been evacuated from dockland Liverpool and was staying at the vicarage with three other boys.

After six months of smiling at her across the street he had finally plucked up courage to ask her out - only as far as the tearooms in the park - and here he was. It was daytime so they didn't require a chaperone, at their ages they were still considered children anyway, although Teddy often pointed out that two boys he knew had lied about their age to join the fight against Hitler. He stood on the doorstep, a pimply faced youth, while her mother hovered protectively in the shadows of the hallway, and she froze. She couldn't speak. The excitement of going out with a boy for the first time proved too much.

That same feeling of giddy anticipation took hold of her now. Speech was beyond her. Theo stood patiently, then she waved him in.

"Cat got your tongue?" he asked as he brushed passed her.

She cleared her throat, coming back to the present. "Don't be so cheeky young man, or there will be no afters tomorrow."

Theo watched her bring the small tray and set it on the table in front of the fire. The cups rattled with her shaky grip but he didn't offer to help. Sometimes you've just got to let people manage for themselves otherwise they become dependents, with no feeling of self worth or usefulness. He found it hard not to leap up and take the tray off her though. The pain in her hands screamed out of every line on her face.

She sat carefully, taking up barely a quarter of the two-seater settee, while Theo reached for his cup from the comfort of the chair. They looked like two characters in a one-act play, inhabiting the stage but not invading each other's personal space. The coloured lights on the Christmas tree flickered gaily, and the heat from the fire wafted the crepe paper streamers. The atmosphere was heavy with unspoken promise.

Theo couldn't remember the last time he'd felt so lost for words. He had a commanding voice, something which had been put to good use on "E" block, where a firm command was worth a thousand slaps round the ear, but now that voice had dried up. Not completely of course, he had still been able to utter the usual pleasantries, but the meat of what he wanted to say just wouldn't come.

Sixty-nine and acting like a pimply teenager, he chided himself. *Come on, be a man. Say what you have to say.* Instead, he sipped his hot chocolate in silence.

"Back in my acting days this might be called a pregnant pause," Delia said absently, as if talking to herself. "I would be on stage, performing one of my deeply meaningful silences, while all the time the audience was wondering if I had forgotten my lines. Once, the prompter had given me my next line in a very deep stage whisper, which could be heard down the street. Very embarrassing."

"And what is your next line?"

"Yes, I think. Depending on the question."

Theo smiled, an indecent thought prompting a very unsuitable question he could put before that answer. His age might preclude the act itself, but the number still had definite connotations.

"You're too old for that," she said, not needing to read his mind. The dirty smile was written all over his face.

Too old? Yes, she was probably right. Suddenly, age seemed very important. Not only his, or Delia's, but the entire population of Darkwater Towers. There wasn't a one of them under sixty, and Theo didn't think any of them had relatives who gave a damn. Too old. Too alone. Too poor. Nobody outside this decrepit block of flats on the edge of an industrial graveyard even knew they existed.

"Have you noticed how quiet it is in The Towers lately?"

The question caught Delia by surprise. "It is always quiet," she answered, avoiding the question. She leaned forward, hooding her eyes against Theo's inquisitive stare.

"Not as quiet as it is now."

"It is Christmas Eve. Some may have gone away. How noisy do you want them to be?"

"Most of the people here couldn't make it down the corridor, never mind away. In any case they have as many relatives as you and I. And that's none."

Delia was flustered. This wasn't what she was expecting at all. The noises that came to her during the night whispered in her ear. Those dark, heart rending sounds that came from the bowels of the earth. Or from Hell itself. It might be quiet as the grave out there during the day, but at night the ventilators were telephones from another world. A world she didn't want to acknowledge existed at all. A world that shared the same space and time as her own. A world that lived in the same block of flats.

"You've heard them as well," Theo said. It wasn't a question. The darkening look on her face was answer enough. "The noises from the air vents."

"They could be the heating."

"The banging maybe. But not the voices."

"The moaning of the boilers, or the whispering of the wind. I have heard wind sound like cats on..."

"And not the screams."

That shut her up. Delia sat in front of the fire, not feeling its warmth. The glitter and twinkle of the Christmas decorations left her unmoved. Instead, the fears she had pushed to the back of her mind stormed forward.

"Délia." His voice was softer, friendlier. "Something is happening. I don't know what. At first I thought it was someone taken ill during the night. God knows we've had that before. But I've been getting a... I don't know... call it a gut feeling. A dark feeling."

Delia sat up, looking into Theo's eyes. "Was this after the letter?"

Theo pondered that. The morning, two weeks ago, when he'd received the results of his medical tests, seemed a long time ago. He tried to remember how he'd felt when sentence had been passed, because that's what had happened. He, Theobald Wolff, male of this parish, had been sentenced to death by cancer, that sentence to be carried out no later than five months from that date.

Had the shock of that letter, sent his mind down a darkly spiralling path? Certainly the sleepless nights had begun around then. And the dreams. No, not dreams in the plural, the same dream over and over. Tim Ransom. Why had he come back to haunt him after so many years? Was the thought of his own imminent death dredging up memories of Tim Ransom's untimely demise? And the reasons for it.

I had nothing to do with that. There was nothing I could have done.

But that wasn't strictly true was it? If he had acted when the taunts started, when the chants of "Beast, beast, beast," had begun to ring through the block...

Theo shut the thoughts out. He was getting away from the point. Had the news of his medical results slipped his mind into a different gear? With the sleepless nights, and the dreams, was he perhaps hearing things more in keeping with his depressed state of mind, than with reality?

He remembered when Tim Ransom had first come back to him. In the hellish cavern of the boiler room. With that, he also remembered Mick McCracken's unusual demeanour.

"Yes," he replied. "It was after the letter, but that has nothing to do with it."

"Are you sure?"

"Positive."

"It's just that, news as bad as that can..." She struggled to be polite. "Well, it can unsettle you."

"Of course it unsettled me, I've only got five months to live, but it hasn't sent my marbles on the loose, and it hasn't started giving me hallucinations." He recalled the look in Delia's eyes when he'd put the question. "It hasn't made me blind to the machinations of the female kind either." He pulled the bottom lid of his left eye down. "Do you see any green in here?"

"I'm sorry?"

"There's no point trying to change the subject. You've heard them too, and it worries you as much as me."

That seemed like a good place for another pregnant pause. The gas fire hissed and popped. Dangling tinsel decorations spun in the thermals from the fire. Theo leaned forward, putting his unused cup on the table.

"And what do you suggest we do about it?" Delia's jaw firmed up, her mouth set in determined fashion.

Now it was Theo's turn to be thrown. He thought about that, and he couldn't come up with an answer. He turned the facts over in his mind, and they didn't prove anything.

They didn't prove anything against Tim Ransom, a voice interrupted, *but he's still dead.* Theo winced at the truth of that remark.

"I don't know," he said eventually.

"Then perhaps you should say what you came here to say." Her voice was low, but pleasant. Changing the subject again.

The reason for him coming here before going to the shops resurfaced. Melinda's words drifted into his head. "...look for someone else after I've gone."

He had come here to ask Delia if she would consider spending the rest of their days together, maybe not as man and wife but more like companions. Close friends. He had even thought some small ember of romance might be fanned into a gentle flame. All that seemed a long way off now. The mood had been soured by his heavy-handed insistence that dark deeds were afoot. Or at least that something not quite right was happening in The Towers.

He couldn't tell her how he felt. If he'd found it awkward when he'd come in, he found it impossible now. "There wasn't anything special," he lied. "I just thought I'd pop in to see you before I left."

"Are you going on a trip?"

"Only to the shops. And Carl Stensel's."

"Then, I will see you when you get back," she finished.

Theo got up and was about to offer to wash the pots. He stopped himself in time, not wanting to take away too much of her independence. In any case, washing up wasn't his strong suit, as a glimpse round his flat would prove.

"Sorry if I upset you," he said, and with that the spell was broken. Apologising was another thing he wasn't very good at, but it was like a magic word to Delia. If a smile could make the world go round, an apology could stop it grinding to a halt. She patted his sleeve as he opened the door.

In that moment he almost told her the reason for his visit, but he didn't. The time had passed, and as she said, she

81

would see him when he got back. With a sad little smile, he stepped into the cold grey hallway, and waved goodbye.

CHAPTER 8

The corridor's bare concrete walls soaked up the light, acting like a sponge. They sucked what little warmth there was out of the atmosphere. To Theo, the hallway seemed darker than usual, but he dismissed it as further evidence of his depression.

There was something else as well. A pungent smell. It assailed his nostrils, sickly sweet, and made him gripe. He paused outside the lift doors and took a tentative whiff. The smell of ripe tomatoes, cabbage and rotting flesh was faint but distinctive. He tried to detect where it was coming from. The obvious choice was the garbage shoot. Theo backtracked towards Delia's door, then turned left along the short corridor to the next flat. It was vacant - Delia's being the only one occupied on this floor - but that wasn't what Theo was looking for. Set in the wall at waist height was a two-foot by three-foot metal hatch. It was hinged at the bottom with a handle at the top. Theo yanked the hatch open and looked down the chute, which led all the way to the basement dumpsters. He took another sniff, and...

Nothing.

Well, nothing more than the usual rubbish smells of stale food and off milk. He shut the hatch. No, the smell seemed to be all around, emanating from the very walls themselves. It seeped out of every pore in the concrete.

Theo dismissed it, and went back to the lift. The feeling of disquiet cranked up a notch as the doors opened, but he couldn't put his finger on it. With a groan of complaint the doors slid shut, sealing him in the cold metal tomb, and the lift went down.

If the corridor on the fifth floor was cold and dark, then the ground floor lobby was as chilly as a freshly opened fridge. Grey light filtered through the smoke stained glass of the front doors, keeping the yellow glow of the obligatory bulb at bay.

Theo stepped down the last two feet from the elevator, once the doors had finally struggled open, and stretched his aching legs. He found himself desperately looking forward to the change of scenery and a chat with Carl Stensel, but first he had to negotiate the Torpedo Alley of the front lobby, and Mick McCracken's apartment door.

Theo glanced across at the caretaker's door, remembering the last time he had called there. "Put t' wood in't hole," his father used to say if he left the door open. Or, "Were you born in a barn?" He wouldn't have had to say either today.

The door was closed.

Theo's gaze swung to the door in the corner marked: CELLAR - STAFF ONLY KEEP OUT

A shiver ran down his spine. That door was closed as well, but from the gap at the bottom a dull red glow, like the slit eyes of a demon, stared intently. The Towers' heart thumped with the intermittent roar of the furnaces, sending warm lifeblood pulsing through the pipes.

Something darker dwelled there, Theo was certain of it, remembering the shock of finding Tim Ransom hanging in the coal bunker, only to be replaced by the malevolent stare of Mick McCracken. Was he down there now, searching for another rat to squash with his shovel?

A trace memory flickered into life like a low wattage bulb on a faulty circuit, its dim glow illuminating an idea he must have had but not recognised.

The shovel.

Theo tried to think what significance that had.

Yes, that's what the caretaker had said, brandishing the battered stoking shovel, but the shovel had been clean. Well, not exactly clean, it had been used for shovelling coal for God knows how long after all, but clean of blood. If

McCracken had just splatted a rat, the blade would surely have been covered in blood and gore, or at least had a smear of it.

But no. Just coal dust.

Theo sidled across the lobby, keeping away from the shadowy corner between the caretaker's lair and the boiler room door. Another thought struck him as he passed the boarded up reception window. When Theo had seen the caretaker in the coalbunker he had been staring back at him but his eyes had displayed a curiously vague intensity. They had bulged from their sockets like freshly peeled boiled eggs. When he thought about it now, McCracken's entire body seemed bloated, straining at the cloth of his shirt and trousers even more than usual.

Grey winter light grew brighter as Theo neared the front doors. It lifted the shadows from his mind, making the dark thoughts seem foolish in the full light of day.

A door handle clicked.

Theo's eyes snapped round. Darkness fell on him like a pack of wolves and all the hideous thoughts flooded back. In the shadowy corner a door opened, not the basement door but the caretaker's flat. A head emerged from the doorway, and Theo's heart froze.

The head was gaunt and emaciated. Skin hung in wrinkly folds from the skull like one of those Japanese puppies, and the eyes were sunken hollows. It was Mick McCracken, but it wasn't the Mick McCracken Theo knew and feared. The intimidating bulk was gone, replaced by a scarecrow bag of bones with all the menace of Wurzel Gummidge.

The eyes were the same though. If the eyes were indeed the mirrors of the soul, then McCracken's still held all the mean spirited nastiness they had ever held. They shone with a cruel intensity that was at once intimidating and reassuring. *No matter how much things change they always stay the same.* Whoever had said that hit the nail right on the head.

And yet...

The straggly figure didn't come out of the doorway, merely hanging back in the shadows of the part opened door. A bony hand leaned on the doorjamb for support, drawing Theo's attention to something else that made the small hairs at the back of his neck stand on end.

A smear of blood was just visible in the light from the bulb in the lobby. Not a little smear either, a great big daub of red paint from a double sized decorating brush. The blood had dried to a deep red black, having run down the doorframe in ragged trickles. On the floor, dark red splats dotted the concrete.

Theo waited for the barbed comment, but as in the cellar none came. Those dead eyes simply watched from beneath hooded lids, then the hand withdrew and the door closed. It was cold in the entrance hall, but Theo was sweating. The cold hard stare unnerved him, not so much because of its apparent lack of humanity - which Theo had long suspected - but because of something that hadn't been there before.

Fear.

What's frightened him so much that he's stopped eating, and wasted away so much in such a short time? Theo cringed at the thought. Close on its heels came another one. *If it's frightened him, should it worry the rest of us?* The answer to that one must surely be yes. If something round The Towers had put the wind up Mick McCracken, just imagine what it could do to the herd of geriatrics spread through the other seven floors. A cloud of doubt settled briefly then was gone. Although there was never much activity in the corridors of The Towers, today there was no movement at all. The thought was there for a second then... poof, gone.

The doors beckoned. Theo had never been so grateful of the chance to get out into the real world for a few hours. When he pulled open the nearest door, fresh air hit him like a tidal wave. It almost knocked him over. Pure sweet unpolluted air.

He glided down the three stairs like Gene Kelly, and forged his way through the industrial wasteland towards Carl Stensel's barbershop, a sense of freedom swelling his chest.

In the Land of the Blind, the One-Eyed man is King," Carl Stensel said in way of explanation, pausing briefly in mid snip. Theo looked at the old barber's reflection in the mirror, uncomprehending. *What on earth was the old fart talking about? Who are you calling an old fart?* He thought. *You're no spring chicken yourself.* That thought brought the answer into focus. "In the land of old farts, the slightly less old fart is King."

"That's a bit deep for Christmas Eve," Theo said, but his mind was on the newspaper headline on Carl Stensel's table, and the daub of dried blood outside Mick McCracken's flat. He glanced at the folded paper's message.
FOURTH DERELICT FOUND DEAD

Even the headline struck a chill in Theo's bones. The headline, and the story that went with it. That, married to Mick McCracken's worrying glance as Theo had come out this morning, was sending his mind down a dark passage tinged with madness. He followed it, as the gentle snip snip snip of Carl Stensel's scissors sounded in his ears.

The walk from The Towers proved more difficult than Theo expected. He felt as if a magnet was drawing him back. All around him the scars of demolished factories snagged at his peripheral vision like blackened trees in some enchanted forest. Twisted metal and dusty piles of bricks formed a battleground of good and evil, and by the looks of things, evil was winning hands down.

Theo forged a path through the Black Witch's kingdom, and all the time the hunched black silhouette of Darkwater Towers followed his progress. He tried not to look back, but couldn't help it. One fearful glance was all it took.

It's watching me. Waiting for me to return. And the monster that took Melinda is waiting there for me. That association shook him. He quickly turned away, his eyes seeking out the refuge of the red and green Gents Hairdressers sign. It was round the corner out of sight.

Come on; pull yourself together, Theo told himself. *It's the letter. Ever since that, I've been as jumpy as a kangaroo on speed. Maybe Delia was right. Maybe I am over-reacting.* He tried to tell himself that, but it wouldn't wash. The dark sightless monster that walked the corridors of his body was hungry. It was feeding off him, and soon would whittle him down to nothing. The weight loss might not be as dramatic as with Melinda - she had only weighed five stone when she'd died - but already Theo noticed a slackness in his clothes and a sagginess to his flesh.

It's eating me alive.

That it was, but something else was at work back in Darkwater Towers. Something just as hungry as Theo's personal monster. It was eating the heart out of the place, and whittling away at the pocket of humanity that dwelled there. Eating away at...

Theo saw the cadaverous face of Mick McCracken in the doorway. A skull with flesh. What was wrong with him? It had to be some kind of terrible disease. A disease, which had infected him in the last two weeks, attacking his immune system and playing havoc with his body. If that was the case then maybe it had spread further. Spread through the other residents. That would explain why it was so quiet in the hallways and byways. Even Charlie Brewer had been absent without leave this morning, the little boxer missing his morning constitutional in the elevator.

Another glance over his shoulder showed the black square of Darkwater Towers receding in the distance. Theo turned the corner and it disappeared from view. A sense of relief washed over him.

Not far now.

Another hundred yards and he would be inside the warm cocoon of Carl Stensel's barbershop. He saw the barber's pole twirling slowly in the distance and picked up his pace.

While Theo was approaching Carl Stensel's barbershop, Mick McCracken was approaching Delia's apartment door. The once proud and swollen body of the caretaker - the product of years of over eating and, more importantly, over-drinking - was only a shadow of its former self. It was shrunken and prune like, and the flesh had ragged tears along the fault lines where stretch marks had been pushed to the limit. Blood seeped through the rents.

He vaguely remembered the influx of new life in the cellar, and his body ached for the bloated, full up, feeling it had experienced for a short time after. It wasn't full up now though. Now his body was running on empty, but it wasn't running under his control. Mick McCracken wasn't the captain of his ship any more, hadn't been for quite a while, and the new captain had been busy.

Blood drops splatted on the concrete, leaving a speckled trail from the elevator to the old crone's flat door. He looked down, seeing his body falling apart but not caring. He paused outside the apartment door and his head cocked to one side. For a brief moment his mind was fully there again, and he was appalled at the terrible things he had done. Even for an eighteen-stone bully with little thought for his fellow man, the things his body had done under direction of the new landlord were truly horrifying. If he hadn't been such a heartless bastard in the first place this moment of pause might have driven him mad.

Then the moment passed, and his hand rose to knock on the door. All he knew now was there was someone in this flat he needed. He let the knuckles rap on the door, leaving bloody red splodges on the paintwork, and waited for a reply.

The red and green sign welcomed Theo.
GENTS HAIRDRESSER the letters read. "COME IN AND TAKE A LOAD OFF" is what it said to Theo. Warmth enveloped him the moment he stepped inside the happy outpost. Carl stopped in mid snip and nodded towards one of the three chairs against the wall. For only the fourth time in living memory, Theo wasn't the only customer.

"You've caught me at rush hour," the old barber joked. "The paper is on the table if you don't mind waiting."

"Not at all," Theo said, shrugging out of his overcoat. He hung it on the rack in the corner and topped it off with his hat. The fur bristled with static, making Theo's fingers tingle. *What have I got to rush back for anyway?* He told himself. *Only fear and confusion.*

He felt a pang of guilt as he thought of Delia. *Of course. He shouldn't overlook her and hoped his clumsiness this morning hadn't spoiled things. He didn't think it would.* A little glow of hope sprung up in his stomach. *When I get back I'll definitely pop the question. Perhaps not the question most young lovers asked, but one along those lines.* The glow spread, and a contented smile crept over his lips.

He picked up the Northern Gazette and shook the pages straight. A shard of ice pricked his good humour and lanced into his chest.
"FOURTH DERELICT FOUND DEAD" the headline blared.

"Emaciated corpse discovered on waste land," a by-line read. There was a grainy black and white photograph of a Scenes of Crime officer examining the scene, which was cordoned off with lengths of striped police tape. A tarpaulin was draped over a section of rubble and the skyline was silhouetted against dull grey clouds.

The shard of ice twisted in Theo's chest again and then stabbed his stomach. He squinted at the photograph, shocked by its familiarity. Not the policeman, or the tarpaulin, or the lengths of scene tape. It was the skyline that leapt off the page and grabbed him by the throat.

Mounds of bricks and concrete bulked around the rusting track of the railroad yards, twisted girders pointing skywards in jagged crosses, like tank traps on the Normandy beaches. And behind it all, the sightless monolith of Darkwater Towers jutted black and horrible out of the desolation. Theo felt short of breath and took a deep gulp of air. His hands trembled as he held the paper, and he had to force them to be still. With an effort he calmed his racing pulse, and read.

"The body of a man was found among the debris of North Eastern Railway's former stockyards yesterday. The corpse was emaciated, and had suffered injuries to the throat. Enquiries are being made to identify the man, believed to be in his early forties, who had been sleeping rough in the derelict storage sheds. The cause of death will be determined by a post mortem examination later today.

"This is the fourth similar death in as many weeks, cutting a path through the transient society that scrapes a meagre living in and around the run down areas of the city. The first was discovered ten miles away on the southeast corner of town. That man, known only as 'Batty', was also emaciated and had severe throat and neck injuries.

"In the following weeks two more homeless men were found murdered, one on the former Rover Car Dealership site, the other in the now demolished Diamond Seal double-glazing factory. This fourth incident has prompted a full-scale police hunt, and they feel that someone is targeting the homeless in these apparently motiveless killings."

Theo rifled through the paper trying to find the rest of the story. Carl chatted to the man in the chair, his voice a dull metronomic drone in the back of Theo's mind. Scissors snip snipped constantly. After a few moments he found the conclusion at the bottom of page five, tucked away between a report on the forthcoming Christmas Mass at St Barnaby's Church, and the social column. He read on.

"Police are asking for anyone who has any information to contact them on 0800 6060504. Calls are free and will be treated in the strictest confidence. Shelter is being offered to the homeless at Central House Social Services."

And that was it. Theo closed the paper and dropped it on the table, wondering briefly what had prompted the Northern Gazette to stick those last four lines on page five when, with a little effort, they could have fitted them on the first page. Then another thought struck him concerning the locations where the bodies were found.

The Rover Car Dealership.
The Diamond Seal double-glazing factory.
The derelict rail yards.

The report didn't say where the first body had been found other than it was the south east of the town, but the other three locations were familiar to him. He studied a mental map of the town, sticking imaginary flags in each spot. They described a ragged line north, skirting the edge of town. If you stuck an arrowhead on the top it would be pointing directly at Darkwater Towers.

A face poked out of the mists of his memory. A haggard, cadaverous, face staring out of the shadows. Mick McCracken. The flesh hung off his face like wattles on a turkey, and the eyes were sunken piss holes in the snow. An emaciated face, which had its geographical location just ahead of the tip of the arrow. Theo shivered, a dark oppressive thought forming in his mind. A shadow flitted in front of him, and then the door slammed. He jumped half out of his skin.

"We're a little jumpy today aren't we?" Carl asked.

Theo looked up. The other man had just left, pulling the collar up round his ears as he passed the shop window. Carl Stensel stood before him, scissors in hand. "I promise not to lop off any more of your ear today," he said, evidently recovered from the embarrassment he felt two weeks ago.

"That's good to know," Theo replied, pulling himself together. "Because I can only hear out of one of them now." He stood up, smoothing down his clothes, and went over to the barber's chair.

The knock on the door made Delia jump. In the hours since Theo had left she had busied herself with preparing the meat for tomorrow's Christmas dinner. It was cooked and wrapped and stored carefully in a large covered Pyrex dish ready for warming tomorrow. She didn't think she would be able to eat it though. Her appetite had deserted her over the last hour or so.

It was the noises again. The ones she had attributed to her dreams - her nightmares - during the long sleepless nights of the last few weeks. The banging and the smashing, and the plaintive cries in the dark. Soul wrenching cries of such utter despair that they tore at her heart.

Now there was the knock on her door and she feared that whatever had been happening in the apartments below was going to happen to her. She wished she hadn't been so harsh with Theo that morning, and for a brief moment thought it might be him coming back to start again. She knew what he had been trying to ask her - what woman wouldn't? It was a trait that all women shared, the knowledge of what their men were thinking, and it was frighteningly accurate. She knew, but had said nothing, simply letting him bumble on embarrassingly. She wished she hadn't.

The knock again, heavier this time. No, that wasn't Theo's knock. His had a kind of rhythm to it, a sort of musical tone. Friendly. Not like this one. This one was angry, dark, and malevolent.

Delia went to the door, drawn against her will by that other trait of womankind, curiosity. She looked through the spy hole, then stepped back in shock. A single, bloody, eyeball stared back at her, barely recognizable as the caretaker she had known for so many years.

She retreated into the room, fear crawling up her throat like bile from a bad hiccup. The neatly ordered flat seemed small and vulnerable. In all the years she had lived here, all the time she had lived anywhere, her home had always felt like her castle. This was the place where she could retreat from the slings and arrows of outrageous fortune, the place to feel safe, but she didn't feel safe now. She stood in the middle of the room, in front of the settee where she had shared hot chocolate with Theo, and trembled.

The door banged again. Not a knock this time, an attack. With a sickening feeling of the inevitable, she noticed she hadn't put the chain or the bolts on after Theo had left, and watched helplessly as the lock began to splinter.

In the age-old tradition of the corner barber shop, Theo sat patiently in the hot seat for half an hour while Carl snipped away, even though there was barely enough hair to warrant cutting at all. Theo reckoned that, when it came to it, the old school of hairdressing - not those poncey unisex places - the shortness of your haircut was directly related to the length of story the barber was telling at the time.

Carl Stensel could tell a very long story.

Even now he hadn't quite finished, so he fussed around the edges of Theo's hairline, snipping off an errant strand here, or thinning a tuft of hair there. Theo watched in the mirror.

"You really shouldn't be there," Carl said, returning to his favourite subject, the unsuitability of Darkwater Towers as any kind of human habitation. "None of them should. But you my friend, you're simply too young to be consigned to the scrap heap."

Theo nodded patiently, nearly losing another piece of ear in the process. He'd heard all this before, but now there was an extra sense of poignancy to the old barber's concerns. *No need to worry about me, old friend. Another five months and I'll just be a footnote in the resident's book. So it doesn't matter what kind of rat hole The Towers has become.* He couldn't tell him that of course. That was too personal. Too sensitive.

"You should carry that woman off, and start a new life together."

Snip, snip.

"I may be a supreme physical specimen and a marvel of modern science," Theo replied. "Hair excepted. But even I'm not up to carrying Delia down five flights of stairs and off into the sunset."

"I was only talking metaphorically."

"Use the elevator."

"And there is nothing wrong with your follicles," Carl teased. "There just aren't enough of them."

"Then what have you been doing for the last half hour?"

"Tidying the ones you have left."

Snip, snip. Carl trimmed a few more. "How is the dear lady?" No humour this time. He was well aware of how bad her arthritis had become.

"Her spirits are up," Theo lied. He remembered the sharp tone of voice as he'd left this morning, and the unasked question he was having trouble getting out.

"Is she looking forward to Christmas?"

"Yes."

Snip, snip.

"You must be king of the hill over there."

"I beg your pardon?" The barber was getting a bit oblique for Theo.

"In the Land of the Blind, the One-Eyed man is King," Carl said by way of explanation, pausing briefly in mid snip. Theo looked at the old barber's reflection in the mirror, uncomprehending. *What on earth was the old fart talking about? Who are you calling an old fart?* He thought. *You're no spring chicken yourself.* That thought brought the answer into focus. "In the land of old farts, the slightly less old fart is King." He said to himself.

"That's a bit deep for Christmas Eve," Theo muttered, his mind on the newspaper headline behind him, and the smear of dried blood outside Mick McCracken's flat. A dark pattern was emerging, and Theo wasn't sure if his own depression wasn't responsible.

There was an uncomfortable pause. Theo sensed an awkward question coming. The headline stared at him in reverse through the mirror.

FOURTH DERELICT FOUND DEAD

"You have seen the paper?" Carl's voice was a whisper.

"H'hm." The hairs - what was left of them - on the back of Theo's neck bristled. Something bad was coming.

"The bodies that have been found?"

"I saw that. Yes." Theo held his breath.

"And have you noticed the significance of where they were found?"

"Carl, what on earth are you trying to do. Spook me on the night before Christmas?" Theo tried to hide the fact that Carl had done just that. *Spooked him,* he told himself. No, let's be honest. Coupled with his own dark thoughts, the demon barber was putting the shits up him.

"The sequence and location of the discoveries," Carl continued, ignoring Theo's interruption, "describe a rough line, ending over there." He gestured out of the front window in the direction of the old railway yards.

Emaciated corpses...

Mick McCracken's gaunt features flashed into Theo's mind.

The Rover car dealership.
The Diamond Seal double-glazing factory.
The derelict rail yards.

"Darkwater Towers is over there as well," Carl said.

"I know where it is," Theo snapped. "I've lived there long enough."

The scissors were silent. "Then perhaps it is time you moved on." Concern showed on the barber's face. Concern for a good customer and a friend. "I have travelled the world three times over. The merchant navy took me to many places, and showed me many things. Some nice. Some not so nice." Carl nodded towards the shrunken head beside the mirror, and told Theo about Kuta Lametka and the village in the South Pacific.

The door shuddered, and the wood around the lock began to split. Delia stood, helpless, in front of the fireplace as she watched the pounding attack on the door.

One thud...

The lock shook in its housing.

Two thuds...

The frame splintered and groaned.

Three thuds...

The door banged inwards an inch, but the frame held.

Four...

The spell was broken. Delia turned and fled into the kitchen. Her heart pounded in her chest and her breath was shallow and rapid. She felt faint, light headed, but by taking action she at least felt alive. More banging sounded from the living room as she opened the pantry door. She paused briefly, considering the double bluff of leaving the pantry door open while hiding on the balcony, and then discarded the idea. To be honest she didn't think hiding anywhere would be any use, but instinct was taking over, and instinct dictated putting off the inevitable for as long as possible.

She looked into the cramped space of the pantry. Broad wooden shelves, stocked with every conceivable dry goods from Heinz soups to Mrs Brown's Yorkshire pudding mix, took up the top half of the larder. There were bottles of Heinz tomato ketchup, Hammonds brown sauce, and dozens of packets of Tetley's tea bags.

It was the bottom half she was interested in. A twenty-pound sack of potatoes leaned against the left side, and half a dozen family packs of Kellogg's Corn Flakes stood on the right. A stack of catering sized marrowfat peas stood next to them.

The dark hollow looked deep and threatening. Childhood memories flooded back. Memories of the den she and her friends had made in the hollowed out tree on the edge of the woods near her home. More importantly, memories of the day she had been trapped in there on her own when the overhanging branch had collapsed across the door. Darkness had taken away her most treasured senses and her imagination had filled the cavity with all manner of demons. When the spider crawled over her leg in the blackness she had screamed hysterically until her father had yanked the dead branch away, flooding the den with light and banishing the monsters of her mind.

Now the pantry took on all the menace of that hollow tree. Try as she might, she couldn't go in there.

A splintering crash from the front door forced her hand. She pushed aside the packets of corn flakes and squeezed in behind them, rebuilding the barrier in front of her.

She re-arranged the tins of peas to form a wall between the corn flakes and the sack of potatoes.

In the lounge, the settee was upended with a crash.

The last tin was in place. Delia reached out carefully and hooked the door closed. It wouldn't close all the way. She leaned forward; trying to get her fingers round the edge and nearly knocked a tin of peas over. Her hands were shaking. All around her the roots of the old tree closed in. The spider waited in her mind to crawl up her legs.

She heard her treasured sideboard smash like so much matchwood, and braced herself. The sounds of rage subsided and there was silence. She pushed back against the wall, trying to curl herself up into a ball. The darkness hugged her, just the chink of light from the crack in the door taking the edge off the blackness.

The silence was oppressive.

Where is he?

Seconds stretched into minutes, and there was no sound. No telltale rustles of the carpet to give away his position.

Has he gone? Oh please God say he's gone.

Silence. Hope built up in her, slowly at first, then with gathering momentum. *He's gone. Praise the Lord.* She reached forward, uncurling slightly, and stretched her hand towards the sliver of light. Her fingers flexed as they neared the edge of the door, and...

Suddenly the light was blocked out. The hulking figure of the caretaker stood in front of the pantry door and Delia shrunk back into the dark world of the tree den. The dead branch had fallen and now she was trapped. She waited for the sickly touch of the spider's legs and tried to force back the scream that was building in her throat.

The blackout seemed to last forever, Mick McCracken standing like a statue in front of the pantry, and just when she thought he would turn away and leave the kitchen, the door was wrenched open.

"...and when the head was shrunk whatever evil was contained in it was sealed forever," Carl finished.

There was a long silence, the scissors forgotten. Theo spoke first. "And that's the head?"

"Yes. But that is not why I told you."

Theo waited for the kicker.

"Before we went into the village I had a terrible feeling of dread. I knew something bad was going to happen, but I didn't know what. Ever since then I have had dark feelings occasionally – once, just before the fire that took the other blocks of flats - but have never acted on them. For the most part I haven't known what they meant. Even now I don't know. But Theo, if there is one thing I do know it is that The Towers' time has come. No shrunken heads, no voodoo, just badness. It is there now. Take Delia and leave."

Theo felt numb. On any other occasion he would have passed it off as the ramblings of an overactive imagination. Another tall tale from the master of tall tales. But hadn't he sensed something dark happening himself? Ever since the letter hadn't he entertained similar thoughts? Thoughts of a dark monster stalking him, the monster that had taken Melinda.

Cancer.

Perhaps Carl sensed that. Maybe he was misinterpreting the feelings he was getting. This was nothing to do with demons or shrunken heads. This was simply the shadow of death which was hanging over Theo, and which would take him in five short months. Yes, that was it.

Mick McCracken...

Gimlet eyes stared out of the cadaverous features. Frightened eyes of a man who only ever looked at Theo with undisguised contempt.

The Rover car dealership.
The Diamond Seal double-glazing factory.
The derelict rail yards.
Darkwater Towers.

Suddenly everything Carl was suggesting seemed all too feasible. The noises in the night took on a whole new perspective. The silence that pervaded the corridors during the day now seemed deep and meaningful.

"Go home and get her now," Carl said.

Theo could think of nothing to say. He stood up, shrugging off the protective cloth. The quaint 'oldie worldliness' of the barbershop felt like a de-pressurisation chamber, his head full to bursting with dreadful visions. From the shelves, bottles of Vitalis and tubs of Brylcreem stared back from a bygone age. Red tipped Styptic Pencils completed the picture, along with a card of plastic combs.

Bug rakes, Theo corrected, taking his mind off the awful picture Carl Stensel had painted. He felt that if he stayed here, in this time capsule from better times, then none of it would be true. That he would be safe cocooned here among the hair care products of his generation.

For the next five months. Theo recognised the futility of that. Cancer was on the rampage, and it would take him in April no matter what. Outside the shop window, the sky was getting dark. Glowering clouds were filtering the light out of the day, just as Carl's words had filtered the light out of his day. It was mid afternoon but it was already clear that night would come early.

Christmas Eve.

Theo didn't think he'd ever felt less festive. For the first time since he'd come in here today he noticed the soft jingle of Yuletide tunes from Carl's wireless. Andy Williams rendered his version of White Christmas. The red and green Gents Hairdresser sign brought visions of Santa Claus and

Christmas trees. The candy striped barbershop pole twirled lazily on the wall outside.

Theo's stomach twirled as well. He felt sick and dizzy, and for a moment thought he'd have to sit down again. Carl Stensel's stern look snapped him out of it.

"Go now," he said.

Without thinking, Theo reached into his pocket for the change for his haircut. Even in the midst of this nightmare, old habits died hard. If he was indeed the One-Eyed Man, and that man was King, then this King was abroad from his subjects, and still expected to pay his way.

Carl waved the money away. "Go, my friend."

Theo put his coat on, and crammed the hat on his freshly shorn head. His fingers fumbled with the buttons of the coat, unable to guide them into the holes. Carl stepped forward and fastened them, like a doting father helping his son get ready for school. It would have looked ridiculous under any other circumstances.

No more words were exchanged. Theo opened the door and hovered on the step. He glanced over his shoulder and was suddenly certain he would never see the Polish barber again. He stepped outside, closed the door behind him, and turned left towards Darkwater Towers.

PART TWO

THE ONE-EYED MAN

Here I am, an old man in a dry month...

- T S Elliot

Old men are dangerous: it doesn't matter to
Them what is going to happen to the world.

- George Bernard Shaw

CHAPTER 1

Theo could smell corruption even before he reached the concrete steps at the front of The Towers. It was the cloying, sickly sweet smell of decaying vegetables, thick and heavy and all pervading. If he'd thought the smell in Delia's corridor was bad, then this was ten times worse.

Something really bad had settled into Darkwater Towers. Something bad and dead and rancid. It was like the aftermath of a visit from Rentokil when months later the handful of mice which had plagued you had died and gone to mouse heaven, leaving their rotting corpses behind to remind you. He wondered how many rotting corpses were hiding in The Towers.

The shadowy landscape which had featured in the Northern Gazette, stood out against the overcast sky, the squat toad-like bulk of The Towers hunkering down over it all. Amongst the wreckage of the industrial wasteland it looked like the silhouette of The Alamo, a decaying fortress against the tyranny of men.

What was it a fortress against now?

As Theo approached, he saw the twinkling lights of Delia's Christmas tree through her window. The sight spurred him on. From a window on the first floor a strand of tinsel fluttered in the breeze, and across the top of the lobby doors a decorative banner bade all who entered a Merry Christmas.

Theo paused briefly on the front steps, then took them two at a time.

His back complained but he ignored it. He had only one thought, get to Delia as quickly as possible, and with that in mind he shoved open the door and barged through.

The lobby was empty.

Theo kept to the right, avoiding the shadowy corner where the caretaker's door was thankfully closed. He felt ashamed of his fear of the burly caretaker. *Not so burly now* he reminded himself. In his prime, Theo would have taken McCracken easily and sometimes it was hard to accept the erosion time had inflicted on his body. He kept fit by walking twice a week and he was as active around The Towers as the confines of the block of flats allowed but he couldn't pretend that his muscles were as strong or his stamina as endless as it had once been.

When he and Melinda had lived on the edge of the council estate, he always went out for the bus at the last minute, forcing himself to sprint the fifty yards to the end of the street and the bus stop. He prided himself on being able to put on a fair turn of speed, even at forty-five - but those days were long gone. Melinda had thought it silly anyway.

A click and a bang from the corner startled him. He froze, waiting for the door to the flat or the boiler room to open. His hands shook. The smell of his own sweat - his own fear - disgusted him. He waited.

Silence. Neither door opened, and Theo breathed a sigh of relief. He sidled further to the right, getting as near to the wall as he could. He felt like a chameleon, changing colour to blend in with his surroundings.

When he got across the killing ground of the entrance lobby, he quickly stepped up to the elevator doors and reached for the buttons. He stopped at the last moment. *What if McCracken's on one of the other floors when I call the lift? Worse still, what if he's in the lift when it arrives?* Theo saw the lift doors open, and Mick McCracken step down from the carriage shovel in hand. "I'm gonna squish me some rat."

He lowered his hand and stepped back. Discretion being the better part of valour, he turned to the stairs. It was six floors to Delia's flat, but Theo decided he didn't want to advertise his movement. The stench was like a solid wall around him and he could feel it settling on his clothes and face. He set off up the steps, trying not to suck in too much breath.

By the time he reached the sixth floor landing, looking down the central cavity occasionally to make sure the ailing caretaker wasn't shadowing him, Theo knew there was something badly wrong. He had paused on each floor and cast a wary glance along the corridor from the lift doors.

On three of the floors there had been blood. Not the darkly threatening smear he'd seen on the door jamb outside Mick McCracken's flat, but thick fresh blood. Several of the flat doors were open.

The sight panicked him. What had seemed a fanciful tale, painted by his own depression, now had all the solid bulk of reality. Just what was happening he had no idea, but something was, that was for certain. He prayed he wouldn't meet anyone in the corridors or he thought he might scream out. That total ignominy would be too much, the final humiliation of a once proud man.

He didn't meet anyone. The corridors and stairwell were empty. Quiet as a ghost. Even the tick and crackle of the ventilation system, and the settling noises of the building itself, had deserted him. It made travelling through the corridors even harder, robbing them of their normal ambient sounds like a spectre stealing your soul.

The place was as quiet as the grave.

Theo paused at the newel post and listened for the lift. There was still no movement and he began to feel foolish for not using it himself. His embarrassment vanished when he looked along the corridor to Delia's apartment.

The grey concrete wall was brightened by a flash of red, a broad swipe which trailed wet paint runs to the floor. The floor itself was smeared with a trail of fresh blood leading to the lift doors.

Avoiding stepping in it Theo made his way along the corridor then turned the corner to Delia's flat.

The door was closed. Theo breathed a sigh of relief, beginning to think Delia might have been spared the ravages of the other apartments he'd seen on the way up.

The relief was short-lived.

A bloody handprint stood out on the pristine paintwork, trailing threads of red down to the welcome mat. Theo sucked in his breath and immediately wished he hadn't. The gangrenous smell was like a physical presence. It slid down his throat, thick and snot-like. He retched.

With the toe of his shoe, Theo nudged the door open. To his dismay he noticed the splintered wood of the doorframe. As the door swung inwards light from the window picked out the handprint on the door. It resembled a child's potato stencil hastily adapted as a Christmas decoration. A splayed hand, fingers apart.

It's too big, Theo realised. *Thank God. It's too big to be Delia's.* The fear, which had crawled into Theo's throat, subsided slightly. The sight of that bloody hand had signalled the worst. He had been certain that she was dead. Dragged screaming from her flat while she struggled to resist, splatting one bloodied hand against the door in a final effort to hold on.

But it wasn't her hand. Hope flooded in, but he tried not to raise his hopes too high. The door had been forced. He pushed it all the way open and glanced cautiously inside.

Wind found a gap in the metal window frames and whistled dolefully, making the decorations above the fireplace sway gently, and tickling the tinsel on the tree. The tree lights flashed on and off, painting the corner first red then green then red again. Theo was reminded of the red and green sign in Carl Stensel's window – GENTS HAIRDRESSER

He half expected to see the candy striped barber's pole twirling on the wall.

The carnage brought him back to reality. *Oh Delia*, he thought. *Your pretty apartment.* Theo stood in the centre of the room and sighed a deep sorrowful sigh. The flat was a mess. It looked as if a whirlwind had struck it. The settee was upended against the balcony window, its cushions strewn over the floor. The coffee table was smashed in the fireplace and the mahogany sideboard - Delia's pride and joy - was a tangle of matchwood. The radio was on its side beside the Christmas tree, hissing static, but the tree itself had miraculously survived.

Theo went over and turned the radio off. He noticed more blood on the fireside rug, and a ragged smear on the kitchen doorframe. The wind moaned in the windows and the cool breeze touched his cheek. It felt like he'd been touched by the icy fingers of death and he rubbed at his neck with a gloved hand.

The wind moaned louder, raising goose flesh on the back of his neck. He felt the short hairs stand on end. Two hanging decorations in the centre of the room twirled in the breeze. This was all too much to take. He looked at the wreckage of the coffee table in the fireplace, and noticed the shattered remains of the mugs he and Delia had drunk out of earlier. Suddenly all the strength flowed out of him. He felt tired, and weak, and alone. For only the second time since Melinda had died he felt like giving up.

A whispering moan, almost a sob, filtered through the windows. He turned towards it, then realised that the wind had dropped momentarily. The hanging decorations were motionless, the tinsel strands still.

Again the moan, but not from the windows.

Theo spun towards the kitchen. This wasn't the wind, it was...

"Delia?" He could barely allow himself to believe...

"Delia? Is that you?" The moaning stopped, replaced by a clattering of metal. Theo lunged into the kitchen in time to see the pantry door swing open. A can of Heinz tomato soup rolled across the linoleum floor followed by two more as a huddled figure crawled out of the bottom of the pantry.

It was Delia, and she was white as a sheet.

Thank God. Theo went over and helped her up. She swayed unsteadily, falling against him. He put an arm round her shoulders and guided her into the living room where the chair he'd been sitting in with his hot chocolate was still upright. He lowered her gently into it and went to the airing cupboard for a blanket. Once he'd draped it round her shoulders she found her voice. "Theo," was all she said. "Theo." A bony hand reached out for his.

"It's all right," he said, crouching beside the chair. He supposed it was the most ludicrous thing to say, considering the state of the room, but it seemed to do the trick. Delia's panicked stare calmed down, and he took her hand, patting it gently. She squeezed back, and then said something that took him completely by surprise. "Of course I will marry you. I will be honoured."

The reply to his unasked question from this morning jerked a tear into his eye, and he squeezed tighter. "Good," he said, then leaned forward and kissed her on the forehead.

After a few moments, when colour returned to her face, she told him what had happened.

"When I looked through the spy hole it was Mick McCracken." Delia's voice trembled at the mention of him. They were sitting at the fold-down table in the kitchen, Delia warming her hands around a mug of hot chocolate. It was half past six, and night had fanned its cape over the candle of day, extinguishing it. Through the windows of Delia's apartment there was nothing but dark. Light from the open fridge door was all Theo would allow, spilling over the table like a sea fret but hemmed in by the closed kitchen door.

Theo's first thought had been to get Delia out of the flat straight away but it didn't take long to realise that she wasn't fit for travelling just yet. He considered going down to his apartment while she recovered, then decided against the idea. After all, McCracken had already been here and left, and could be anywhere in The Towers searching for prey. No, best stay until she was strong enough to travel, then head straight for the front doors.

With the kitchen door closed, and making as little noise as possible, Theo had calmed Delia down, first re-arranging the blanket around her shoulders after moving into the kitchen, then making the traditional hot drink. There was no Galaxy Fruit and Nut this time however. Neither had any appetite.

After a few sips she continued. "I barely recognised him," she said. "His face was shrivelled, and his eyes were weeping blood."

The refrigerator switched off with a shudder that made them both jump. Wind whistled through the ill-fitting window next to the cooker.

"He started bashing at the door so I hid in the pantry." She was being brief to the point of circumspection, but Theo read between the lines. He saw the fear in her eyes and didn't need to know more.

"After it had gone quiet I thought he had left, then he opened the pantry door, and I thought he would see me." Her voice quivered close to tears, so Theo put a reassuring arm round her shoulders. When he looked into her eyes he realised she wasn't crying for herself.

"It's all right," he said. "Get it out of your system."

"It was Uriah."

Theo was confused. "What was?"

Delia took a deep breath to calm her tears. "Uriah came to the front door. I think he was bringing another scarf. I heard his voice, then McCracken was gone. I had my eyes closed so I didn't realise until I heard..." This time she did begin to cry. Theo gave her a length of kitchen roll, and waited.

"McCracken must have been restricted because I heard him shuffling out of the living room. It was a slimy, sickly noise, and when he called to Uriah his voice was breaking, gurgling, as if his vocal chords were rotting. I couldn't move. I was too frightened. When you came in, I thought he had come back. Until you called..."

The tears came again, and Theo held her tight. "That's it, let the tears come - get them out of your system." To his own ears, the words sounded puerile and inadequate, but Delia calmed down and looked into his eyes. "I meant what I said you know?"

"Well, you'd better wait until you're asked," he joked. Then kissed her forehead again. "Come on. It's time we got out of here." He helped her up then cautiously opened the door.

The living room was a sea of shadows, dotted with islands of greater dark. He guided her through the wreckage of her home towards the open door. Cold grey light filtered in from the corridor, glittering off the blood trail on the floor. He waited in the doorway; listening for any sound that might indicate the caretaker was coming back.

Silence. Except for the moaning wind.

Theo prepared to step out into the corridor when a touch of déjà vu hit him. A previous trip to the lobby popped into his head, and a conversation with another resident of Darkwater Towers.

Charlie Brewer had told him about a noise in the cellar. The possibility of big bad Mick McCracken coming a cropper in the boiler room had amused them both, but the Good Samaritan in Theo had reared its ugly head. He had no choice but to go down there and check he was all right, even though he didn't want to.

Now Uriah Lovelycolors' safety had been called into question, and before Theo set off for the front doors of The Towers and escape, he knew he would have to check on him first.

With a sinking heart he edged along the corridor towards the stairs.

CHAPTER 2

Uriah Lovelycolors lived on the floor below Delia's and three doors along from Theo's, so it wasn't exactly a major detour for them to call in there on the way out.

The old man was eighty-five - and looked every day of it. He had been the first resident of the newly formed retirement home at Darkwater Towers. He had chosen apartment fourteen because that was the age he'd started work, something he had always been keen on. Work was more than a means of earning money to Uriah, it was an end in itself and the worst thing that ever happened to him was retiring. After fifty-two years of labour in the clothing trade, first as a tea boy and finally as Section Head at Park Clothing Company Limited, suddenly finding himself with nothing to do had been like a cold shower. A shock to the system.

Like most of the other residents, a severe shortage of capital and a lack of concerned relatives forced him into that old people's home from Hell, but despite that handicap he had always kept himself busy. If he hadn't he might as well have turned in his shield and checked out early. The eccentric's mind may well have wandered extravagantly over the past few years but it was knitting which saw him through the melancholy that gripped him like an iron fist.

And it was knitting that had almost saved his life. Theo reasoned when stepped through the old man's door.

It was nearly eight o'clock, and night had already sucked the heart out of the block of flats. The corridors, which had never been exactly busy, were now inhabited by spectral shadows as black and impenetrable as the heart of the demon. A heavy pungent stench hung in the air reminding Theo of hot summer days at the bottom of town when the smell from the abattoir hung over the streets like a warm blanket.

The journey to Uriah's apartment took twenty minutes, Delia hanging onto Theo's arm with all the tenacity of a Titanic survivor's grip on the last lifeboat. They were inseparable. In the course of the journey he felt he'd known her a lifetime. Now that the question had been answered, even before it was put, the prospect of sharing the future with her filled him with purpose. Despite the shortness of time left to him, he was determined to make the most of these last five months, but first they had to get out of The Towers.

Why don't I just take her out the front doors now? He asked himself. *Straight away. No detours.* All the way down here he'd put that question. And all the way down here he knew the answer. *I am what I am. I'm Popeye the sailor man.* Or in his case, *Theo the Good Samaritan man.* As much as he wanted to, he simply couldn't leave without checking on the old eccentric first. As they approached Uriah Lovelycolors' door he was certain he had wasted his time.

The trip might have taken Theo and Delia twenty minutes, but Uriah must have covered the distance much quicker. Adrenalin, that good old "fear flight or fight" drug the body could produce at will, must have given the old man speed he hadn't known he possessed. That, allied to McCracken's chronic condition, had kept him just in front of the game, allowing him time to get into his flat and lock the door.

It had made no difference.

The knitting, which was Uriah's life, had almost done the trick. A heavy knit scarf was tied round the door handle, its red and green wool recalling Carl Stensel's red and green 'Gents Hairdressers' sign and the festive colours of Santa Claus and Christmas trees.

The scarf was a futile effort. The door hadn't so much been smashed open as blown apart. Half of it hung forlornly from its hinges while the lock and handle section was still fastened by the scarf. Between the two was a gaping hole that couldn't have been more devastating if a cannon had been wheeled up and fired at it. Splinters of wood were everywhere. A faint smell of smoke fought to be recognised over the smell of putrefaction.

"Let's go," Delia pleaded, squeezing Theo's arm.

"In a minute," he said. "I just have to check."

"No, you don't." She was desperate now. "Please. Let's go."

For a moment he almost did as she asked, and later wished he had, but it wasn't in him to just up and go without seeing if the old man was alive or dead. *'I am what I am...'* Sometimes it was a curse.

Theo looked deep into Delia's eyes and saw the love he'd always hoped for reflected there. It wasn't the dewy-eyed look of the love-struck teenager but the knowing, considerate look of mature love. In that moment he realised how much he'd missed that in his life since Melinda died. The joy of waking up next to a woman you were completely at ease with, and totally committed to. He leaned forward and kissed her on the forehead.

"Yes I do." He held her face in his hands and gently massaged her temples with his thumbs. The motion calmed her slightly. He was going to tell her to wait here but that would have been totally redundant, so he simply turned away and stepped through the door.

The gloomy interior of the flat was even worse than Delia's. McCracken's whirlwind temper had unleashed a destructive force the likes of which Theo had never seen before.

Every piece of furniture was trashed, not just upended but destroyed. The two-seater settee and single chair of the cottage suite were just so much splintered timber, their traditional cushions ripped apart. Fluffy white stuffing and pre-shaped foam was scattered across the floor like fresh snow. Uriah's worktable and sewing machine were in the fireplace, the table resembling a cannon-swept foredeck on a ship of the line. It was peppered with holes and smashed beyond recognition. The sewing machine was a lump of twisted metal, dusted with plaster where it had hit the wall, chipping away the masonry. A bookcase with glass doors lay across the entrance to the kitchen, the glass gone, twinkling on the carpet like early morning frost, and the wood stripped of its veneer. More glass crunched beneath his feet, smashed from the pictures on the walls, and...

Theo realised the bulb had gone as well, the floral lampshade hanging from the ceiling, empty. What light there was came from the kitchen. It twinkled off the festive covering of broken glass and cushion filling, forming deep pools of black in the corners of the room. Light and dark. The sharp contrasts seemed almost film-noirish, and Theo's head spun back to those heady days of black and white. Humphrey Bogart walking the night in Casablanca. Boris Karloff lurching along the cobbled streets towards Dr Frankenstein's castle. And...

Everything in life wasn't black and white. Everything in Uriah Lovelycolors' apartment wasn't either. The light from the kitchen might well have picked out shards of brilliant white, and cast the blackest of shadows, but there was another colour as well.

Red.

He had seen it on the way down of course, the split splat trail of blood from Delia's apartment. He had even noticed the bloody handprints on the remains of the door, but all that faded into insignificance compared with the flood of colour before him now.

He tried to rationalise it, telling himself that the colour was highlighted in the glare of the kitchen's overhead. His feet felt like lead as he approached the kitchen.

Eight feet...

The fallen bookcase hid most of the floor.

Six feet...

The living room became a dark picture frame for the kitchen interior through the door.

Four feet...

Red. Bright gleaming red. The floor was awash with it. Not dark congealing red but bright, effervescent, life giving red.

Two feet...

Blood was everywhere. Theo felt faint at the sight of it. The smell of it too, so thick it formed a sharp metallic taste in his mouth. He stood for a full two minutes on the threshold of this hellish vision, then stepped over the bookcase.

Delia stood on the landing and wondered what was keeping him. Her back ached and her heart pumped a throbbing pulse into her temples - the beginning of a tension headache. She backed away from the door and leaned against the banister rail, steadying herself with a fragile hand.

Theo's crunching footfalls had stopped fifteen minutes ago, and she was torn between calling to him or going in after him. Fear clamped her throat shut. Not simply fear of what she might find, but fear of being heard by someone other than Theo.

Wind sighed around the stairwell, raising gooseflesh on her arms. She peered through the opening, noting the upturned furniture and the shredded cushions. In the back of her mind she replayed the sickly dragging of McCracken's footsteps through her apartment and she felt sick. She tried to shut her mind to the sound but she couldn't. Instead she overlaid it with the sound of Theo's silent proposal. Silent in voice but loud and clear in both their hearts. The thought should have cheered her, but it only strengthened her fear.

What is he doing? She agonized.

A window banged in the breeze, echoing through the stairwell, and Delia felt a stab of panic shoot up her throat. She was rooted to the spot. Welded to the banister. The wind grew stronger, battering the northwest corner of The Towers, and she felt cold and lonely, and vulnerable.

Somewhere in the distance she heard the lift begin to move.

Uriah Lovelycolors was lying round the corner in the kitchen. He was broken practically in two, his throat shredded by vicious cuts... and he was smiling.

Theo stepped gingerly over the bookcase, careful not to slip in the oil slick of blood, and felt his heart sink. He had expected Uriah to be dead of course, the sheer level of destruction in the living room left that without doubt, but this was even worse than he had anticipated. Even worse than Tim Ransom.

The shiver that ran down Theo's spine was only partly due to the gruesome scene in front of him. His mind skipped between the two deaths, both terrible in their different ways, and both the fault of Theobald Wolff.

My fault? Now come on you can't lay that on me. He almost spoke out loud.

Theo knelt beside the twisted corpse, finding a patch of clean floor away from the blood. His conscience examined the circumstances, admitting as it always did his responsibilities over Tiny Tim's death and extending that train of thought to this latest turn of events. *Could he have prevented the death of Uriah Lovelycolors?* He asked himself the question.

How could I? I didn't even know anything was wrong.

Liar! The ferocity of his own reply shocked him. If he hadn't known there was something amiss at the Towers then he had certainly suspected, he had even confronted Delia about it earlier today, but the question was, *what could he have done about it?*

Nothing, that's what.

Just like you did with Tim Ransom. You knew then but did nothing - just let things take their course even though you suspected he was innocent. Knew he was innocent. Now you've done the same again, let events run on without even trying to stop them.

The bitter taste in Theo's mouth was as much shame at his own inaction as the dry metallic taste of Uriah's blood. Ever since the letter he'd felt something was wrong around the Towers, noises in the night, a stillness during the day, and that strange encounter with Mick McCracken in the basement. What it had all meant he still didn't know, but there should have been enough to prick his curiosity, raise his suspicions, or at least get him wondering.

Back in his days as head warder he would have smelled trouble long ago, and acted on his instincts...

Not always you didn't.

...but after so many years in this dead and alive hole those instincts had been dulled. He had begun to doubt his feelings and mistrust the senses, which had once stood him in good stead. Now he simply went with the flow and did nothing about what he suspected, that badness had settled in at Darkwater Towers, and more than likely taken Mick McCracken with it.

Theo looked down at the Mona Lisa smile on the old man's lips, preparing to get up, when Uriah's eyes opened and the dead man spoke.

The landing outside Uriah Lovelycolors' flat was empty. Even the wind held its breath as it realised Delia had gone. The lift droned up towards the top floor, clanking an occasional protest, and left the clean uncluttered landing without even the slightest sign of a struggle, because there hadn't been one.

Theo leaned closer to make out the old man's gibberish. Uriah's ramblings had never been easy to understand but now, when he spoke, a terrible gurgling noise came from the wounds in his throat, and tiny speckles of blood spat down his shirt.

"...get inside. Hee hee hee." The laughter dissolved into a racking cough, blowing out flaps of skin below the jaw. "Couldn't do it."

"You couldn't get inside where?" Theo asked.

Uriah shook his head, opening the wounds, and almost making Theo sick. He didn't think he could watch much more of this, but he couldn't just leave him. The old man's eyes were glazing over, losing focus. Fear had dumped so much adrenalin into his system it must be the only thing keeping him alive, dulling the pain.

"Wants... all," Uriah managed. "Us all... inside." He gestured weakly to his chest with an arthritic hand, then to his mouth. "Inside..."

Theo looked around him for something to cover Uriah with. Instinct told him to keep the old man warm, but his heart knew it was already too late.

If I'd only acted sooner. Noticed the signs.

You did notice the signs; you just didn't do anything about them. Same as before. Theo pushed the voice aside. He might well have sensed something happening throughout The Towers but there had been no evidence to say what it had been. That being the case there was nothing he could have done to save Uriah, or anyone else.

In the back of his mind though, that simply wasn't enough. Guilt was a funny thing. Sometimes you felt it even if it wasn't reasonable. Theo knew damn well he wasn't responsible for this mess, but he wished he had taken some action earlier, even if there was no clue to what that action could have been.

He reached for the kitchen towel beside the door and suddenly a hand clamped on his wrist. Uriah made a supreme effort, his eyes showing renewed purpose, and formed each word carefully. "It... wants..." Blood spat from the ragged curtain of flesh that had been his throat. "Do not... let... it... in..." He once again gestured to his mouth. "I saw..." Uriah coughed weakly, "its eyes."

Theo felt the old man's grip weaken, and then the hand fell away. Uriah's eyes were fading out. "Didn't... get... me..." he whispered, smiling. Then he died. Theo pulled the towel from the rail, draped it over Uriah's face, and pushed back from a kneeling position to a crouch. His knees protested loudly, hiding the shuffling noise from behind him. He massaged his thighs, preparing to get up, when he felt a shadowy presence step into the doorway. The moan sounded cold and dreadful, then a hand grabbed his shoulder.

Theo spun round, almost cricking his neck, and stifled a scream. Shock stabbed into his heart. The figure was draped in shadow, light from the kitchen seeming to draw back from it. Theo overbalanced and put a steadying hand onto the floor, squelching in the tacky blood.

"Oh my goodness..." the figure exclaimed; Delia then stepped forward into the pool of light. Theo's heart triphammered in his chest and he was about to snap back at her when he saw the shock on her face. He struggled to his feet and ushered her into the calming darkness of the flat, away from the brightly lit kitchen and its gory secret. He said nothing, mainly because the traditional "everything will be alright" seemed so inadequate. He simply placed a reassuring arm around her shoulders and guided her through the carnage of the living room.

"I heard the lift coming and I was frightened," Delia explained in a quiet voice tinged with panic, "so I came in for you. I didn't expect... oh poor Uriah." She began to cry, her body shaking as the shock caught up with her. Theo squeezed her shoulder.

A thought struck him. "Where did the lift go?" he asked.

"To the top floor."

They were nearing the front door, or what remained of it, and Theo paused beside the shattered door lock. Apart from the constant whistle of the wind the landing was quiet. Having fulfilled his Good Samaritan duties there was only one thought in Theo's head: *get to the ground floor and out the front door, but that was down five flights of stairs. In Delia's state he didn't think she would make it. The other alternative was the elevator.*

Theo stepped onto the landing and listened. The lift was stationary but that wasn't what he was listening for. He knew where the lift was, the top floor, what he wanted to know was where on earth was Mick McCracken?

The loose window sounded a rogue scent downstairs, flapping loudly in the wind. Theo ignored it, listening for movement upstairs. There was none, just the sighing of the wind and the occasional twang of the lift cables. Then he heard it. Somewhere high above in the north west corner a window smashed, followed by a heavy scraping noise as something was dragged through one of the empty apartments.

That was all Theo needed. "Come on," he said, urging Delia forward. Her shakes had eased but she was still trembling. He led her towards the lift doors and pressed the call button.

CHAPTER 3

The cold grey tomb of the lift drew in around them and took them down, Delia huddling in the lee of Theo's protective arm, still trembling while Theo kept a watchful eye on the floor indicator. The black finger crawled past four and seemed to take an age inching through the voids between each of the floors.

Delia looked up at Theo and squeezed his waist. "I feel like we're the last passengers on a doomed liner," she said, raising a glimmer of a smile. The shock had worn off now, but she was still shaky. The sight of Uriah Lovelycolors' broken body had been bad enough, but the wait for the lift had been worse. From the moment Theo had pressed the call button, time had gone into slow motion.

The motor had whined into life and the lift began its journey from ten to five, but what made her skin crawl was the noise on the top floor. The dragging noise stopped immediately, followed by sounds of a crashing headlong dash through the northwest apartment towards the lift shaft. Delia watched the floor indicator above the lift doors, willing it to move. It didn't, and the crashing noises grew nearer the central core. She held her breath, shrinking into Theo's side, and finally the pointer slid from ten to nine, then downwards. Thudding hammer blows sounded on the tenth floor doors.

Now, in the relative safety of the elevator car, she allowed herself a smile. The sigh, which accompanied it, was pure relief. They were on their way down to the lobby, and that dastardly Mick McCracken was stuck on the top floor. Yes, it definitely felt like they were the last survivors on their way to the lifeboats.

"Won't be long," Theo said, squeezing her shoulder.

Delia nodded. "If this was a liner, the Captain could marry us now."

Theo looked down into her eyes. It seemed absurd that he'd found it so difficult to pop the question. In the light of subsequent events it was the least of his worries, but it was still an important one. He found himself wondering about her, suddenly realising he knew very little about her life before he and Melinda moved in.

"How long have you lived here?" he asked.

The question caught Delia by surprise. She thought about that. "Ooh, going on fifteen years," she replied. "Why?"

"Just wondering. Was your husband with you back then?"

"Oh no. He had run out long before my money did."

"No relatives to help you out?"

"Had you?" Her face reflected the stony reality of loneliness. "Would any of us be here if we had any alternatives?"

"No. I suppose not."

"At least you had Melinda to keep you company." Delia saw the sadness flood his face and wished she hadn't mentioned her.

"You know, sometimes I feel awfully guilty at having brought her here for her to spend her final years..." His voice faded. "Nobody should have to end their days in a place like this."

Delia waited, sensing there was more he needed to say.

"It was all my fault. Our savings were supposed to tide us over but I... Silly really. I thought I could better the return on the interest by investing."

"Did you lose it all?"

"Just about." He listened to the walls tick their approval. The Towers would love a hard luck story like this. "And she died here because of it."

"You didn't give her cancer."

"No."

"And you did all you could to make her comfortable at the end."

"Everything except what she wanted."

"That's nonsense and you know it."

Theo looked into Delia's eyes, realising just how important she had become in the years since Melinda's death. In the years leading up to it as well. She'd been a good friend when they'd both needed one, and a shoulder to lean on after.

"Did I ever tell you what she said just before she died?"

Delia didn't answer, not sure she wanted to know.

"She made me promise to look for someone else after she was gone. To make sure I didn't spend the rest of my life alone. I never did though. Couldn't get over losing her." His eyes bore into hers, tears welling up. "But I didn't have to look after all, because you were there all the time. I just couldn't see further than the end of my nose."

The floor indicator crawled past three, the cables groaning overhead, and moved down towards two. The thundering blows on the tenth floor lift doors started again, bringing him back to the present. The reality of his situation came back to him. Even if he survived tonight, at best he had five months to look forward to but at least he was certain now he wanted to spend that time with Delia. Melinda would have approved.

The lift shuddered on its track, groaning under the strain. The cable hummed and cracked, echoing down the shaft.

Theo's voice was tight. "I still haven't asked, have I?"

"No." Delia felt very young, like a schoolgirl on her first date.

"If my knees didn't ache so damned much..."

"Oh stop going round the houses," she asserted. "If we get out of here tonight, then tomorrow I will marry you."

"Tomorrow's Christmas Day. There won't..."

"By all that's holy, Theobald Wolff, I don't believe I've met anyone so standoffish. If we can't find a Minister on Christmas Day then it will be a poor show."

Theo smiled, and stood back from her, holding out both hands. She took them willingly, ignoring the pain in her swollen fingers.

"In that case," he said. "Will you marry me?"

She paused for effect, looking deep into his eyes, then the lift shuddered to a halt. The banging upstairs stopped. Her mouth tasted dry and harsh and panic forced her into Theo's arms. He enveloped her in a protective cocoon as they both shot a glance at the floor indicator.

It hovered just above the ground floor.

The doors didn't open. Fear swelled his throat, making it difficult to swallow; then he remembered how long it had taken the doors to respond on his trip to check on Mick McCracken in the basement. The cables twanged and echoed in the blackness above, and the wind moaned its warning down the shaft.

Theo pressed the "doors open" button. Still nothing. Far above, the pounding stopped, as if the caretaker was listening to what was happening in the cold grey cubicle ten floors below. The prospect of being drawn back up to the tenth floor, into the waiting arms of Mick McCracken, spurred Theo on. His fingers beat a tattoo on the control panel.

Delia sagged beside him, and it was only with an effort of will that she stopped herself sliding to the floor. She looked pale and fragile. One look at her sent Theo's fingers into overtime.

'Ping...'

The doors sighed and began to open while upstairs the banging started again. Like a snail going uphill they inched wider. Delia straightened beside him, hope shining in her eyes. Freedom was only thirty feet away. She could see the smoke-stained glass of the front doors across the lobby, and felt the comforting warmth of Theo's arm around her shoulders.

Two feet. Three feet. The gap widened, and now the entire entrance hall was visible. Night sucked the life out of the grey concrete enclosure, showing through the wired glass like a solid presence. Delia stared at it longingly, then realised there was something missing.

The floor wasn't there!

Is there no end to this nightmare? She thought. From the gaily-twinkling lights on her tree to the bloodstained door of her apartment this Christmas Eve was spiralling down through fear, to despair, to insanity. Looking out through the elevator doors was like looking at one of those clever diagrams where the stairs climb round the castle walls, never getting anywhere but simply rejoining themselves. The madness continued. Darkwater Towers was turning into just such a diagram, all routes leading down but not going anywhere except back on itself.

The floor doesn't exist any more, and neither do we, she thought. *We've slipped over into the Twilight Zone without noticing.* Delia remembered with trepidation some of that show's spooky black and white stories. They had never been her favourite viewing but she had felt drawn to them on those endless nights when sleep wouldn't come. Now they had become her personal nightmare.

Except it wasn't hers alone was it?

"Theo, where has the floor gone?"

Delia was shocked by his response, reinforcing her belief that the nightmare had taken over. He laughed, and then jumped down from the lift doors into nothingness.

"Theo!" she screamed. First his feet disappeared into the void, then his legs, and finally his body...

Thunk. The sound jolted her back to reality. Theo didn't vanish before her eyes, but merely stepped back from the lift to reveal he still had both legs and both feet. She still couldn't see the floor but she did hear the reassuring sound of his footsteps on concrete.

"The lift's broken," he explained. "Won't go all the way down."

Delia allowed herself a laugh, but it sounded on the edge of hysteria. With an effort she brought herself under control, fighting back the urge to laugh and cry at the same time. This wasn't the Twilight Zone after all, it was just Darkwater Towers. The strangeness, which had descended on her, was simply disorientation, and the oddities stopped there. She was back in the here and now, in an elevator of an almost dead block of flats, and just over there was the way out. The way to freedom.

She felt better.

Theo held out his hands to help her down when suddenly the Twilight Zone sucked her back. Her head spun and she felt sick.

Somewhere in the almost dead block of flats a telephone rang.

Theo heard the telephone ring as he reached out for Delia, and it threw him almost as much as her. Apart from on his shopping expeditions, he hadn't seen a telephone in years, let alone heard one. Certainly none of the residents had a phone, they could barely afford to eke out a living, never mind splash out on such luxuries as a telephone. Didn't have anyone to ring anyway, or they wouldn't have been here.

It rang again, one long melodious ring, then silence. His hands faltered.
Delia stepped back from the edge of the lift, fear etched on her face. In this ten-storey mausoleum Theo hadn't heard a telephone ring unless it had been on the television, and he hadn't watched that too often. His mind raced. *What could it mean?* He didn't know, but one thought shafted into his mind like an arrow. *If there were hardly any phones in The Towers,*

and hardly anyone left to answer one even if there were, then this call must be coming from...
...outside.

Theo stretched his hands out to Delia. "Come on, quickly." Urgency added a harsh edge to his voice. He waggled his fingers impatiently, but Delia backed away into the far corner of the elevator. The telephone rang again, and Delia's swollen hands came up to cover her ears. Panic flashed in her eyes and Theo could see she was on the ragged edge. He tried to keep the impatience out of his voice as he attempted to coax her forward. "It's all right Delia, it's just the phone." He stilled his fingers, holding his hands with the palms upwards, trying to give a calming signal he didn't feel. If that was someone from outside then he could call for help, if he got there before they hung up.

Delia lowered her hands slightly, her eyes meeting Theo's. Focus returned but she still looked shaken. She took a faltering step forward.

"That's it. Come on."

She approached the lip of the elevator floor.

"Come on," he urged. "We'll answer it together."

She began to reach down for Theo's hands, then the telephone rang again. The single tone rang out across the lobby, echoing off the bare concrete and ringing in his ears. Delia cowered back. Theo's head snapped round as he tried to place where the phone was. The sound of it stayed in his eardrums like a faint trace light on a retina after a bright flash.

Whoever was ringing must be calling from the outside, he couldn't get that thought out of his mind, and - *if they were from the outside then they could get help.* Up until now he had been set on getting out of here, and that was still the priority, but second to that was calling for the cavalry. He spun back to Delia who was backing all the way into the corner again. *What to do?* He wanted to get her out of the lift, but he needed to find the telephone and answer it. Send out a distress signal and hope that, unlike the Titanic, someone would take notice.

The single long ring echoed out again. It was definitely on this floor, so that narrowed it down to the caretaker's flat or the reception desk. Theo turned towards Mick McCracken's door. How ironic that the call which could save his life would come to the lair of the man who was trying to kill everybody in The Towers. He looked pleadingly at Delia, but he couldn't wait any longer. "Hold the lift," he called to her, and then set off towards the sound of the telephone.

Delia saw him go and her heart sank. The sour taste of panic dried her mouth, and her ears rang to the sound of a thousand telephones. In this dead black tower it seemed that every flat had a phone, and every phone was ringing.

Her hands throbbed as they covered her ears, but neither the pain of the arthritis nor the fleshy mufflers could keep the sound at bay. 'Rrrring'... The sound cut right through her, sending jagged shards of panic into her heart. She became short of breath, and her knees began to shake.

The Christmas lights. Think of the Christmas lights. Delia drew on the memory of the decorations in her flat. She once again saw Theo stringing the lights out to check them before draping them around the tree. She could smell the drinking chocolate and taste the first square of Galaxy Fruit and Nut. Outside the windows of her apartment the wind howled gently, highlighting the friendly warmth of the fire and the colourful glow of the lights.

It was working. She didn't know how long it had taken, time seemed to have lost its meaning here in the Twilight Zone, but the ringing in her ears had stopped. She lowered her hands, sparking a fresh bout of pain as the blood rushed in, and listened.

Silence. Only the wind's soft music sounded quietly through the cables over her head. The light of the floor indicator panel shone dully above the doors, and for some reason that seemed important. She wondered how long Theo had been gone, and was about to take a step towards the front of the lift when a cold shiver ran up her spine. Something else was working through the silence around her. Above her. She could feel it more than hear it. A soft repetitive breath. A sigh. It came every couple of seconds, counter-pointed by a rhythmic pulse like a heartbeat of the dead.

Someone was listening. Delia tried to remember what else was missing. What other sound had vanished along with the demonic ringing of the telephone. It came to her in a flash, together with the reason the floor indicator was so important.

"Hold the lift," Theo had said as he'd gone looking for the telephone.

Delia's heart came up into her mouth. The noise, which had struck fear into her all the way down from Uriah's apartment, was the constant banging on the elevator doors on the tenth floor. Now the banging had stopped, and she was certain the caretaker was listening to her every move through the glass against the wall of the elevator shaft.

"Hold the lift..."

Too late she realised what was happening, and before she could reach for the "hold" button the doors slid shut. High above, the motor kicked in, and with a groan from the cables the lift jerked once, then began the journey back up to the top floor. In the distance she thought she heard Theo call her name, then the sound of the elevator swamped her.

When Theo had turned his back on the lift doors a sense of déjà vu flooded over him. Approaching the caretaker's apartment took him back to a few days ago when he'd come down here to check if Mick McCracken was all right. It was another ironic twist that didn't escape him. On that occasion he had hoped the burly caretaker would answer the door and therefore save him going down into the basement. Now he prayed he would not.

The door loomed large with its dark smear of dried blood, and fear of what might be on the other side tightened his throat. Off to his left a malevolent glow showed under the cellar door. Without thinking he raised his fist to knock, then stopped. Whatever lurked in there didn't need Theo announcing himself. He lowered his hand.

Inside the flat the telephone rang again. Theo remembered why he was here and threw a nervous glance at the ceiling. Somewhere up there the bloodied shell of Mick McCracken was stalking the corridors of the tenth floor. If nothing else, that meant he wasn't in here waiting for Theo. He reached for the handle and took a deep breath. Behind him the lift doors stood open, throwing a sliver of light across the concrete. His hand tightened around the handle, turned it, then pushed open the door.

Blackness surged out at him.

He almost stepped back, not because of the dark but because the smell which assailed his nostrils made him gyp. Rotten cabbage and a bunged up toilet couldn't have smelled worse. God, something awful had died in here, or McCracken had the worse case of the runs imaginable. Theo reached to the left of the door for the light switch, hoping it was in the same place in all the apartments. It was. He flicked the switch but nothing happened. The darkness laughed at him.

As he stood in the doorway Theo realised that the room wasn't in total darkness. Against the wall to his right was a four-foot fish tank. The twelve-inch fluorescent shone dully, running off the tank's back-up battery. A glance at the wall socket showed why. A single black snake slithered from beneath the tank, but its square black head lay motionless on the carpet. The tank wasn't plugged in. Theo went towards the plug and winced as his feet crunched on broken glass, sounding loud in the silence of the apartment. He realised why there was no light. All the bulbs had been removed and smashed. Avoiding the shadowy bulk of the furniture Theo reached for the plug and clicked it in place. The fish tank flickered twice then shone with an eerie green glow.

The room leapt into a kaleidoscope of stark contrasts. Bright sharp edges and deep impenetrable shadows. Theo expected to find it trashed, furniture upended and smashed just as it was in Uriah's apartment, but it wasn't. The settee and two chairs appeared to be in their normal position, and the TV and hi-fi didn't look out of place. A pair of dark grey trousers were neatly folded over the back of the settee and a freshly ironed shirt hung over the armrest. A pile of magazines, 'Engineering Weekly', were stacked and squared off on the coffee table next to an unfinished crossword, which was folded back beside Webster's Dictionary.

It was in total contrast to how Theo expected the big man's apartment to look. Webs of shadow crept in from the walls, sucking what little light there was out of the room. The only sign of discord, apart from the broken light bulbs, was the large ornate mirror above the fireplace. It was smashed, shards of silvered glass hanging out of the frame at crazy angles. Green light from the fish tank splintered off the edges. Against the back wall a smaller mirror had suffered the same fate.

A bloody handprint stood out against the wall next to the mirror, and strings of bloody mucus decorated the shards of glass in the frame. Time slowed down and it seemed an age before the telephone rang again. He scanned the shadows, trying to find the phone. Next to the kitchen door was a full-length wall unit with display shelves. As the reverberations died away a glint of green light picked out the dial and hand set.

For the first time, Theo wondered what the hell he was going to say when he answered it. The rotting garbage smell hung heavy in the air, and he tried not to breathe deeply, taking only shallow breaths, but the stench still formed a taste in his mouth. He went quickly to the phone but was afraid to pick up the receiver. It rang again. *What to say? What to say?* The thought ran through his brain like a lost child in a Christmas Store. Then he picked it up.

"Hello?" It sounded stupid but it was an automatic response. Silence from the other end.

"Hello? I need help. Can you get the police straight away?" Now the verbal log jamb was broken, Theo's old training kicked in. Important things first. "I'm at Darkwater Towers near the old railway yards. I need the police and an ambulance. More than one. Someone's been attacking the residents and he's still in the flats." Theo paused, waiting for the inevitable questioning backlash.

Silence down the line, then a soft rasping breath, almost gurgling. Theo's blood turned cold. He thought he detected the beginnings of a laugh before the caller hung up. Realisation hit him like a hammer blow, and he spun for the door.

Delia...

Theo ploughed through the apartment towards the lobby. Then he heard the lift motor start up and knew it was too late. As he passed the settee something caught his eye and almost stopped him in his tracks but he was too far-gone in his dash for the elevator. A pair of black sightless eyes watched him go.

His breath came in short panicky gasps as he came out of the door into the lobby. Cool air, almost fresh after the cloying stench of McCracken's flat, washed over him then the sight of the lift doors closing slapped him in the face. "Delia!" He shouted, almost a screech, as he was dashing across the lobby. The doors closed with a sigh and the floor indicator began its upward journey. Theo slammed his hands against the doors and cursed.

CHAPTER 4

In that moment, Theo could have cheerfully died on the spot. All his will to live evaporated in a flash. The floor indicator ticked away like a metronome from Hell, counting down the seconds to Delia's fate. Theo didn't need to watch to know which floor it would end on. It was obvious, and that would be the end of that.

The letter flashed its message in his brain. *Cancer* ... The doctor's prognosis curled into his bones. *Five months at the most...* The inevitability of it all was a weight too heavy to bear. Melinda's plea for him to end it all, and his failure to help in her hour of need was a bitter pill he had never been able to swallow. Now he had failed again. Failed to prevent this from happening even though he had sensed the wrongness of the place, and failed to protect the only other person he had ever cared about. *It goes back further than that though doesn't it? Tim Ransom. You failed to do the right thing then as well.*

Rage welled up inside him, souring his palate and drying his mouth. He slammed his hands into the doors again and swore with primeval force. Tears of anger stung his eyes. He turned and stared across the lobby at the front doors. Freedom waited just twenty paces away. Outside, the night beckoned him, and he went willingly, all his will to resist gone. He reached the doors and put a shaking hand on the handle. A nagging thought surfaced in the kaleidoscope of his mind, joggling for attention amongst the shattered pictures of his past. *A pair of cold black eyes.* The significance of them, and even where he had seen them simply wouldn't come, and all he could think of was getting out. His hand tensed and he prepared to open the door.

NO... Not Melinda's voice, not even her essence, but something stronger. A deep-seated instinct that was as much a part of him as his heart or his lungs. The same instinct that wouldn't let him ignore the caretaker's plight in the cellar or Uriah's danger in his flat. The Good Samaritan in him came to the fore, and wouldn't let him run out on a friend. Wouldn't let him run out on anyone. It was something that had always been in him, a voice that wouldn't let go. He had ignored that voice once, and tragedy had followed. In the end, that might have been the test which had strengthened his resolve, but the bottom line was, *he couldn't leave now. Not without Delia.*

Theo turned back to the lift. The metronome tick-tocked all the way up to the tenth floor. High above him the motor ground to a halt, and he held his breath, expecting to hear what was going on up there. His mind raced, trying to get a handle on what he should do next. He checked the time, but his watch was broken, the glass cracked with the hands frozen at nine fifteen. It must have smashed when he'd hammered on the lift doors.

Ten floors up. Ten flights of stairs. He knew he could make it, he was after all the One Eyed Man of Darkwater Towers, but what condition would he be in when he arrived? Certainly not in any fit state to take on even an ailing Mick McCracken. Not bare handed anyway.

That clicked another thought into place, pointing the way to his next move. Good Samaritan or not, he wasn't a fool, and only a fool would go up against the demon caretaker unarmed. In Darkwater Towers that meant only one thing. Newton Wimer.

It was another touch of irony that the gun Theo had considered suicide with only days before, should now be his last hope for salvation. He thought about that as he made his way up the main stairwell, careful to stay against the wall so he couldn't be seen from above. He thought about the possibility of his death as well. Not possibility, certainty, because he'd already been given notice to quit this life. Notice and date of termination, more or less.

"...five months at the most."

Yes, he was going to die, possibly screaming for someone to end it all for him just as Melinda had, but he found the prospect of dying tonight too much to take. The only comfort he could find was the thought that positive action might balance the books for his previous failures. His refusal to help Melinda was like a corkscrew twisting in his heart. It turned and twisted and bit deep into his conscience. Despite a lifetime of being on the right side of the law, the good side of life's creatures, he had continually allowed pain and death to overshadow him. Melinda, Tim Ransom, Uriah Lovelycolors...

...and Delia?

He picked up the pace, ignoring the stitch in his side, and took the steps two at a time. He knew he wouldn't be able to keep that pace up, but the pain in his side took his mind off the pain inside his head. He didn't know if he would be in time, or if he could do anything if he was, but he was damn well going to try.

Outside, the breeze stiffened, howling round the exposed northeast corner of The Towers, and somewhere downstairs a window banged its tattoo as the wind forced its way in. Theo reached the fourth floor and paused. Another sound was drifting down the hollowed out heart of the tower block. Spiralling down the staircase to greet him. He was forced to smile at this final irony as he considered a bleak and humourless future practically devoid of hope. From an upstairs flat the cheerful strains of Jingle Bells rang out gently.

The Major's door was closed but Theo could hear the strains of "Silent Night" quite clearly. It sounded out of place under the circumstances but somehow comforting. Life went on, the world went on, and it was Christmas Eve after all.

The seventh floor landing was cold and uninviting but Theo found it hard to open the door. It felt like he'd been standing outside doors he didn't want to open for most of his life, an outsider looking in, an intruder waiting for his turn. Every door held a secret, and every secret was surrounded with an aura of fear and dread and danger. Something about the last door he'd gone through tried to force itself into his mind but it wouldn't come. The warning wouldn't register. The wires were down.

"Silent night... holy night...
All is well... all is bright..."

No it isn't, Theo thought. *It was neither silent nor holy, and everything most definitely wasn't well.* The gloom of the corridor negated the "all is bright" as well, or had he heard the lyrics wrong? One of Melinda's gripes had always been that he listened to the tune of a song but never the words. It used to drive her mad when a beautiful love song would be reduced to a tuneless whistle as far as he was concerned.

Whatever. He was stalling. Never mind the song, it was time to open the door. "Take the money... Open the box..." Michael Miles couldn't help Theo take his pick this time. The game show host was pushed to one side, and Theo reached for the handle. His breath was coming in deep, lung filling gasps despite the stench. The stairs had taken their toll.

"*Open the box...*"

So he did. One quick turn and the door swung inwards, and Theo stepped into the orderly world of Major Newton Wimer retired.

It was the very fact that this was such an orderly world that caused Theo to lower his defences. As he closed the door quietly behind him he felt safe for the first time that evening. The fire blazing in the hearth was warm, the lights bright and clean, and the gentle lilt of Christmas Carols lulled him into a false sense of security. It was a mistake anyone could have made.

The urgency of his mission was still there, but the imminent danger he'd felt ever since his return from Carl Stensel's barbershop diminished. Carl Stensel. Something niggled but wouldn't come. With the door firmly closed at his back he let out a sigh of relief. Nat King Cole and a heavenly choir filled the room with 'Oh Tannenbaum' from the Major's CD player.

The revolver. Theo set his mind to the task, searching the walls for the Enfield .38. He noted that the coffee table was thankfully free of weapon parts, so at least it wasn't in the process of being stripped and cleaned. That meant it must be on display. He stepped towards the fireplace, eyes flicking from the Royal Artillery shield across the framed campaign medals to the Browning above the fire.

Cancer...

Déjà vu tried to drag Theo back to the day he'd put Delia's Christmas decorations up.

Five months at the most...

He remembered Melinda's face as she'd pleaded with him to end it all, and more recently the despair which had settled in his heart while the Major had left the room. The gun had seemed like a perfect opportunity to finish it. *Stop the bus; I want to get off. If the Major had just been a bit longer...*

Something creaked behind him and shock screamed up his throat. Every hair on his body, from his arms to the back of his neck sparked to life. He turned round slowly, certain he would find McCracken waiting to pounce. The room was empty.

If the Major had just been a bit longer... Theo remembered where Newton Wimer had gone, the bedroom, and it was the bedroom door that was partly open. The creaking noise came again, from the other side of the bedroom door.

"Major," Theo called, realising it was the last thing he should have done. He'd climbed seven flights of stairs, careful not to make any sound that might give him away, and here he was, just three floors below McCracken's last known position, shouting through the door. There was no Christmas tree in the apartment, but the glow of the fire and the bright clean lighting coupled with the constant lilting music player brought the festive season alive. It calmed his nerves and camouflaged his voice.

Theo was torn between his need for the gun and that pain-in-the-arse Good Samaritan instinct that demanded that he check the bedroom out. The nightmare vision of Uriah Lovelycolors' broken body still burned in his mind. The possibility that Newton Wimer might be in the bedroom and in need of help, was too strong to ignore. He quickly glanced round the walls, marking the Enfield's position next to the framed campaign medals, then he bypassed the settee on his way to the bedroom.

What did the old man keep in there? The thought intrigued him even as he dreaded what he might find. He approached the door silently, the music covering his footsteps, and reached for the handle. The creaking had stopped but that didn't reassure him. He was certain he'd heard it, and it was a noise that struck a chord from his past. He felt cold, and fought the urge to shiver. A cold dark recollection was forming in his brain, and it wasn't a pleasant one. He suddenly didn't want to go in there.

Theo's hand rested on the neatly painted panel of the door and paused. No creaking. After a second he plucked up courage and pushed gently. The door was heavier than he'd expected, and only moved a few inches. He pushed harder. The door swung open, revealing a neatly folded bedspread and the foot of the single bed. A mahogany blanket box snuggled at the bottom and next to that was a small writing desk with fold down cover.

Theo stayed where he was, glancing round the floor for telltale signs of the bloody carnage he'd found downstairs. There were none, and he breathed a sigh of relief. He pushed the door fully open and stepped over the threshold. The bedroom was empty. The head of the bed was as neat as the foot, the sheets turned down and the pillows squared off at the top. A dark wood bedside cabinet and lamp stood next to the bed, and beside that a large double wardrobe.

Other than that, nothing. Theo cleared the door and he felt it brush past his shoulder as it began to swing shut. The creaking noise sounded again, only this time he knew where he'd heard it before. His throat clenched, keeping down the scream he felt coming.

The creak... creak... of straining rope counterpointed with the jangle of keys in his ears. A large heavy bunch of keys. He instinctively selected the solid flat metal one with the triangular head and opened the cell door. He knew he should have checked earlier, especially after what the other warders had said, but he hadn't. He looked down at the razor sharp creases in his grey uniform trousers, then up at the door. This wasn't the open-barred cell door of so many prison movies; this was a solid metal door with a peep hole and drop down hatch. He turned the key and twisted the handle, then pushed. At first he thought Tim Ransom had escaped, then he felt the weight of him dragging on the door.

Theo spun round, sucked in his breath, and looked straight into the dead black eyes of Tiny Tim.

Shock dumped into his system, sparking every nerve. The six and a half foot giant wasn't so much hanging, as slouching behind the door. His neck had stretched a good twelve inches and he must have died slowly as the ligature tightened round his throat. His tongue was a thick black sausage and his eyes were bulging and bloodshot.

And the head... It seemed to have shrunk at the top almost as much as it had bulged at the bottom. Rolls of flesh had ridden up the neck as the noose stretched it, pushing the chin up and squashing the face down to meet it. The top of the head looked depleted of mass, the skin dark, shrivelled and prune-like. He must have been hanging there for a good eight hours. That would put it before evening check out but after...

Theo pushed the thought to the back of his mind. The responsibility was clear, as were the culprits. The snarling jibes of his colleagues still rang in his ears, and the fact that he hadn't enlightened them only made it worse.

Now there was the problem of what to do next? Own up to his tardiness, and condemn those responsible, or close ranks and cover his back?

The decision wasn't an easy one; it was one that would haunt him for the rest of his days. Even now, as his mind played tricks on him, the argument with Melinda that night still hurt. Over something as petty as folded towels on the banister rail as well. It was the only time he had ever swore at her, and Melinda's deep, calm, understanding of his reasons were uncanny. She had tapped into a vein that ran straight to his heart. She understood without having to ask that something terrible had happened at the prison, and hadn't questioned him when he decided to take early retirement, even though it left them short on their pensions.

That was why he'd loved her so much. Still did. And it was the reason looking into the shrivelled black face of Newton Wimer brought it all back. *How long had he been dead?* Theo wondered. *A good eight hours.* That would put it before Theo should have delivered the shopping and after... Yes, things had a tendency to come back at you. *What goes around comes around.* Theo would normally have called for the shopping list before leaving, but he hadn't today. Today he'd had fatter fish to fry. More important matters to attend to. More personal. He thought to himself, *having ignored the Major I still haven't managed to pop the question to Delia, have I? So a selfish act had once again resulted in...*

Stop it! Theo clamped down on the run of his thoughts. That was getting him nowhere. Newton Wimer was dead, and there was no getting away from that. That left the reason he had come here. The gun. Theo pondered the idea of cutting the Major down then decided not. The Enfield. That was uppermost in his list of priorities now. He could mourn his bad judgement another time, but for now there was Delia to think about. He gave the Major one last glance then pulled the door open. Aside from the scratches on Newton Wimer's throat, something he hadn't noticed when Theo's mind whisked him back to 1982, something else seemed nigglingly familiar. The cuts to Uriah Lovelycolors' throat had been more pronounced, but that wasn't it. The thing that was staring him in the face went back further than that. And deeper.

...*in the face. Black face.*

A curl of fear fluttered across Theo's neck, bristling the hairs behind his ears. A slow dawning realisation spread over his face. A realisation that begged more questions than it answered.

Shrivelled black face. Dead eyes.

Someone else was abroad in Darkwater Towers. Someone who had left something in Mick McCracken's apartment.

No. Not a shrivelled face, a shrunken head. Dead black eyes that stared back at him with malevolent glee, and twisted lips that smiled coldly. Kuta Lametka. That head had stared blankly at him on countless occasions beneath Carl Stensel's mirror. Tonight it had watched him from a crease in McCracken's settee, but what could the diminutive barber be doing in The Towers? And why hadn't Theo seen him?

The newspaper story slipped into his mind. The story, and Carl's insistence that the pattern of bodies led right to Darkwater Towers. The rope creaked, forcing a strangled groan from the dead man's mouth.

Then Theo heard another sound...

...the door to the flat being opened.

Adrenaline flooded Theo's body like a sensory overload. He moved faster than he would have believed. The gun was near the fireplace but the door was open six inches and widening. He flew across the room, banging his thigh on the arm of the settee, and grabbed the tall narrow bookcase, pulling it over in front of the door. It toppled with a crash of falling books and slammed the door shut.

A roar of anger sounded from the landing, chilling Theo to the bone. It wasn't so much a roar as an angry gurgle, like someone shouting through a glass of water. He didn't wait to hear any more. With agility that belied his years, Theo dodged between the settee and the easy chair, and made a beeline for the Enfield. Behind him a wet slapping thump pounded on the door, driving Theo on. The CD player paused between its festive offerings, holding its breath.

Then his hands were on the revolver. His fingers felt stiff and unresponsive, betraying the years of inactivity since his Army days. Another salvo of banging sounded on the door, and Theo's hands began to shake. The doorframe splintered. *Is it loaded?* He searched anxiously for the cylinder release, the gun quivering like a frightened puppy in his hands.

Click. The barrel broke forward and five golden discs winked gaily in the firelight. The sixth chamber was empty, a safety feature Newton Wimer had always observed. Never leave the hammer on a loaded chamber. The sixth bullet was tied neatly in the knot of the lanyard.

The doorframe creaked and split, the cracking wood sounding like a whiplash. Theo nearly tipped the bullets out on the floor, but narrowly managed to snap the cylinder shut. Splintering wood became a constant accompaniment to

"I'm dreaming of a White Christmas..."

Christmassy songs still emanating from the stereo. Then the heavy thudding sounded nearer, more urgent. Theo spun round and saw the gap in the door was nearly a foot wide. The bookcase was leaning into the room. A blood spattered hand reached through the gap, trying to dislodge the bookcase. Now Theo could taste panic in his mouth like a dry electric charge. He raised the Enfield, sighting along the top, and squeezed the trigger.

It didn't move.

Shit... The safety catch. He quickly tilted the side of the revolver towards him, searching for the gnarled grey knob. He found it and slid it forward. Now the door was coming all the way

"...just like the Christmases we know..."

The bookcase was tilting crazily. Theo raised the gun again, backing away from the horror before him. The bloodied hand slapped at the bookcase. Keeping both eyes open, as he'd been taught all those years ago, he sighted along the barrel. Just up and to the left of the hand, square on the door. His hands steadied, he held his breath, and squeezed. Click...

Bastard... the empty chamber. Theo cocked the hammer with his thumb, barely moving the barrel from its target, then a hot coal popped loudly in the grate. He shot a terrified glance at the fire and snubbed the back of his legs against the chair. The combination of shock and being brought to a sudden halt did it. He overbalanced and sat hard on the edge of the chair. If he'd landed plum in the middle he might have still got off a shot, but as it was he sat awkwardly on the left hand arm rest and tilted the chair over. His arms flew out for balance and the Enfield struck the wall, twisting his wrist back on itself.

The gun went off. It roared like a cannon and pain exploded in Theo's left arm. A bloody flower bloomed on his sleeve, and fire ran·up into the shoulder. The fingers of his left hand felt numb with shock, reflexing out into rigid pikes. His right hand reacted in concert, unable to help itself, and the gun dropped to the floor.

The doorframe gave with a final splintering crack, and Theo was up and running despite the pain. Next to the fireplace was the kitchen, and along the back wall, the Major's bedroom. No escape through either of them. That only left one option, the fully glazed door onto the veranda, but that would still leave Theo seven floors up on a cold wintry night.

Without looking back he knew he had no choice. Keeping his left arm as still as he could he snatched at the brightly polished brass handle and prayed that Newton Wimer didn't keep it locked. He didn't. The door swung outwards and Theo hustled onto the balcony, slamming the door shut behind him. The veranda was as clean and tidy as the rest of the Major's apartment. In the left hand corner, against the balcony wall, was a tool tidy, several shelves fitted with various sized drawers for screws and nails and whatever else the old man felt he needed. On the right was the pigeon loft, and that's what Theo was looking for. It was four feet wide by two feet deep, and stood three feet high on four stubby legs. It was the bunk up he needed to reach the next floor.

The cold wind cut like a scalpel as Theo reached up into the darkness for the balcony rail. Seven floors down, night blanked out the swathe of industrial wasteland, a black carpet of tangled metal and dusty masonry. Only the gaily-coloured light of Carl Stensel's barbershop sign showed in the distance.

Everything else. Nothingness. He could be looking out across a hole cut in the fabric of the universe, only the stars above and the red and green "Gents Hairdresser" sign below shedding any light on the world. Nothing else existed.

Except the balcony rail.

Theo tried to concentrate on that, but his mind kept returning to the cosy warmth of the barbers shop, and the shrunken head next to the mirror. That red and green sign which had reminded him so much of Christmas now only represented blood and slime. He felt betrayed, and foolish, and deeply afraid.

A crash came from inside the flat as the bookcase was thrown free. No time. Theo stood on the rickety pigeon loft and thrust upwards. His aging joints complained. Pain flared in his left arm and fresh blood began to flow. The ten-story block of flats seemed to be a mile high. Bing Crosby crooned about a White Christmas on The Major's CD player, then that too was sent crashing as a twisted shadow lurched towards the balcony.

The pigeon loft shifted under Theo's weight as the shattering of the coffee table sounded inside. The shadow made a beeline for the veranda door. Theo's good hand reached up, and dried wood splintered underfoot, the pigeons fluttering restlessly.

Balcony rail. Where's the bloody balcony rail?

The door trembled at McCracken's approach. But was it McCracken? Doubt clouded his judgement. Another element had been introduced. A darker element in the shape of his old friend Carl Stensel and the story of Kuta Lametka. Concentrate. He forced the thoughts out of his mind and reached up for the rail.

Got it. Theo grasped tight on the cold hard metal and shoved off with his foot. The pigeon loft leaned over, its sides splitting with a crack and then Theo lunged out into the clear blackness of the night. He hung for a second and then grabbed with his other hand, ignoring the pain, swinging up with the momentum from the loft.

Pigeons exploded into the cramped space of the veranda.

Theo's legs hooked over the next balcony's floor and he pulled himself up. Sweat broke out on his face despite the cold wind. "Aaargh...." He banged his arm as he landed on the disused veranda. Below him the door burst open.

No thought, just action. Theo was up and moving before the pigeons cleared the pigeon loft. The door in front of him was frosted with starlight. He twisted the handle but his hand had lost all its strength.

He tried again.

Locked.

There were curses from below, then the pigeon loft was kicked aside.

The bloody doors don't lock, Theo chided himself. *Wrong way.* He quickly turned the handle the other way and pulled the door open. Then he was inside, away from the bitter wind and into the eighth floor apartment. The shadowy interior was streaked with shafts of moonlight, throwing dappled patches on the dusty floor. One of the patches shifted then solidified, and Carl Stensel stepped forward.

No. This is isn't how it happened, Theo's fevered brain tried to argue, but the evidence was right there in front of him. There was something wrong with the picture though. It was Carl Stensel alright, but he looked... taller. Fuller as well. His eyes were bloodshot, and tiny stretch marks across the scalp line had started to bleed.

Theo took a step backwards, the Stensel thing followed, then Theo noticed it was holding something. No, not holding, dragging. Like a park keeper clearing leaves into a sack which he pulled around behind him. This wasn't a sack though. He grabbed at his chest as pain stabbed into his heart. Tears of pain and anger welled up in his eyes. "Nnoooo..." he screamed as he recognised the baggage Carl Stensel was dragging.

Delia Circelli's lifeless body was slumped on the floor, the once neatly primped hair held tightly in the barber's fist. He dragged her towards Theo like a caveman bringing home the kill. Blood trickled from the corners of her mouth, and her eyes stared blankly. She seemed smaller than in life, the skin wrinkled and shrivelled.

Emaciated corpses...
The Rover car dealership...
The Diamond Seal double glazing factory...
The derelict rail yards...

Theo was out on the balcony now, the icy wind flapping at his collar. Stensel dragged Delia's corpse into the doorway, blood dripping from the split ends of his fingers.

FOURTH DERELICT FOUND DEAD

Fourth derelict, but how many more in Darkwater Towers? Theo's head was spinning. He felt faint, and weak, and very very cold. The balcony began to sway, and Stensel's bloody hand reached out for him. That was the last straw. Theo stepped backwards one last time, fetching up against the balcony rail. As the hand made to grab his shoulder he twisted away from it and overbalanced.

Cold black night engulfed him as he plunged over the rail. One sickening crack against the edge of the veranda then he was cartwheeling down the side of The Towers. The starry sky swapped places with the red and green hairdressers' sign, spinning in a dance of death, then he mercifully passed out as the ground rushed up to greet him.

PART THREE

A TALL DARK ROOM

Nor aught avail'd him now
To have built in Heav'n high Towers; nor did he 'scape
By all his Engins, but was headlong sent
With his industrious crew to build in Hell.

- John Milton

A blind man in a dark room - looking for a black hat
Which isn't there.

- Lord Bowen

CHAPTER 1

Theo's eyes flew open and his left leg kicked out instinctively, almost tipping him off the battered leather chair. His breath came in short sharp gasps and he wasn't sure if he'd screamed or not. The nightmare vision of Carl Stensel dragging Delia by her hair was etched on his retinas, but as reality slowly reasserted itself it began to fade, like the pain in his left arm, which was now just an uncomfortable ache.

His head twitched on the folded sheet of the examination table. Lead weights were fastened to his eyelids, forcing them to close again. With an effort Theo forced them open. He could smell the stale dust of the bed sheet and his mouth tasted dry and sickly, as if he'd coughed up some phlegm and swallowed it down again. The furry caterpillar that was his tongue licked his lips but there was no moisture left. The dehydrocodeine tablets had soaked it all up.

After what seemed an age he lifted his head, but it wouldn't turn right. He had been unconscious for

...*how long? How long have I been out?*

Several hours with his head tilted to the left and the muscles in his neck had seized up, barely able to face front never mind anything else. He sat up, stretching his back, which was thankfully not as bad. During his years as a prison warder he had done his fair share of night shifts, much of the time between rounds spent catching as much shut-eye as he could. He had learned the art of sleeping sitting up, using whatever was available for added comfort. Sometimes that meant leaning back against the wall, or sometimes simply sitting bolt upright until his head lolled forward, waking him up, but as head warder more often than not it meant leaning over his desk, resting his head on his folded arms. Two quick stretches had always straightened his back, and that was the case now. His neck would take a while longer.

Theo turned to the sink and turned on the cold tap, cupping his hands to scoop up the cold clear water. He drank eagerly, slaking his thirst, and then splashed handfuls of water over his face, rubbing it into his eyes. That done, he began to rub his neck, twisting it slowly up and down, then left and right. Muscles creaked and the bones grated but eventually he felt much better.

Antiseptic light glared off the medical room tiles, contrasting with the dark depressing thoughts, which ran through his mind. The sadistic twist of his memories told more about his state of mind than the tripping effects of the DF's. The thought that Carl Stensel might be involved in this - because after all, what other reason could he have for being in Mick McCracken's apartment - sent his mind reeling.

The fluorescent buzzed frantically overhead. Somewhere in the tall dark room, which had once been a bustling tower block, a window continued to bang in the wind. Water dripped disconsolately from the tap, and Theo turned it off. What was he to do next? His options were limited, and indeed his responsibilities reduced to next to nothing. As far as he could tell, the flats had been stripped of life. His Good Samaritan urges had proved nothing, saved no one, and the person he had returned to rescue had been lost. Delia Circelli was probably as dead as the rest of the residents by now. That left the way clear for him to leave.

Theo flexed his neck to make sure it was mobile again then stood up. His legs were stiff, reflecting the amount of exercise he'd put them through over the last few hours. He once again wondered how long he'd been unconscious, and glanced at his watch. The frozen face - shattered at nine fifteen - reminded him of how close he had come to getting Delia out. Anger rose in his throat, swelling his chest in that old army way Melinda had loved so much, and burred between his clenched teeth.

Escaping with Delia had been his primary goal when he'd come back from the barbershop. Escaping alone didn't have quite the same ring to it.

Cancer...

Melinda had once told him how lucky they were to be spending the rest of their lives together. It was about the time they'd booked into this heartbreak hotel, and Theo suspected it was aimed at lifting his moral at a time when it most certainly wasn't high. That might well have been the case but the fact of the matter was she was right. They had weathered their fare share of matrimonial storms, and there had definitely been plenty of low periods, but those had been more than compensated for by the sheer pleasure of being in love with a woman who loved him. If living together for the rest of their lives was the worst they could expect, then that was pretty damn well good enough.

...at the most five months.

With Melinda gone, he had finally realised how much he cared for Delia and after the doctor's letter his hand had been forced. Melinda could be very persuasive, even from beyond the grave, and the promise he'd made at her deathbed had looked to be coming true. With so few days left to him, the quality of those days became very important. Delia was that quality. Now she was gone too.

That left the way clear for him to leave...

It did. But for what purpose? What quality of life could he expect now? With no one to share those final days what was the point? The anger turned up a notch. His future had been snatched away at the last minute. If that wasn't enough, the terrible deaths he had witnessed deserved a better reward than Theobald Wolff skulking off into the night.

He looked around the medical room, remembering the phone call that had decoyed him away from the elevator, and a plan began to form in his mind.

Twenty minutes later, Theo slipped quietly out of the medical room into the hall, his pockets bulging. He turned left, ignoring the locked door to the car park, and was immediately swallowed by the shadows creeping off the walls. After the brilliant light of the medical room it was as though he'd stepped into some medieval dungeon. Keeping his back to the wall he edged towards the lobby.

He didn't know how long he'd been out of the picture, so that threw up his first problem. What had been going on while he was unconscious, and more importantly where was McCracken now? Until he knew the answer to that he'd have to be very careful. The demon caretaker could be waiting round the next corner, or could it be the demon barber? Not Sweeney Todd, but Carl Stensel?

Theo remembered Carl's tale of the village in the South Pacific, and the untimely end of Kuta Lametka. Was he more involved than he'd admitted, or was it sheer coincidence that the same thing was happening here, so close to Carl Stensel's tonsorial emporium? He didn't know, and until he had an answer the keeper of the shrunken head should be treated with suspicion.

The corridor came to an abrupt left turn into the lobby. Theo waited silently, listening for any sign of movement. The wind had strengthened, buffeting the front doors and breathing seductively through the floors above. He held his breath, trying to pick out any sound not connected to the wind or the normal settling noises of the flats. After a few minutes he risked a quick look round the corner.

The lobby was empty. Shadows haunted the far reaches, soaking up what little light there was like the soul collector sucking up lost spirits. The elevator doors were closed, and Theo strained his eyes to see the floor indicator. The lift was on the seventh floor. Good, that meant the ground floor should be safe. Theo stepped round the corner, staying close to the wall. If there were going to be any surprises he didn't want them coming from behind. He quickly checked the basement door, and it was closed, then the caretaker's door. That was where the telephone was but it wasn't where Theo was heading. The thought of going in there filled him with dread, not just the bloody hand prints next to the shattered mirrors, or the rotting cabbage smell of dead flesh, but the shrivelled dead eyes of Kuta Lametka. No, the caretaker's apartment had its part to play, but not yet.

Across the lobby, past the elevator, the main stairwell was shrouded in a cloak of darkness. Only the bottom two steps were visible like cold grey slabs in the mortuary. Opposite them were the double doors of the front entrance, and next to them was Theo's destination, the reception office, its half glazed door closed to the world for more than three years. A hatch and window faced onto the lobby, its broad sill the only contact point the residents had with the authorities that ran The Towers. A small brass reception bell stood on one side and a pen-on-a-chain on the other. Dust built up in the corners giving the whole thing the air of a ghost town.

Theo hoped it hadn't been stripped of its equipment. If it had, then he would have to go to plan "B", only he had no idea what plan "B" was. One last glance at the floor indicator to make sure the lift wasn't moving, and then he strode purposefully across the lobby to the office door. He remembered the medical room, and prayed that this door was open as well. He grasped the handle and turned it.

The door wouldn't open.

He tried again, and then turned it the other way. The door still wouldn't open. Theo cursed under his breath, then considered kicking the door in, discarding the idea immediately. The noise would not only send a signal to whoever was listening, but he probably wasn't strong enough anyway. As a rule, doors don't kick in as easily as in the movies, and almost never by someone who's nearly seventy.

He looked around the foyer, hoping for inspiration, or better still; a crowbar, but found neither. He tested the door with his shoulder, only succeeding in aggravating the ache in his left arm. It didn't budge. Not even a shudder. Tools. He needed tools. Something that would give him enough leverage to prise the lock. He wondered about the caretaker's flat, and then remembered where the fat man kept all work related items.

The boiler room.

Theo looked at the door marked, CELLAR - STAFF ONLY KEEP OUT, then back at the office door, then over to the elevator doors. Three doors, all closed, and Theo wanted two of them to stay that way. It was just his luck that the one he wanted to open was the only one that was locked. The floor indicator hadn't moved, still arrowing the seven, and the lift motor was silent. He weighed up the time-loss versus energy-saved, and voted with his feet. Time didn't seem to be the most important issue any more, his five months were whittling down and Delia was beyond help, and he was going to need all the energy he could muster before the night was done. So, the cellar it was.

He was sweating by the time he reached the bottom of the stairs, the twin furnaces roaring their approval. It was like Hell re-visited, and Theo felt their malevolent stare follow him across the rust streaked floor. The pressure gauges and fuse boards hummed, and fire glinted through the furnace viewing windows, throwing dancing red and gold light across the walls.

"What you doing 'ere?"

McCracken's greeting was as fresh in Theo's mind as if he was standing here now. The disgusting bulk of the man standing in the entrance to the coalbunker was so real he could smell stale sweat, and taste the fear he was so ashamed of. McCracken wasn't here though. It was just another trace memory, and Theo searched the floor space with his eyes. Tools. Where did he keep his tools?

"Had to splat a rat first though..."

The shovel leaned casually against the wall of the coalbunker, its shadow dancing across the doorway.

"Had to splat a rat..."

This time Theo noticed the flat blade of the shovel, and remembered the moment of unease as he'd climbed the steps on his last visit. Rat splatting would most definitely leave its mark on the shovel that did the splatting, and this shovel didn't have that mark. He thought back, dragging at the subconscious memories stored in the back of his mind. No, it hadn't borne the mark then either. It wasn't important now, but it was another indication of the signs Theo had missed. Another reason for reproaching himself for not doing something to stop this whole thing at the beginning.

Just like...

Theo slammed the thought away. He'd spent too much time on the fiasco of Tim Ransom's death. Now was the time for positive action, not re-hashing the mistakes of his past. The shovel. He went over and picked it up. It was a broad bed coal shovel with a sturdy shaft, but Theo didn't think it would do for forcing the office door. He put it down and looked around. There was a small tool set and a torch on the shelf next to the fuse boards but he could tell from here it was too small to hold anything useful. He was drawing a blank, and his heart felt heavy with disappointment.

Then he noticed the service door into the lift shaft. It was heavily riveted metal; about four feet tall, with a single large handle similar to those on a submarine. The door looked like it was rusted shut, but on closer inspection Theo saw that the hinges were worn smooth and shiny, and the door seal had an eighth of an inch gap. It was the only other door in the basement, and it was his last chance.

The handle was stiff and Theo needed both hands to move it. Ignoring the pain from his arm once he got going he withdrew the bolt in one smooth movement. He pulled the door open and peered inside. It was as black as pitch, making the coal cellar look like Blackpool illuminations. He went over to the shelf and picked up the torch, flicking it on and off to test it. It worked. Back at the door he bent to look inside, switched the torch on, and played the beam around the musty interior.

The room wasn't a room at all. It was the workspace beneath the lift shaft so that necessary repair work could be carried out to the bottom of the elevator. It was eight feet by ten feet, with greasy runners up the two narrow sides for the counterweights. Shining the torch upwards produced a dizzying pattern of concentric squares, each one smaller than the last. The beam picked out the doors to the lobby, followed by each floor up to five until the beam could reach no further.

Theo shivered. Somewhere up there in the darkness the elevator was resting on the seventh floor, waiting to carry its nightmare master to whichever floor he desired. And even further up the rotten core of Darkwater Towers, somewhere on the tenth floor, that master had been spending an awful lot of time. Theo wondered briefly what he'd been doing up there, then decided if it kept McCracken as far away from him as possible, then the tenth floor would suit him just fine.

Something else caught his eye, and he realised why the lift couldn't reach the ground floor any more. The elevator tracks, one in each corner for the guide wheels, had come loose just above Theo's head, and two six-foot lengths had fallen across the shaft. The six inch wide girders formed a cross, wedged against each other, preventing them falling into the inspection pit. It meant that the rollers of the lift couldn't settle below the ground floor so the doors could open level with the floor.

Wind played whistling games in the shaft and the cables twanged and echoed. Thick oily sweetness filled Theo's nostrils, together with the sour smell of damp. It seeped into his bones and told him he'd been in here long enough. One last sweep with the torch and he was stepping out of the door, backing out so as not to bang his head. That's when he saw the metal bar, a long ago discarded off-cut from one of the narrower beams. It was three feet long, flat at one end, and just the job. Theo pulled it away from its cobwebby bed in the corner and stepped back into the warmth of the boiler room.

Without pausing to close the door, he headed back to the steps.

The bar did its work in two minutes flat, chewing the wood around the lock and bending the bolt. The door flew open; Theo was in the office. He pushed it shut behind him and surveyed the room. To his left was the reception window with its broad flat sill, the dull stained windows shut firmly on their runners.

A tall narrow bookcase stood to the right of the door, the top shelves filled with assorted books. A "Collins Dictionary and Thesaurus" leaned casually against a battered copy of "A to Z of Building Maintenance", which in turn dwarfed an unreturned library copy of Stephen King's "Four Past Midnight". On the next shelf down was a well-thumbed stack of "Forum" and "Fiesta - Reader's Letters". The bottom two shelves held half a dozen cardboard box-files marked 'A to E,' and 'F to I,' and so on.

The only other piece of furniture was the desk, a square black MFI self-assembly job with all the personality of a pop-up picture book. It said everything about the owners of Darkwater Towers, cheap, barely functional, and not built to last. There was something missing, and Theo began to panic. Damn, they've taken it out. When they closed the office up they took it out. The top of the desk was thick with dust, a pink blotting pad barely visible next to a discoloured pen-tidy. Apart from that the desktop was empty.

Theo glanced across at the reception window. No, it wasn't there either. His heart sank, then he noticed the wire coming through a hole in the wall next to the reception window. It snaked down to the floor and disappeared behind the desk. He leaned over and saw that it ended abruptly at the right hand drawer. The telephone snuggled quietly in its bed of papers as Theo opened the drawer, relief flooding over him. It dinged softly when he put it on the desk and picked up the receiver. Please God, let it be working, he prayed, putting the receiver to his ear.

A soft purring sounded through the earpiece. Theo racked the phone, then looked through the drawer it had come from. It was time to call for the cavalry but first he wanted...

A new sound intruded into the little room, a sound he was becoming all too familiar with. The elevator motor. He tried to think how long it had been running but didn't have time to go out and check the floor indicator. He knew which way it was going anyway. Down. He scrabbled through the papers, discarding the BT phone book, searching frantically for... There it was. A small green leather bound notebook with "Telephone Numbers" embossed in gold script on the cover. He flicked it open, skimming past the emergency numbers and the "talk sex" lines, and noting thankfully that the numbers he wanted were there.

The elevator sounded closer. Theo put the book in his back pocket and picked up the telephone. His mind raced, wondering how much time he had. He didn't want to be caught like a wasp in a killing jar in this single door office, but he couldn't pass up the chance to ring the police. His fingers keyed in 999 and the line went dead. Of course. This was the reception telephone. He dialled 9 for an outside line, then 999 again.

The dialling tone sounded in his ear.

One ring... two rings...

The lift stopped and the doors opened.

Three rings...

Theo heard the thud of feet hitting concrete from the raised lift floor.

A cultured voice answered, "Emergency services. Do you require Police, fire or ambulance?"

"Police, I'm at..."

Then the footsteps were at the door. There was no time. Theo tried to keep hold of the receiver but it slipped from his grasp. He grabbed the office chair and wedged it under the door handle. A disembodied voice called in the distance, "Hello can I help? Hello... Hello..." The receiver swung from its cord beside the desk.

The door bulged with the weight of a shoulder but the chair held. Calmness settled over Theo, and suddenly every movement had purpose. He pulled the desk to reinforce the chair, then went to the reception window. The left-hand glass slid silently in its track and Theo sat on the sill with his back to the opening. The door banged again, moving the desk and chair six inches into the office. This was all about timing. There would be none of this Die Hard rubbish here. No diving head first through the window as the villain crashed through the door, Theo would break his neck if he did that. And there was no point climbing out of the window while McCracken was still outside either. Timing.

Theo tried to remember where he'd left the bar he'd used to jemmy the door. He was sure he'd leaned it against the wall, and prayed McCracken hadn't picked it up. The door bowed inwards, almost dislodging the chair. One more push and it would be open. Theo braced himself.

A gust of wind from the ill-fitting office window swirled dust around the desktop like a silent disapproving ghost. It played across the blotter then fell silent, waiting.

The telephone handset swung slowly to a stop. For a brief moment all was still, all was quiet.

"'Twas the night before Christmas and not a creature did stir..."

Theo held his breath. For a second he was sure McCracken had abandoned the door and was sneaking round behind him. Any minute now he would feel the caretaker's rancid breath on his neck, and...

The door slammed open, smashing the chair and throwing the desk against the far wall. Theo reached up, grasped the lintel of the reception window and swung his legs up and out. He darted round to the door, slammed it shut and grabbed the bar from against the wall. He slid it under the handle, then twisted it sideways, snagging it across the door jam. It wouldn't hold forever but it would give him time.

The grey slabs of the bottom two steps peered from under the shroud of darkness in the opposite corner, and the elevator doors stared blankly across the foyer. Theo had a head start, but it wouldn't be long before the monster escaped the office and was in pursuit. No, the stairs wouldn't do, and the elevator would show its destination for all to see. He needed to get upstairs but not that way.

The door handle jerked but held. *No time to lose.* Theo turned left and hurried round the corner into the medical room corridor. Behind him the office door reverberated with the blows from within. Along the corridor and he was once again swallowed by the shadows. His hand felt in his trouser pocket, searching for...

It's gone. I've lost it.

Then his fingers touched the cold metal of the key and he fished it out. The single light guided him to the end of the corridor and the door to the service stairs. Wood splintered from the lobby and the iron bar rattled onto the concrete floor. The office door was open. He hoped McCracken was heading in the obvious direction after checking that the elevator hadn't moved. The main stairwell.

With shaky fingers he unlocked the door to the service stairs, certain he would feel the caretaker's hand on his shoulder at any moment. The darkness behind him seeped into his mind, bringing out night terrors to drag his eyes away from the door handle. The handle itself began to twist and slither, hissing like the serpent it had become. Flashing teeth grinned at him and the forked tongue flicked out. Footsteps echoed from the corridor behind him.

Fear dried his mouth, and his hand hesitated over the handle's scaly skin. *There's nothing behind you*, he told himself. The footsteps drew closer. The snake nipped at his fingers. His eyes were drawn to the sound behind him.

THERE IS NOTHING BEHIND YOU!

The footsteps were silenced, and the snake snapped back into a door handle. Theo's breathing sounded loud in his ears, but it was the only sound he could hear. He opened the door and stepped into the gloom of the service stairwell.

CHAPTER 2

Theo's plan was incredibly simple and totally insane. Most of it was in place in his mind, and the mechanics of it were almost complete. There was just one more thing he needed, and only one place he could get it. His own apartment on the fifth floor.

After locking the door of the stairwell behind him he waited, letting the cool darkness wash over him. He remembered how that darkness panicked him when he first came down here. How the bulb blinking out after discovering the door was locked had driven fear up his throat. Now, after almost vapour-locking in the corridor, the cloak of darkness was calming. He basked in it momentarily.

The darkness still hid demons though, demons in his mind. The nightmare scenario he was part of, poked and prodded his subconscious. McCracken... Uriah... The Major... Horrendous visions from a nightscape that went on forever. The blood and the smell and the silent screams that had infested The Towers over the last two weeks, they all came out of the darkness, fed by the calming inactivity as he paused at the bottom of the stairs.

Don't think about it just get on with it. Theo tried to close his mind to the visions that assailed him, but there were two more that could not be denied. *Delia Circelli... and Carl Stensel.* What had happened to one, and what part the other played, wouldn't go away. The only way to silence the whispers was to act. He'd already stood aside far too long, uncertain about what to do, or even what was happening. Now he had a plan of action, as crazy as it was, he felt better.

That plan meant returning to his apartment. Theo pushed away from the door and took the steps two at a time, climbing up towards the welcoming light of the first floor landing and beyond.

Theo had a scare when he reached the fifth floor landing. As he carefully closed the door behind him, a loud bang rattled his teeth and he scurried back into the stairwell. His heart thumped fit to burst and his hands were shaking.

The bang sounded again, then again, then stopped. Stringy tendrils of wind sighed through an open door several floors above him, touching him with icy fingers. The wind gusted twice, and the bangs returned. Twice. Theo calmed himself, realising the window that had been banging intermittently, had been banging here on the fifth floor. He opened the door slightly and peered out.

The landing was empty. Theo's flat was in the opposite wing, along this corridor, past the elevator and main stairwell, and along the far side of The Towers. As he prepared to steal his way across there he had another fright.

He'd locked the door this morning but he couldn't remember where he'd put the keys. It seemed a lifetime ago since he'd set off with his shopping list, breaking his journey in the cosy warmth of Carl Stensel's barbershop. At that time his life had been tilting down the gentle slope towards death by cancer, a thought marginally less intimidating than asking Delia to marry him.

When he'd left his apartment, he had an orderly life, a romantic interest in Delia, and a friend in Carl. Now that life was turned upside down. In twelve short hours his perceptions had been stripped away to show the jagged underworld, which had always existed, hidden beneath the humdrum routine of everyday life. He patted his trouser pockets, only coming up with the loose change in his left pocket and the key to the stairwell in his right.

The main stairs and the elevator doors slid past him in a fog as he approached the north wing, still rummaging. He knew the keys weren't in his jacket pockets before he filled them from the medical cabinet, and he never put them in his back pocket, already bulging with the small telephone book from the office. That only left his inside pocket - no, just his wallet - and the small stamp pocket opposite that.

There they are, thank goodness. His fingers touched the cold metal key ring just as he saw he wouldn't need them. A sharp pain stabbed into his chest, and for a moment he thought his problems might all be solved by a swift and massive heart attack. He rounded to corner to his apartment door, only to see it wasn't there any more.

Like Uriah Lovelycolors' flat, the door had been decimated. Not just smashed open, destroyed. Splinters of wood were strewn across the hallway like an abandoned game of pick-up-sticks, and the handle lay untidily beneath the twisted hinges. A bloody smear snail-trailed through the doorway, balanced by a single footprint every three feet. Whatever was stalking through Darkwater Towers was limping badly and leaving a trail a blind man could follow.

"In the Land of the Blind, the One-Eyed man is King..."

He didn't know why he hadn't noticed it before - probably too pre-occupied looking for his keys - but he should have seen this coming all the way from the elevator. Theo paused in the doorway, looking into the epicentre of a blast of nuclear proportions. His apartment - Melinda's more than his, he always felt - was totally destroyed. It took the wind out of his sails, and depressed him more than anything else he'd seen tonight. This was deeply hurtful, and very, very personal. It was how people felt when an intruder violated the sanctity of their home. And more than anything that had been stolen, the feeling of invasion took something more: their privacy.

Theo felt a whimper climb into his throat, and bit it back. A cold wind took away the cloying dead-flesh smell from the landing, and the window banged again. All evening that window had been beating a tattoo throughout The Towers, sounding an unnerving heartbeat through the dying tower block. Now it only sounded infrequently, like the fading pulse of a man on his last legs. All the time Theo had been listening to it, he'd never thought it would be his window in his apartment sounding his last rights.

He entered the apartment and took stock.

The grandfather clock, rescued from Melinda's parents when they died, was just so much matchwood in the corner, and the Philips television which could only receive three channels wouldn't even get those now, its tube a smoking hole in shattered glass. The settee was upside down. The wood effect of the gas fire was punctured and twisted. And through the kitchen door, the fold-down dining table was legless and flapless, the unwashed breakfast things he'd felt guilty about this morning strewn across the linoleum. The kitchen chairs were snapped in two, canted at an awkward angle against the cooker.

Theo felt hollowed out, as if someone had used one of those apple corers to scoop his insides out, core and pips and everything. The little flat hadn't been much but it had been home, and it was the last place Melinda had lived. For that reason alone it held a certain nostalgia and for that more than anything else he felt violated, abused, and downright pissed-off.

Melinda...

Forgetting the reason he'd come back here, Theo spun round towards the dark wood dresser that stood under the window. Surprisingly it was still in one piece. Melinda stared angrily from beneath beetled brows. There was no mistaking that look. It was the look she reserved for days when Theo left his clothes over the bedroom floor, or when he left the breakfast pots in the sink for the entire day, or when he screwed the towel up in the bathroom instead of straightening it to dry.

No. Not that day. That day she had been annoyingly restrained. Theo remembered his reaction, and shame once again coloured his cheeks. He looked into his dead wife's

eyes, and saw her expression change. The hard-edged anger gave way to sadness, and that slipped into compassion for Theo. This was his home as much as hers, and she sensed the hurt behind his grim expression.
WE WILL NOT DIE,
UNLESS WE ARE FORGOTTEN...

No, she wasn't forgotten, never would be. Her face in the photograph didn't change at all, but he sensed her mood, and knew just how she would have felt. Anger first, then sadness, then that typical Good Samaritan streak would kick in and she'd feel sorry for Theo. That's the way she was, and only now he realised that's where he got it from. It wasn't in his genes and it wasn't something he'd picked up from the do-gooders at the prison, it was Melinda. The simple kindness, which was deep rooted inside her, had rubbed off on him during their years together. He was a better man because of her and that doubled his sadness. If he was a better man through knowing her, how much less of a man was he without her?

Melinda's picture gave him strength. He touched it gently, thankful that among all the destruction, her common decency had been left untouched. On impulse he picked up the gilt edged 6 x 4 inch frame and kissed her softly, then slipped it into his inside pocket. He stuck out his chest, in that old army way she loved so much, and snapped "come on" to himself, banishing the self-pity which had been creeping up on him.

In the corner by the door, something else had escaped the carnage. Theo walked over to it and looked down into the wastepaper bin. Besides not washing the pots as often as Melinda would have liked, he also hadn't emptied the bin in over two weeks. In truth there wasn't much in it anyway, most of the rubbish going in the bin liner under the sink ready for the garbage shoot. A crumpled piece of paper stared up at him.

Cancer...
... at the most five months.

He bent to pick it up, smoothing out the creases and read the message again. Two weeks ago he had resigned himself to a gentle slide into illness and death, feeling it would be a release from a life devoid of hope, or happiness, or peace.

Now, with the end staring him in the face a lot sooner than expected, he didn't want to give it up. The urgency of the situation sharpened his senses, and the danger heightened his awareness. This was the feeling people got during the war, when imminent death made them live each moment to the full because it might be their last. Theo knew tonight might be his last, and he intended to make it count.

He opened the left hand drawer of the dresser. Neatly folded handkerchiefs hugged the corner beside regimented socks and two curled up leather belts. He pushed the socks aside and reached to the back, fingers questing. They aren't here. He bent to look, pulling the drawer further out. Light fragmented and starred on metal. His fingers touched cold steel, and he pulled the heavy pair of HMP transport handcuffs out of the drawer.

Now he was ready. He ran over the plan in his mind, ticking off each item in his pockets and weighing the cuffs in his hand. They should do the trick. Then Theo noticed a strange shape reflected in the window, and electricity coursed along the white highway of his bones. He turned back into the apartment, and watched Carl Stensel limp out of the kitchen, leaving a trail of blood on the lino.

For the second time in half an hour Theo thought his problems would be solved by a swift, massive, heart attack. Pain clamped his chest, squeezing with an iron fist. He rubbed it with his free hand and the pain eased.

Kuta Lametka...

The shrunken head might well be wedged in the folds of Mick McCracken's settee downstairs, but Carl Stensel's head didn't look much better now. The barber looked pale and sickly, his eyes bulging eggs in red-rimmed sockets. Flecks of blood stood out on his cheeks.
Emaciated corpse discovered on wasteland...
Emaciated bodies. Theo recalled the story in the Northern Gazette, the gruesome discoveries, the location of the bodies, and the direction they had been heading. Following on from that he remembered Mick McCracken's fat and bloated body in the cellar, and then the shrivelled face as he looked out of his flat when Theo had returned.
Shrivelled face... shrunken head.
Kuta Lametka...
The dead black eyes of the shrunken head had watched Theo read that paper in the cosy warmth of the Gents Hairdressers. The Gents Hairdresser had brought that head to Darkwater Towers where the, once fat, caretaker had become a shrivelled prune. And now the hairdresser was becoming a shrivelled prune himself. Theo tightened his grip on the handcuffs, holding one end so the other swung loose. He braced himself for the assault.

Dead black eyes. Bulging eggs in red-rimmed sockets. Theo watched those eyes for any change that would signal the attack, but all he saw was sadness. Carl Stensel stared back at him, blood leaking from a split in the corner of his right eye, and his head tilted to the left. His eyebrows raised in the middle in comical apology. Theo faltered. Something wasn't right. The ogre that stood before him wasn't as imposing as he'd expected. A modicum of sympathy filtered into his resolve.

The barber staggered to his left, holding out a hand to steady himself on the door jam. Blood seeped from between his fingers. The sudden movement sent another spark of electricity through Theo's body and he stepped back against the dresser.

"I tried to..." Carl Stensel began, then the hand slipped, leaving a bloody print on the paintwork as he toppled over onto the living room floor. Theo acted immediately. Despite his fears, that old Good Samaritan instinct came to the fore. Melinda's photograph in his pocket would be smiling approval. The instinct, which had rubbed off from her, took charge, and Theo forgot about the handcuffs and went to Carl's side. The old barber was sprawled across the carpet on his side, mouth working silently.

Theo crouched beside him, not sure where to get hold, then a hand of iron gripped his arm. The hairdresser's eyes glared at him, and his mouth formed words as clear as mud.

"...tried to warn you," he said, then passed out.

CHAPTER 3

Wind howled under the door of the laundry room, and Theo wedged the towel across the bottom to form an improvised draft excluder. Carl was sitting, swathed in blankets, against the boiler in the corner, a mug of thick black coffee warming his hands. The DF's Theo had given him with the coffee were beginning to take effect, numbing the pain and controlling the shakes which threatened to spill more coffee down his front than in his mouth.

The taste of bad-news-to-come soured Theo's taste buds like an attack of bile burped up and swallowed down again. He stood over Carl and waited. Along the corridor the loose window in Theo's apartment banged in the wind, and he wished he'd closed it before leaving.

After Carl had collapsed, Theo had soaked a cloth in warm water to revive him, dabbing it gently over the old man's face until he spluttered awake. That done he had examined the wounds, shocked at their severity but puzzled by their nature. Carl's hands had narrow splits running the length of his fingers. They oozed blood in a steady dribble. His eyes were sore, the upper and lower lids red and swollen. Tiny fissures between the eyelashes squeezed pinpricks of blood onto his cheeks.

All that looked painful enough, but his feet must have been the worst. If his hands had split, then his feet had split big time. Blood soaked through his socks and shoes, and the involuntary wince when Theo touched them showed just how much they hurt. Walking on them must have been hell. Theo brought sterile dressings from the first aid box (which Melinda had insisted they keep in the kitchen) and more warm water. He cleaned the blood from Carl's hands and wrapped them in clean white bandages. Within seconds, fresh blood seeped through. There was no way to close the cuts and short of getting an ambulance, dressing them and dishing out painkillers was the best Theo could do.

Amid the carnage of his apartment Theo suddenly felt vulnerable. After finding Delia hiding among the ruins of her kitchen, Theo had made hot chocolate and sat her down at the kitchen table, reckoning that if McCracken had already been there they would be safe. He didn't feel that way now. The level of destruction showed a more concerted effort than the damage in the other apartments, and there was something else. Even before all this started, McCracken didn't like Theo.

Don't think he appreciates you getting extra supplies for us wrinklies.

He wouldn't appreciate a good shit if he was constipated.

Charlie Brewer had been right, but this was more than that. Theo felt the caretaker had targeted him for a reason, and that meant if he'd missed him once he might try again later. That left the problem of what to do about Carl. He couldn't just leave him, and by the looks of him he needed serious attention. Theo listened at the door and decided to risk a slight delay. The kettle boiled in two minutes flat, and Theo filled the Thermos flask with strong black coffee, then he gathered as many blankets as he could carry and got Carl to his feet.

That was half an hour ago, and now the gents hairdresser seemed to be coming round. Theo absent-mindedly touched the ear that had nearly turned him into Van Gogh.

"Well Carl," he said. "This is the longest you've gone without talking since I've known you."

Carl managed a weak smile, holding the mug tight between both hands.

Satisfied that the door was sealed from the wind, Theo walked over and sat beside the barber. The fifth floor laundry room was as austere as the rest of the tower block, dull grey walls over terracotta tiles. A single Hotpoint twin tub stood next to the door and a rack of floor-to-ceiling open lathed shelves for drying were fastened to the wall beside the boiler. Gentle heat gave the little room a cosy air and the low wattage bulb above the door barely kept the shadows at bay. Carl was just a shadowy pile of blankets with a head and arms in the corner, and Theo wasn't much more.

It was safe. Or as safe as you could get tonight in Darkwater Towers.

Theo looked at the barber. Carl stared back, any hint of a smile banished from his face. "Over here the one eyed man might be king," he said, "but I thought you might need glasses to see a little better."

"Let's cut the cryptic crap shall we," Theo said quietly, his voice low and dangerous. "Just tell me what's going on."

"I told you about Kuta Lametka," Carl started. "Well, I think something similar is at work here." His hands were steady around the mug, and his voice had regained some of its strength.

"I don't understand. What has an island legend got to do with a string of deaths leading to Darkwater Towers?"

"It was, as you say, a legend before we arrived, but don't forget, I witnessed its continuation. And don't forget the bodies. They were in the jungle leading to Sol Benita, but they were not shrivelled and emaciated because of the heat."

Theo leaned his head back against the wall as he tried to remember the story Carl had first told him in the warmth of the gents hairdressers. Heat from the boiler took him back, but as Carl repeated his tale Theo's mind took him further. Carl's voice droned on, crossing every "t" and dotting every "i", and the heat did a magical thing. It carried Theo from the draughty laundry to the warm leather of the barber's chair, and from there to the steamy heat of the South Pacific.

Dense foliage crowded around him. Sweat flowed down his neck, soaking into the collar of his cotton shirt. In the distance a monkey called in a chattery voice, and all around him the constant buzz of insects made his head spin. Then, as they parted the leaves in front of them, the village of Sol Benita came into view.

The smell of fear was thick and heady, like a narcotic spread across the jungle leaves. It wasn't just the bodies they had encountered on the trail from the shore, it was something else. Carl could taste it as clearly as the salt from his own sweat.

Death was in the air.

Carl threw a nervous glance at his shipmates. Joe Westerman's imposing bulk brushed the trees aside with arrogant self-confidence but the boson's eyes betrayed his unease. Grizzle-chinned and wide as a gun carriage, Joe could outface Rambo and out-eat Desperate Dan. If something had got him spooked it had to be serious. Abhir Kuskas was a different matter. The ship's purser - nicknamed Abacus because he could count the hairs on your belly as if they were coins of the realm - would look nervous if he'd won the lottery, let alone seeing the corpses they'd encountered in the jungle behind them.

The one who gave Carl some confidence however, was the one he'd have least expected. Harold Beauchamp, the Emily May's Supply Officer, was a bookish, bespectacled, white-as-a-sheet, pimple of a man. The crew called him 'Beau Geste,' not because he shared the splendid ideals of the French Foreign Legion, but because they all reckoned he'd had his funny bone removed. No jests from him. He wasn't at sea because he could navigate, or because he could cook, or because he had a natural instinct for the vagaries of the oceans. He was here because he could count, get the best deals going, and scrounge like a good-un. None of these were qualities to instil confidence in a rag-tag crew who were scared shitless by the things they'd seen since leaving the ship, but against the odds he had.

Five miles behind them, the tramp steamer Emily May rode anchor in the bay, while Captain Hanson and the rest of the crew made running repairs after the storm. The party of six who ventured to Sol Benita were considered lucky. They not only escaped the punishing labour of refitting a 200-ton cargo ship, but there were the benefits of a beer or three, and the chance to meet the natives. The women especially, who were renowned for bestowing their favours on visiting crews.

Right now, Carl didn't feel lucky at all. A monkey screeched sharply to his left, making his skin crawl, then Joe parted the leaves and Sol Benita came into view. As they came out of the trees, the village elder (or chief) came over to greet them. He was a short man with a pot-belly, wearing an incongruous mix of blue sarong, a Nike tennis shirt, and a New York Yankees' baseball cap worn back to front. He waved his hands vigorously and jabbered like the monkey in the trees. Carl didn't understand a word of it but knew what he was saying.

Go away. Danger. Get out.

His mouth tasted sour and dry. The sweat on his back turned cold and the shirt plastered across his shoulders felt like a cold damp towel. Joe Westerman looked nonplussed - which wasn't unusual - and backed off a pace as the elder advanced on the group of sailors. Abacus stepped behind the protective bulk of the boson. Only Harold Beauchamp stood his ground, and for that, his stock went up in Carl's eyes. He held his arms out, palms down, placating the village elder, who slowed his excited jabbering. His voice lowered until he was talking normally. Carl still didn't understand a word of it.

"What's he talking about Beau," he asked, standing shoulder to shoulder with him. He kept the quiver out of his voice, but only just.

Beau listened patiently to the village elder's story, then turned to Carl. "Come with me," he said. Then to the others, "Stay here. Don't touch anything." He set off across the compound towards a large domed building that stood out among the wooden shacks and the Mercantile Marine Store and Bar. Carl fell in step beside him, the village elder simply watching them go.

"What is it?" Carl tried again.

"I don't know." Beau looked even more dour than usual.

"Come on. He must have said something."

"He said plenty. None of which made any sense."

The open ground opposite the store's front porch and walkway was dried mud. Normally the arrival of a shore party would attract the curiosity of the villagers. Children would circle them; waiting for cast-offs, and girls would flaunt their ample curves, plying for trade. Today no one came out. None of them even stuck their heads out of the door to see who was there. Today, the village was silent as the grave. The only sounds were the insects chirruping in the dense foliage, and flies buzzing noisily around their heads.

Beau led Carl between the store and a ramshackle outhouse, into a clearing the size of a squash court. The domed building towered above them, and Carl noticed something strange about it. All the windows on this side were boarded over with heavy timbers, and the double doors were nailed shut. The cold towel on his back turned into an ice pack, and the small hairs at the nape of his neck bristled.

Then a plaintive cry that was neither human nor monkey sounded from inside of the building and Carl almost turned and ran.

"All he'll say is, It is caught. It is caught."

Carl watched Beau's face in the flickering glow of the oil lamp. This threw an eerie shadow across the boardwalk in front of the store, turning the Supply Officer into a grotesque monster crawling across the floor. All around them in the gathering gloom of early evening the jungle noises began to recede, closing down for the night. Only the constant buzz and chirrup of the insects sounded in the heavy atmosphere.

"<u>What</u> is caught?"

"He didn't say. Not with any sense anyway. But whatever it is, they're all afraid of it, that's for certain."

Carl sipped his lukewarm beer. The hard wood of the bench pressed grooves into his buttocks, but he didn't want to get up. Getting up would be an indication of upcoming action, and tonight he wanted none of that. Harold Beauchamp sat next to him in silence, sunken eyes staring unseeing at the boarded shut building across the compound.

A bottle smashed on the wooden floor in the bar, sending shock waves through Carl's chest. Joe Westerman, Abacus, and the rest of the crew were inside, taking Dutch courage. No thought had been given to submitting the order for supplies and the deck hands stuck close to Joe, seeking reassurance from his bulk. For all his strength however, he was out of his depth here. The only man who seemed to have a handle on what was going on was Harold Beauchamp and he wasn't letting on.

Sweat rolled down Carl's face, stinging his eyes. He wiped a stained cotton sleeve across his brow. The beer was warm and gassy, leaving an unpleasant taste in his mouth but it did give him something to do. Took his mind off the village elder's heated dialogue with the supply officer. Carl had stood and watched, not understanding what was being said, but understanding it was bad. Beau had retorted with venom, disgust sounding in his voice and, without looking at Carl, had stalked off to the Mercantile Store.

Not knowing was bad enough, but the thing that stuck in Carl's mind, even years after, was the look in the eyes of the strong young man who was introduced to Beau that evening. He stood erect and proud, exuding a dignity borne of many years as the village's protector. He was dark-skinned and well muscled, probably twenty-five to thirty years old, Carl never found out which and in all the conversation that followed the only thing Carl understood was his name.

Kuta Lametka.

Now, as Carl followed Beau's gaze towards the domed building that had become a prison for... something... he waited for the supply officer to explain. The man he had always thought of as a weak-willed waste of bunk space knew what was about to happen, and Carl sensed it was something terrible. Slowly, night crept over the village, splashes of light flickering in the windows of several of the mud huts. Apart from the village elder and Kuta Lametka, no one else had showed their faces but those lights showed that the village wasn't as deserted as it seemed.

Carl finished his drink and set the glass on the floor. He glanced at his watch. Eight thirty. Full dark. As if Carl had broken the spell, Beau stood up abruptly. "It's time," he said.

"Time for what?"

"I'll tell you on the way. Un-holster your side arm."

Carl couldn't believe they were going to do this, yet as he kept station outside the nailed up doors, it sat right with the dread feeling he'd had ever since they entered the jungle this morning. He'd been sailing the South Seas for long enough not to interfere with local traditions, and definitely not to question native superstition or legend. But this was going to be hard.

In the flames from the torches either side of the doors, he felt very alone. Beau hadn't returned from checking that all the windows were still secure, and the rest of the crew had been banished to the bar, something that hadn't taken much persuading. The demented cries from behind the nailed up doors had stopped as if the source of the beastly noise knew something was afoot.

Kuta Lametka waited at the far end of the small enclosure, taking communion, or whatever-the-hell stood for that there, from the village elder. He was preparing himself with a stony face that could not hide the fear in his eyes. The indefinable IT which had infected and discarded all those bodies on its way through the jungle waited inside the Council Chamber, residing in the human vessel of the village elder's only son. For three weeks it had been penned in, locked up inside the most important building in Sol Benita.

They had waited for it to grow weak, for the host's body to wither and die. The village elder had cried over his lost son, but those tears were long gone. Now his son was dead, and all that remained was the shell, the husk, devoid of grain or the slightest trace of human spirit but before that body died something else had to be done and that was...

Carl's fevered mind pushed the thought aside. It was too ghastly to contemplate, and glancing over at the frightened face of Kuta Lametka only made it worse. A rhythmic drumming started inside the chamber, faint at first, then gaining strength. The ceremonial council drum. The beat pulsed and ebbed, growing louder then softer, but always keeping the beat. Carl's heart pounded in his chest, and the rhythm of the drum matched it. It drew him on. Fear flared his nostrils. His breath grew short and anxious.

From the darkness to his left a shadowy figure emerged. A hand fell on his shoulder like a hammer blow, and Carl jerked back, heart in his mouth. Beau patted his shoulder again, more gently, trying to reassure the man who would later become the Gents Hairdresser to Darkwater Towers.

"You know what to do," Beau said, drawing his service revolver.

Carl nodded, his pistol already in his hand.

Beau turned and signalled to the village elder who shambled over to the front of the building, his legs stiff and unresponsive. Kuta Lametka followed. The young man's eyes were closed, lips murmuring a silent prayer. Inside, the drumbeat grew louder. That was good. It meant they knew where IT was. Beside the drum. The large bowl of the drum was mounted on a platform in the centre of the room, in full view of all the council members' pews. Beau raised the claw of the ship's packing tool, and prised out the first nail.

The drumbeat stopped.

Carl held his breath. Beau looked up from the second nail. Kuta Lametka paused in his mutterings. Then Beau was attacking the nails. One by one they screeched out of the heavy wooden door, scattering on the floor like spent cartridges. Carl braced himself, raising the pistol.

Within minutes the door was free. Beau dropped the crowbar in the dirt of the yard and reached for the handle, pistol cocked and ready. Carl moved to one side, letting Kuta step into the gap. One final glance around, then Beau yanked the left hand door open. Carl caught a fleeting glimpse of the council chamber, lit only by two flickering torches either side of the drum, then Kuta walked into the room and Beau slammed the door shut, sealing his fate.

They stood outside the door for a full two minutes. Then the screaming started. Carl lunged forward but Beau, displaying strength you never would have guessed, held him back. "No. Not yet."

"You bastard," Carl yelled. "We can't just leave him like that."

"We can, and we have to. You know that."

Beside them, the village elder wept quietly, canting awkwardly to one side, a broken man. The screams were replaced by a disgusting choking noise, like a man drowning in porridge, then the room went quiet. The jungle surrounding the village exploded - a cacophony of noise - monkeys chattered and screeched, wild birds cawed, and the combined force of the evening insects chirruped and buzzed, disturbed by the happenings in the council chamber.

"Now. While it's weak." Beau pulled open the door for the second time and stepped inside, gun raised. Carl followed, keeping to the right while Beau took up a station on the left. The village elder stood between them, limping slightly. Flames from the torches licked at their faces, glinting off the smooth metal of their pistols. It tried to keep the shadows at bay, but failed miserably.

Carl waited for his eyes to adjust to the dark, feeling like a child again, cowering in the blackness of the ghost train tunnel. Any minute he expected to feel the soft touch of cobwebs on his face, and hear the scream of the corpse rising from its coffin. Neither came. He simply stood, frozen to the spot, and watched as flickering light picked out angles and lines around the council chamber.

The room was perhaps twenty feet across, and fifteen feet high at its peak. From the blackness at the edges Carl could see shadowy benches running the circumference of the circular building. The council pews hugged the wall, forming a circle, every seat facing the centre. The rest of the floor space was empty until it reached the platform with the heavy drum.

Empty? No, not empty. Light flickered on a shiny wet patch on the floor in front of them and then a more solid shadow formed beside it. The village elder whimpered softly as he recognised the cast off shell of his son. Beau moved forward slowly, and Carl kept pace with him, glancing around the gloom nervously. Apart from the body on the floor there was nothing.

Darkness closed in around them, heat from the constantly burning torches pricking beads of sweat on Carl's face and neck. A rancid, bad-meat smell steamed from the heavy atmosphere, making it hard to breath without choking.

It lined his throat, and flavoured his mouth. He wanted to spit it out, but couldn't raise enough moisture, his mouth bone dry.

As they stepped round the body on the floor Carl caught a glimpse of its sunken features. Even though he'd seen the same thing several times on the journey through the jungle it still took his breath away. The body lay in an untidy heap; partly covered by the blanket it had wrapped itself in. The hands were curled into claws, bony fingers barely contained in shrivelled folds of flesh. The torso seemed to have fallen in, shrink wrapped over a skeleton that stuck out in bony shards, ribs here, hips there, shoulders across the top. Then there was the face. That was what had provoked Carl's response. Parchment leather features were wrinkled and sucked in on a skull that looked far too big. The eyes were rimmed with tiny rips in the flesh, staring blankly out of an emaciated frame that was barely human. The throat carried the scars of his attempts to tear out whatever had possessed him, but the corpse bore witness to his eventual failure.

There was something else, but Carl didn't have time to work it out because they were now past the corpse, heading for the only place the beast could be hiding. The drum on the platform in the middle of the room. Fear seized him, and the gun began to shake in his hand. He tightened his grip as he approached the platform.

Eight feet...

The drum was just a musical instrument.

Six feet...

Now it looked ominously like a giant squat toad.

Four feet...

The frame which held the drum, spread across the platform, hiding a dark rectangle of unseen space behind it. Plenty of room for someone to hide... or something. His hand steadied, and he kept the barrel pointing squarely at the base of the drum. To his left, Beau did the same. Somewhere behind him the village elder stayed close.

A niggling doubt fluttered across Carl's mind. The emaciated face wandered across his mindscape. Then Beau was climbing onto the platform, and Carl steadied his aim, ready for whatever might come bounding over the drum. Beau moved left, around the drum base, pistol cocked and ready. He sidled behind the squat black toad, and...

Nothing. Beau relaxed his grip on the pistol, resting his gun hand on the opposite shoulder like a down market James Bond. His head leaned forward and he scraped his chin across the back of his hand. He let out a sigh that was three parts relief and one part fear. "He's not here," he managed.

Carl felt madness creeping over him. The pent up fear of whatever-the-hell was loose in here screwed his stomach into a knot of muscle. *If it wasn't behind the drum then where...* His head snapped upwards, alerted by a sound in the shadowy roof space. Beau whipped his pistol into straight-armed aim.

That niggling doubt returned. Even while he aimed at the ceiling it persisted. Something was wrong.

High up in the blackness the sound came again. A creaking noise followed by dropping twigs and straw. Carl panicked. His mind was torn between what he heard and what his mind was telling him. Fear tightened his face into an ugly grin. More straw fell from the unseen roof beams, and he squeezed the trigger.

Click.

Carl's mouth voiced a silent scream, his vocal cords frozen. His fingers fumbled for the safety catch, snagging it off. All at once the discordant note in his mind leapt into clarity. It wasn't the drum and it wasn't the ceiling; the thing they sought wasn't hiding behind the door, as they'd come in.

...whimpered softly as he recognised the cast off shell of his son.

The cast off shell it might be, and emaciated it certainly was, but it shouldn't be taking up so much room under the blanket. Carl snapped his attention from the rafters to the floor just in time to see Kuta Lametka rise from the folds of the blanket.

There was no doubting it was Kuta Lametka, but he wasn't the same man who had come in a few minutes earlier. He rose from the floor, then just kept rising. He must have grown at least a foot since the change and filled out too. His face had spread but the skin that covered it hadn't been able to cope. Ragged stretch marks ran down both cheeks and the nose and eyes had torn as the nostrils and eyeballs bulged outwards. Blood ran in tiny rivulets down his face and the eyes not only bulged they glowed with evil intent, pinpricks of red sparking in the irises.

The village elder stood dumbfounded, unable to believe what he had feared and expected but never experienced. Kuta moved forward, closing the gap to the elder with incredible speed. Carl swung the pistol down and aimed squarely at the monster's chest.

"Nooo. Don't kill him," Beau yelled, dashing down from the platform. He lunged at Carl, knocking the gun aside as the explosion sent the bullet smashing into the pews. Carl was too far-gone, the plan sent flying out of his head in his panic. The village elder had turned to stone. Only Harold Beauchamp remembered what they had to do, and here as well his stock went up.

"Not yet," he screamed at Carl, then to the elder. "The sword. The bloody sword." At last the council member, who barely had time to grieve over the loss of his son, snapped out of his trance. He struggled to draw the curved blade of the ceremonial sword from beside his right leg. Miraculously his limp was cured. Beau lowered his pistol to Kuta Lametka's knees but he was too late. With a flash of fingernails turned into talons, the beast struck out, snipping the supply officer's hand clean off. The fist, still holding the revolver, slapped to the floor, and the gun went off. The sound exploded in Carl's ears and he was suddenly back with the game plan. Blood gushed from Beau's severed wrist but before he could attempt to staunch it the talons swung back, taking out his throat and half his chin. His head lolled forward into the cavity and he died in a spreading pool of blood.

It mustn't be killed outright while it still has its head.

Of course not. Carl remembered what Beau had said on the porch outside the Mercantile Store. "If it is killed the essence will invade the nearest subject. The only way to prevent this is to..."   Carl was in control of himself again. He quickly aimed and fired twice, blowing out Kuta's kneecaps. The swollen native dropped like a stone, the shattered legs giving way. He fell forward, breaking the fall with his hands. For just a moment he leant like that, his head bowed with pain. The village elder saw his chance. He swivelled to one side, making room for himself, then swung the sword in one mighty blow. The blade caught Kuta across the back of the neck and crunched bone as it sliced through the swollen flesh.

Lametka let out a roar that was instantly cut off. The head dropped to the floor and rolled to one side. Carl snatched the leather bag from his belt and dropped it over the snarling face. He nudged it in with his foot then tightened the drawstring. The mouth still moved against the leather and the head felt hot. Carl fought back the vomit that rose in his throat. To his left, Beau twitched twice then was still. The oppressive heat in the council chamber made Carl's head spin. The room began to sway. In front of him the torch flames did a lazy dance, then the drum seemed to be rolling off the platform. Phantoms swept out of the shadows, mingling with the blood and carnage on the floor, and carried Carl away. Then, as the village elder took the leather bag from him, Carl passed out.

"I don't know how long I was out," Carl said, his drink forgotten. "When I came round the head was in a jar, and that was almost worse. It had already begun to shrink, so it was more or less normal size again, and it just had a look of surprise on its face."

Wind howled in the corridor outside the laundry room, trying to force its way under the door. Theo sat in silence.

"It was Kuta Lametka again, apart from the splits, but the evil thing was still inside. I could see it behind his eyes. It was trapped, and once the pickling process was complete that was that. The village was free of the badness. Two days later we took the supplies to the ship, but nobody mentioned what had happened. We said Beau had had an accident and buried him there. The village elder made a big thing of it. Quite a ceremony. Afterwards he took me to one side and gave me the head. It was completely shrunken by then, just as you saw it at the barbershop. He wanted it taking as far away from Sol Benita as possible."

Carl lapsed into silence, and Theo could see he was close to tears. He shifted his position against the wall, trying to get his mind round the strange tale he had just heard.

"And then?" He asked.

"Then?" Carl's eyes came back into focus. "Then I lost my appetite for travelling. When I got back to England I left the Merchant Navy and reverted to my old trade. Cutting hair was my first job and it will be my last." He looked at Theo meaningfully. Heat from the boiler made the room feel cosy and warm, but Theo felt anything but cosy. He was trying to discover what relevance Kuta Lametka had to the events unfolding at Darkwater Towers.

"And you think the same thing is happening here?" Carl put his mug on the concrete and huddled beneath his blanket.

Fear was etched over his face, but there was something else. Sadness. And guilt.

"This thing is a disease. A living thing yes, but only as alive as bacteria or germs. It infests the host and then controls it. Uses it as a vessel to carry it from one place to the next."

"But why did it come here?"

Carl looked at his feet.

"What?" That guilty look was worrying Theo.

"It is a disease, but it is not alone. There are others, kin if you like. I think they are linked."

Theo didn't like the way this was going. "And?"

"When I brought the head here it was to get it as far away from Sol Benita as possible. I don't think it was far enough."

That shut Theo up. It seemed incredible that this thing had come all this way to... to what? Avenge its kin? Reclaim its kin? It was just too fantastic for words, but was it true? There was something else leading on from that. That guilty look clung to Carl's down turned face. "Then this is about..."

"Yes." Carl looked up. "If I hadn't brought Kuta Lametka here..." His voice faded away. Unable to say what was plain to see. "And I don't think this is the first attempt." Now the guilt was so thick it almost moved Theo to tears.

"What do you mean?" he asked.

"Well. A few years ago..." Before he could finish, Theo's head jerked towards the door. The towel wedged across the bottom kept the draft out, and it muffled some of the noises from the landing. It didn't dampen all the sound though, and now the distinctive whine of the elevator motor could be clearly heard. Theo listened with bated breath as the lift stopped, and the doors opened just twenty feet away along the corridor.

CHAPTER 4

Before Theo had left Moor Grange School, when he was thirteen or so, he had broken the school record for the hundred yards dash. When the staff panic alarm had gone off in "E" wing, many years later, he had come pretty close to breaking it again, but when the bell dinged at the end of the corridor, signalling the arrival of the elevator, Theo reckoned he'd blown that record into a cocked hat. He was at the laundry room door in a nanosecond, aching back or no aching back.

Carl struggled to his feet but a combination of the comforting heat from the boiler and the energy sapping powers of the painkillers left him weak and drowsy. He leaned against the wall for support.

Theo slid the rolled towel away from the door with his foot and listened intently. There was no immediate sound from outside so he opened the door an inch and peered through the gap. Down the corridor to the right, Theo's apartment was just out of sight. The familiar sound of McCracken's laboured steps came along the corridor. They seemed to be heading for Theo's flat, no doubt checking again to see if the ex-prison warder had returned. Theo thanked his lucky stars that he'd insisted they come along here instead of waiting in the kitchen.

The footsteps grew louder, and Theo nudged the door almost shut. One eye glared out through the gap, and he saw something that froze his breath in his mouth. When he'd attended to Carl's wounds he'd cleaned and dressed them as best he could, but blood had continued to seep through the bandages as he'd led Carl to the laundry room. As he looked out now, he could see the smeared trail leading from his flat right to the door. The footsteps stopped outside Theo's apartment.

He closed the door, and looked frantically round the laundry room. Carl was in no condition to make a dash for it, and the trail of blood lead right to their door. Theo racked his brain for a solution. The room was stark and grey and empty, just the Hotpoint in one corner and the boiler in the other. No hiding place there. That only left the wooden shelving along the left hand wall. The pine frame stood floor to ceiling, each shelf constructed of three by one planking spaced six inches apart for airing. The shelves were four feet deep and eighteen inches apart. On the middle shelf was a pile of neatly folded sheets and towels, ready for collection.

Theo calculated size and weight, then glanced over at Carl. A thin pool of blood had begun to settle at his feet, and the bandages were stained a dull red. Theo quickly took the spare dressings from the First Aid box, unwrapped them then, scattering the wrappings on the terracotta tiles, he smeared the pool of blood into a trail towards the door, stopping a couple of feet short. He took a towel from the shelf and laid it between Carl and the shelving.

"Come on," he said. "Stay on the towel."

Carl saw what Theo was doing and moved as quickly as he could. Outside, the footsteps started again, and Theo switched off the light.

Theo held his breath as the door opened. Light from the corridor bled into the room, dull, grey and listless. It reached the corners but only just, and picked out the rust spotted Hotpoint and the insulated padding of the boiler, but for a moment the dull red smear on the floor blended with the terracotta of the tiles.

A shadowy figure stood in the doorway, its head then cocked to one side as if deep in thought. Theo could just about make him out between a gap in the barricade of towels and sheets on the second shelf.

Theo was curled up, knees drawn to his chest, and Carl was wedged behind him against the wall. Theo was relying on the theory of parallax view, hoping that from the side the six-inch gaps between the lathes would form a solid block to McCracken's sight line. There were only enough towels and sheets to block the front of the shelf, and if McCracken decided to lean in and look down he would be able to see their pathetic attempt at concealment.

The figure waited in the doorway, staring at the blood on the floor. Theo hoped that the blood would say - they have left this room, dragging blood behind them, but then they noticed that and dressed the wound properly before leaving. It was a thin hope, but it was all they had. Theo squinted through the gap, holding his breath. His heartbeat so loud he was sure McCracken would hear it. Cold air wafted in through the door. Carl's leg began to tremble behind him.

The figure stood there for what seemed an age, tall and still and silent. Tiny footsteps crawled up Theo's forearms, pricking the hairs up and raising gooseflesh. Suddenly he thought. *Something was wrong. Tall and still and silent. Still and silent certainly, but tall? No, not as tall as before.* Theo tried to remember how much the caretaker had shrunk when he'd last seen him in the doorway of his apartment. The face had sunk and the frame had become emaciated as his life force was being used up, but he had still appeared tall.

The shadowman paused a moment longer, then reached in and flicked on the light. Fear shrieked through Theo's body, and Carl jerked involuntarily behind him. The light was blinding, but not as revealing as when the figure stepped into the room. It wasn't Mick McCracken at all. It was Charlie Brewer.

Theo felt relief flood over him. The diminutive boxer stood looking at the bloody smear and discarded medical wrappers, then turned towards the airing shelves. At least someone else has survived, Theo thought, and was about to call out when a hand clamped over his mouth. Shock jumped up his throat. Momentarily he had forgotten about Carl lying cramped behind him. Then anger surged forward. *What the hell are you doing?* He yelled in his mind. *It's Charlie.*

Theo stared out through the towels, and for a brief moment Charlie stared right back. Their eyes were locked like the proverbial, "their eyes met across a crowded room" and Theo was glad the little boxer had seen him. Then he saw something in those eyes he recognised. Something he had seen earlier but not realised, and something Carl had only just finished mentioning. There was a glint of red in those eyes and, now he thought about it, they were bigger than before. Bulging. Tiny splits, fresh and sore, showed around the rims, and beads of blood pricked out. The cheeks too were stretched and taught, ragged tears visible in the bright light of the laundry fluorescent. That glint of red had showed in McCracken's eyes when he'd last seen him, and according to Carl it had flashed in Kuta Lametka's eyes as well.

Those terrible eyes stared right through Theo like x-ray vision and he thought he was caught. Then the eyes swivelled to the right, checked the washer and the boiler, and seemed to make a decision. The room was empty. The prey had gone. With more spring in his step than Charlie Brewer had exhibited for many years, the new demon of Darkwater Towers turned and left, not bothering to switch off the light or close the door.

Footsteps receded along the corridor, and Theo's mind screamed in turmoil.

CHAPTER 5

A kaleidoscope of images swirled round Theo's tortured mind. Mick McCracken splatted him a rat in the tropical heat of the basement. Charlie Brewer entered the circular forum of the council chamber with Carl and Beau, while Delia banged rhythmically on the stretched skin of Kuta Lametka's upturned head. And Melinda wandered serenely through the corridors of Darkwater Towers while snowfall outside signalled Christmas Day, a crumpled letter from Theo's doctor in her hand.

It was the vision of Melinda that dragged him back to reality. He felt into his inside pocket for the reassuring shape of the photograph.
WE WILL NOT DIE,
UNLESS WE ARE FORGOTTEN...

The message burned through the cloth of his coat and warmed his fingers. Until a few weeks ago the prospect of spending the rest of his life alone had seemed unbearable, then the Black Spot of the test results had marked him, setting the time before he would be re-united with Melinda in the hereafter. Those things had been certain, set in stone by the Great High Poombah himself. 'Your time is up, come in number sixty-nine...'

Now he didn't know what on earth to think. The orderly existence, which was his life at Darkwater Towers, had been thrown into Destiny's tumble dryer. Up was down and down was God-knows-where. Slowly his head stopped spinning but the heat was still on. The dryer rolled to a stop, and he was once again cramped up with Carl Stensel on the wooden shelving of the fifth floor laundry room. The boiler pumped out heat despite the door being open.

The first order of business was whether to stay or go. Suddenly the little room seemed incredibly unsafe, the cosy warm feeling of sanctuary gone, but logically speaking it was probably the safest place to be. It had already been searched so that should stand for something, but Theo remembered that his apartment had already been searched as well, and that hadn't stopped It returning. McCracken or Brewer - or whatever the hell It was - seemingly wanted Theo badly. As he struggled out of the confined space, the obvious place to hide and regroup was the last place he wanted to be. Also there was something he needed to collect, something that was central to this whole mess, and he was only just realising its importance. There were still a lot of questions to be answered, and Carl Stensel was the man to answer them, but this wasn't the place.

Theo helped Carl out of the shelf, listening carefully at the door. The elevator clanked and whined, climbing the floors again to the tenth. Theo made a mental note to check out what was so important up there but that was for later. Now, with the coast clear, it was back to the service stairs and déjà vu time all over again. He felt for the key to the ground floor access door in his pocket, and helped Carl along in silence.

The old barber didn't ask where they were going. Theo reckoned he probably knew anyway and, as they entered the narrow stairwell, Theo vowed this was the last time he would scuttle downstairs with his tail between his legs. If he truly was the One Eyed Man, then this tall dark room he knew as Darkwater Towers was his kingdom, and by God it was time to fight for it. The fifth floor door closed behind them, and it was once again down the darkly lit stairwell to the ground floor.

It gave Theo a perverse sense of pleasure to be plotting the demon's downfall, while sitting in the heart of its lair. The stench, which had filled McCracken's apartment, had faded but not gone altogether and, as they sat in the small kitchen drinking the caretaker's coffee laced with a good measure of Bushmill's Irish Whisky, it felt like the last day of the Alamo in reverse. He wasn't sitting here waiting for the final assault by General Santa Anna's troops, but planning a final assault of his own. Sitting in the middle of the Formica clad table was one of his main weapons. The shrunken head of Kuta Lametka, which had been wedged in the corner of Mick McCracken's settee. How it got there was the question Theo had just asked Carl.

The old barber sat with both hands flat on the Formica top, an image that was a million miles away from the man who had a red and green Gents Hairdresser sign in his shop window, and a traditional candy-stripe pole outside. His whisky-laced coffee stood forlornly between his hands, and his brow furrowed as he marshalled his thoughts.

"As I said, I came to warn you." A gust of wind howled in the lobby, as if called upon by the BBC sound effects department for a spooky radio play. Theo expected to hear a clap of thunder, but it never came.

"Warn me of what? Kuta Lametka?"

"That yes. And the corpses and the caretaker and..." Carl looked sheepish, "other things."

"But how did the head get in here?"

Carl waved him down. The effort seemed to drain him and he sagged forward. Theo thought he was going to collapse over the table. "That is not important. What is, is how it works. Remember the corpses in the jungle, emaciated and sucked dry? It's the same here. The Rover Car Dealership. The Diamond Seal double-glazing factory. The derelict rail yards. *And* here." Carl ticked them off one by one. "Emaciated. Sucked dry of their life force. The trail of them led through the jungle to Sol Benita, and they led through the urban jungle to Darkwater Towers. The bodies were discarded when their usefulness was over, or when a better one became available. They are like runners with the Olympic torch, the flame passes on when each runner is spent."

Theo remembered the empty husk of the village elder's son, dumped on the floor of the council chamber like a used raincoat after the storm. The kitchen darkened with each word Carl uttered. The story sucked the light out of the room just as the demon sucked the life force out of its victims. Except it wasn't like that at all. The energy wasn't sucked out of them, it was used up while the demon inhabited their bodies, as if it ran on double power and ran the batteries down too quickly. That was what Carl was trying to say, Theo was certain of it.

"And McCracken?" Theo asked, knowing the answer already.

"Used up. Spent."

Theo remembered the gaunt face that had stared out of the caretaker's apartment door when he'd returned from the barbershop. Yes, he was pretty much spent then.

"And now it's in Charlie." It wasn't a question. Theo recognised the bloated look of the diminutive boxer, the red-rimmed eyes and the stretch marks down the sides of his face. He had seen it before in the boiler room on the day of the rat, if there had ever been a rat. McCracken first. Charlie next. *Where did that leave...* "

Did you see any of the others when you got here?"

"No."

"The bodies across town, they must have been picked at random, but here only two have been taken. Where have all the others gone?"

Carl thought about that before answering. "I don't know but I can guess."

Wind rattled the kitchen window, and the sound turned Theo's blood to ice. He thought he was beginning to read the pattern, and wasn't sure he wanted to hear the answer to his question.

"This is a lonely place. An isolated place. In the city there can't be too many places like it. Somewhere with a ready supply of people who will never be missed because nobody cares about them anyway. To come all this way, across many continents, The Towers must seem like a blessing from above."

"Or below," Theo muttered.

"Yes. A place where no one will be missed, except that they are all missing."

"Spares?"

Carl nodded slowly. That strange guilty look crept over his face again, but before he could continue, Theo changed the line of questioning.

"You said it had come for the head. Why come here when it was at your shop all the time?"

"It has come a long way. Thousands of miles. I think a few hundred yards out isn't bad after such a journey."

But that didn't sound right. Theo thought the barber was keeping something back, and that guilty look had something to do with it.

"When I came here tonight," Carl continued, breaking Theo's chain of thought, "it was McCracken who stalked the corridors. Charlie Brewer must have only recently been taken, but he won't last as long as McCracken. McCracken was strong, the ideal choice, but before It leaves here *It* will need a stronger vessel than any of the others can provide."

Theo's skin puckered into a thousand tiny goose bumps.

"I thought I heard you in his flat, stupid of me really but I am past my best. He caught me beside the fire and..." Carl appeared to be having difficulty getting this bit out. "McCracken was already weakening. I must have seemed like a gift to him, save his larder for later, and It tried to get inside me. It swept down my throat but somehow I managed to keep it out. I don't know how. I think some people are harder to infect. Uriah Lovelycolors was one, which was why he had the cuts to his throat; he ripped the badness out of himself.

The Major too. Hung himself while he still had some control. McCracken though, he was a big weak fool. Easy meat."

The Major? Uriah? Theo couldn't remember how much of tonight's events he had shared with the hairdresser, but he was certain he hadn't gone into such detail. Doubt slithered into his mind like the serpent in the Garden of Eden. He stared more keenly into the eyes of his old friend. The cuts around his eyes still looked sore but the bleeding had stopped, and the ragged stretch marks had crusted over. Was there something else behind those eyes, something other than sadness and caring and... guilt? *Why guilt?*

"We struggled," Carl continued. "Ordinarily he would have been far too strong for me, but his strength was waning. I managed to get out and he was too, dizzy... winded... I don't know which. Maybe when It has to re-enter a subject It has to gather Its strength again. Whatever, anyway It couldn't follow me. The only place I could think of was your flat, so I waited there for you."

Theo listened with only half his mind; the rest was weighing the words carefully, sifting them for grains of truth and hints of a lie. Something was wrong but he couldn't put his finger on it. Something was giving the old barber recriminations. They say guilt sits heavy on the shoulders of the honest, and Carl had been an honest man for as long as Theo had known him.

"The head must have fallen in the struggle. Luckily it got wedged between the cushions until you found it."

Another thought struck Theo, but it wouldn't come out fully formed. It was something Carl had said earlier in the laundry room. It niggled at the back of his mind like one of those maddening itches between the shoulder blades you can never reach to scratch. Try as he might, it just wouldn't come. He set his mind on another problem.

"If the others are being kept for later, does that mean they are still alive?" Theo couldn't keep the hope out of his voice. For the first time since his narrow escape from the reception office he allowed himself to believe he might still save Delia. The germ of an idea, sewn in the laundry room, began to grow, despite his doubts about Carl. The possibility of rescuing Delia simply added weight to the pot.

"Possibly," Carl said. His eyes, avoiding Theo's at all costs, stared at the mug between his outstretched hands. "They may be alive, or they may be being kept alive. The two are not quite the same."

The wind outside strengthened, but the sounds inside Theo's head drowned it out. The clunk and rattle of the lift doors and the electric whine of its motor. He had heard that sound so often that it was almost as prevalent as the settling noises of The Towers or the pounding of his heart. Just lately though, those elevator noises had been coming from a different direction. Not the regular runs between the seventh floor to the lobby and all points between, but a more distant outpost, well into enemy territory.

The tenth floor.

If the missing residents of Darkwater Towers had indeed been spirited away, they wouldn't have been spirited far. Theo's first choice would be they were in the ogre's second home, the cellar. That was where Theo had first encountered the radically altered Mick McCracken, and it was the nearest place to his apartment. But if they were being kept as 'stock' for the demon's private larder, then the need for a refrigerator was more likely, and the tenth floor was much cooler than the boiler room. Theo watched the old man opposite, gauging his reaction. He was dying, there was no doubt about that, and more importantly Carl himself knew it. Theo could see it in his eyes. Since receiving the test results he had become acquainted with that look, the sad eyed, hollow-stared look of a man who knows his time is running out. So far he had only told Delia - who else was there? But his next step would be a difficult one. He decided there was no easy way round it, so best be blunt.

"You're dying," he said, watching Carl's eyes carefully. They closed slowly then opened again. His chin lowered once in a half nod. "So am I."

To this Carl's eyes hardened. He was about to speak but Theo waved him down. "The same thing as Melinda. I got the results a fortnight ago. At best I've got five months."

Carl's face ran the gamut of emotions. Shock flicked his eyes wide open, sadness weighed them down, then something slithered behind the hang dog look and was gone. Guilt again? Finally tears welled in those sore red-rimmed eyes, and he asked, "Are you sure?"

"As sure as I can be, but that's not the point," Theo took a deep breath, because what he was about to propose would mean the end to both of them. "The fact that we are going to die makes us the most dangerous people for McCracken. Brewer - I mean." Theo remembered something he had read in one of Melinda's arty-crafty books, 'A Dictionary of Quotations.' She had always goaded him into reading more educational books, but he had resolutely stuck to his Stephen King and Robert Ludlum. It was a quote by George Bernard Shaw. Theo recited it now.

"Old men are dangerous: it doesn't matter to them what is going to happen to the world."

"Now who is getting cryptic?" Carl gave a painful smile.

Then Theo outlined his plan, and preparations for the final assault of The Alamo were under way.

Half an hour later they were on the move again. There had been no recent movement from the elevator, and a quick glance at the floor indicator in the lobby showed it was still on the tenth floor. Carl was limping badly, but in view of what they were planning to do, that didn't matter too much.

So long as he could make one last trip to the seventh floor that was all that mattered.

Theo touched the photo in his pocket for comfort and looked out through the wired glass of the front doors. Earlier he'd contemplated opening them and running off into the night, but now he had a new purpose. He was going to die anyway, so it might as well be tonight.

Before he turned back to the stairs, he saw movement out in the blackness beyond the doors. Stuttering white ghosts drifted down from the night sky, and it began to snow.

CHAPTER 6

By the time they reached the seventh floor it was snowing hard. Theo could see the heavy flakes through the landing windows, more purposeful than the spectral butterflies outside the lobby doors, bigger too. It reminded him that this was Christmas Eve and it might even be Christmas Day by now. He began to check his watch, then realised it was broken. 'Nine fifteen' the frozen hands said. *What time was it? What did it matter?*

Theo paused for a moment on the landing, letting Carl catch his breath. He stared out at the swirling white curtain of snowflakes. It was going to be a White Christmas, here at least, even if that didn't count for the festive wager.

White Christmas. Theo could only remember that happening twice before, once when he was a ten year old schoolboy waiting with bated breath for the magical hour of five o-clock, the earliest he dared get up without being sent back to bed, and listening to the soft quietness of the world outside. When he'd finally got up, the excitement of seeing through the kitchen window the garden blanketed with virgin snow had almost overridden his desire to open his presents. Almost but not quite. He'd got a Hornby train set that year, plus some Meccano - his favourite.

The second White Christmas years later had been much better. He was married to Melinda and they had just about settled into their apartment at Darkwater Towers. The rail yards had still been open then, and the fluffy white covering was scarred by the wicked black lines of the rails, so choked with oil and grease that the snow wouldn't settle on them. Melinda had looked out from their balcony and, despite the scars, had breathed a happy sigh. The world was white and soft and pretty, and that was something they hadn't been able to say for a long time. Theo came up behind her, enclosed her in his arms and nibbled at her neck. She laughed and swivelled in his arms to face him.

"Want to build a snowman?" She asked.

"Want to play snowballs?" He countered.

Her hand snaked between his legs in a shocking change of character and gently squeezed his balls. "If you like," she laughed crudely, "but what about your favourite number?" They went back to bed, and that was the only time she had ever initiated his favourite position. It was the best Christmas present he ever had. Beat the Hornby hands down, even with the figure eight track. The figure sixty-nine track was much more effective.

Looking back, that was the happiest Christmas of his life. Three weeks later she began to feel ill, and after tests discovered she'd developed cancer. She never saw another Christmas.

Now the snow was back again. The derelict railway yards would just be so many snowy hillocks and the rails, no longer choked with oil and grease, would undoubtedly disappear under the soft fluffy blanket. Theo wondered if he would be alive to see it, and found he really wasn't bothered if he didn't ever see it again. His lasting memory of a White Christmas would be making love to Melinda, and that seemed right and proper.

The landing was cold and harsh. Theo's breath plumed in front of him in a tight white cloud. Carl leaned against the railing next to him, looking paler and sickly. Blood had begun to leak down the side of his face where the stretch marks had split. He favoured his left leg, and Theo noticed the right foot had left a splodge of red on every second step, the wound forced open by his efforts to reach the seventh floor.

"Are you ready for this?" Theo asked. A silly question really. *Were you ever ready to be a human sacrifice?* He doubted if the village elder had asked Kuta Lametka that question because the answer would always be 'no,' but 'a man's gotta do what a man's gotta do.'

The look in Carl's eyes told their own story. Sadness was replaced with fear but overriding that was a steely look of determination. He was ready as he was ever going to be. Theo glanced at the elevator doors, closed and silent beside the stairs, he then helped Carl away from the railing towards Newton Wimer's flat.

The plan was simple, but now they were about to put it into operation it seemed completely stupid. Theo felt for the handcuffs in his belt and then, reassured that they were still there, scanned the flat for the CD player, which had been knocked aside the last time he'd been here. He found it among the debris of the coffee table. The casing was cracked but apart from that it looked to be in working order. The CD rack underneath it had spilled its contents across the floor, but after a few minutes of searching he found the disc he wanted.

Once he had set up the player against the back wall it was time to search for the other things he needed. Carl straightened an upended chair and sat heavily. Theo went to the front wall above the fireplace. Miraculously the wall decorations had been untouched during McCracken's rampage through the apartment. He had been intent on reaching Theo after all and, despite smashing his way through the furniture, had little time for more wholesale damage.

The Browning was still mounted on the wall next to Newton Wimer's campaign medals but that wasn't the gun he was looking for. He looked down at the beige carpet, so neatly kept while The Major was alive but now covered with splintered wood and broken glass from the coffee table. He couldn't see it and tried to remember where he'd been standing. Then the sudden agonising pain of the gunshot wound to his arm pricked his memory.

He moved over towards the overturned armchair, the one he had backed into before he had toppled over, dropping the revolver. With one foot he cleared away the debris and shifted the chair to one side. The Enfield .38 was under the chair. Theo picked it up and broke the barrel. Five golden discs winked up at him, one of them dented by the hammer and stained by the discharge. His arm ached in sympathy. He clicked the revolver shut and checked the safety catch was on, then he slipped it into his jacket pocket. Four bullets left. That should be plenty for what he had to do. Carl wouldn't be a moving target after all. Now there was only one thing left. He went over to the wall cabinet and looked through the glass doors. Trophies glinted back, highly polished every week whether they needed it or not. He was looking for the familiar egg shape on its stand, and for a moment he thought it had gone, then he saw it. The case must have taken a knock when McCracken headed for the veranda door, and the ugly black pineapple had nudged over on its side. He opened the doors and picked up the grenade, weighing it in his hand.

Wind blew the curtains away from the open balcony door, sighing into the room like a long lost lover. The cold made his hands tremble. Or perhaps it wasn't just the cold. He looked over at Carl, sitting and waiting patiently in the chair and his heart went out to the ex-sailor turned hairdresser. The balcony door banged, startling Theo into action. He was in danger of winding down, instead of gearing up. Flurries of snow had already drifted through the door, forming a shallow wedge across the carpet. Theo pushed the door closed, shutting the cold out. The curtains died, hanging limp and lifeless and silent.

That struck a chord. Theo turned towards the bedroom. That would be the ideal place for him to wait, offering a good view of the radiator and also of the apartment door. Theo didn't think he could cope with Newton Wimer's swinging body again though. He might have exorcised the death of Tim Ransom, but the blue-black face of The Major was something he could do without tonight.

The only other vantage point was the kitchen. He went over to the door and pushed it open, listening all the time for any sounds from the floors above. The kitchen was untouched, as neat and as regimented as The Major had left it. After the muted tones of the living room, all greys and beiges, the little kitchen was a riot of colour. The narrow fold-down table had a freshly ironed red and white checked tablecloth, which matched the chequer-board red and white linoleum floor tiles. The base units and wall cupboards were bright yellow with white, marble-effect worktops. Theo thought he'd walked into the set for 'The Big Breakfast.'

In the living room, Carl coughed, holding his hand over his mouth. Theo looked out from the kitchen door as Carl pulled his hand away. Speckles of blood dotted the palm. Theo felt a heavy sadness for the old barber who had been his friend for as long as he'd lived at Darkwater Towers, and who had helped him through the depression following Melinda's death. Now that the time had come, he wondered if he'd have the courage to do what had to be done.

"Kill me. For God's sake kill me..." Melinda's deathbed plea swam through his mind.

"If you love me, then please make it stop..." That too. *If he'd had the power then, would he have used it? Could he have put a gun to his wife's head and pulled the trigger? Blamm... All over. The pain gone forever. Could he?*

And could he do it now for his friend?

He fingered the revolver in his pocket, the metal cold and hard and dangerous. This was much more than simply pulling the trigger to end his suffering though wasn't it? Much more. Carl might not be as dear to him as Melinda but he was much closer than Kuta Lametka. Theo felt the weight of the shrunken head against his chest, and hitched the string around his neck to ease the pressure. His hand shook, fingers unsteady.

No, not Kuta Lametka. Not a beheading either. Theo cringed at the thought of the simple plan he had devised in Mick McCracken's ground floor apartment. Chopping the head off and pickling it hadn't worked, so more drastic measures were needed. Not pickling the head, which held the demon's breath, but destroying it completely. In Theo's other pocket, the hand grenade pressed against his hip.

Theo ignored the graphic picture that flew into his head at the touch of the ugly grey pineapple. He went over to Carl and sat on the chair arm. His left hand rested gently on his friend's shoulder. They sat like that for a long moment, neither speaking. Then Carl looked up, sadness filling his eyes. "I am so very sorry," he said, and Theo thought he meant for bringing the head here in the first place.

Theo nodded, patted him gently on the shoulder, and then drew the heavy-duty transport cuffs from his belt.

Wind rattled the balcony door, trying to get in. Through the glass Theo watched dancing white demons cavort in the blackness, heavy white moths attracted by light from the flat. Carl's chair was next to the central heating radiator along the back wall, his right hand firmly handcuffed to the inlet pipe. The heating was off - Newton Wimer had never liked the dry heat central heating produced - and the metal was cold against Carl's skin.

The gloves were off. It was time to put up or shut up, to shit or get off the pot. The showdown was here and the big hand was nearing high noon. Theo felt a shiver of anticipation and the icy hand of fear. Carl sat patiently, looking like he didn't have a care in the world. He had made his peace with God and was ready to meet him.

Theo held his hand out in front of his face, watching the outstretched fingers. They didn't tremble. He was ready. He went over to the jury-rigged CD player, then threw one last glance around The Major's apartment. This would be his killing jar, just like the one he'd placed on the out-house roof to catch wasps as a child. Carl was the jam in the bottom, and Theo the lid, waiting to slam it shut once the wasp flew in to investigate.

Now he had to draw the wasp in. He had to waft the jam's aroma up the stairs to the tenth floor. The bedroom door was closed, as was the glazed door to the balcony, but the front door was tactically open. Theo selected the track on the CD and pressed play. The orchestra struck up the opening refrain, then Bing Crosby began to dream of a White Christmas. Theo touched the photograph in his pocket, remembering his last White Christmas, then turned the volume up. Bing's voice swelled, sweeping out through the open door and onto the landing.

Theo walked purposefully across to the kitchen, nodded at Carl, then stepped inside. He pushed the door to leaving a two-inch gap and then drew the Enfield. He clicked the safety catch off and waited, his eye to the gap. From here he could just about see the floor space between Carl's chair and the front door.

"I'm dreaming of a White Christmas..."

The gun felt heavy in Theo's hand.

"Just like the ones we used to know..."

Sweat on his palm made the grip slick and hard to hold. His breath came in shallow gasps.

"...when the treetops glisten, and children listen..."

The shrunken head of Kuta Lametka felt like an evil talisman against his chest and in effect it was. This entire mess began with the bringing of that head to the barber's shop down the road. What did Carl mean, "I don't think this is the first attempt"? The thought popped into Theo's head from nowhere, then slid away again. The weight of the gun in his hand and the sight of Carl waiting calmly for his end drove it away, but the taste of that question persisted. Dry and bitter and unpleasant.

"...to hear sleigh bells in the snow."

Bing Crosby crooned on, the sound drifting up the stairwell at full volume until it was an echoing whisper batting off the bare concrete walls. Whatever stalked those cold grey corridors was certainly aware of it by now, and hopefully the smell of the jam would draw it into the killing jar.

Theo's eyes stared until they hurt, unable to blink despite the water building up under his lids. They flicked round the room, taking in each item like the metronomic tick-tick-tick of the clock, counting down to the showdown.

Carl in the chair, small and sad.
The clear space of the killing ground.
The open door to the landing.

The metronome ticked on, and Theo's eyes followed the cycle.

Carl in the chair. The open space in front of him. The door to the landing.

Sweat beaded on his forehead, running down and stinging his eyes.

Carl, the open space, the door...
He flexed his fingers round the pistol grip.
Carl... space... door...
He swallowed but his mouth was dry.
Carl, space, door. Carl, space, door. Carl, space, door.

Theo's head began to spin, his eyes wavering in and out of focus. Bing Crosby faded back in, belting out the last line of the song. The music swelled to a crescendo as Theo's eyes flicked through their cycle. Carl, space, door. Carl, space, door.

Then the music stopped. It was like that frozen moment when the two gunfighters have strode manfully up the main street to face each other, then, just before they draw their guns - silence. Wind buffeted the balcony door. Carl sat like stone in the chair. The killing ground waited, and the door gaped open invitingly. Theo could hear his breath rasping between gritted teeth and his heartbeat thudding loudly in his ears. The CD player clicked off, making Theo jump.

Silence apart from the wind. Only it wasn't silence at all. There was another sound. A sound that had become an integral part of this Christmas Eve. The oily whine of the elevator motor hummed in the background, then it stopped and the musical ding echoed through the block of flats as the doors opened on the seventh floor landing.

Theo wiped his gun hand on his trousers and got a firm grip. He drew back the hammer with his thumb, the metallic double click sounding loud in the gaily-coloured kitchen. His eyes were glued on the apartment door. Nothing else mattered any more. Just that cold hard rectangle.

He strained his ears for the oncoming footsteps but only heard the elevator doors groan shut again. *Now It would be coming. Will it still be Charlie Brewer or has it moved on?* He didn't think it would have yet. Charlie's body might not be as strong as McCracken's had been, but it would certainly last the night out.

Kuta Lametka burned into Theo's chest like a bad case of heartburn, reminding him why all this was happening. His eyes flicked through the cycle one more time. Carl, killing ground, door. In that single glance his mind recorded every detail as if it might be his last. Carl sitting, head bowed, in the armchair, his hand cocked by the handcuffs like a pantomime gay boy. The jury-rigged CD player, its usefulness over now that the signal had been sent. The cleared space of the killing ground, nothing obscuring Theo's line of sight for that final shot.

And there was the gaping mouth of the apartment door, where any moment now the demon of Darkwater Towers would walk into the trap. The killing jar would suck him in then Theo would slam the lid down with a bullet to the heart. Then the demon would be out, searching for the only other vessel it could inhabit, Carl Stensel. Once inside it would be trapped, fastened by those handcuffs to the radiator like a wasp stuck in the jam. All Theo had to do then was keep his distance, kill the barber and slip the hand grenade into the slack jaws.

All he had to do? In all his sixty-nine years he had never been asked to do anything as remotely disgusting as this.

"Kill me. For God's sake kill me..." Melinda had begged. Yes, he had been asked, hadn't he? Only that time he had failed miserably. He couldn't afford to fail again. His hand tightened around the revolver and his eyes sharpened. Every ounce of concentration was focussed on his view of the grey rectangle of the landing.

He is coming. I can feel it. Theo thought, then screwed up his courage, flexed his fingers, slipping his forefinger into the trigger guard. Hairs on the back of his neck bristled, raising goose flesh and cooling the sweat on his skin. Was it the heightened state of fear or the gusting breeze from the balcony? He didn't know, but it sharpened his senses, cranking them up to fever pitch. Everything in the apartment was as still as the grave, just the gentle swish of the full-length balcony curtains sighing in the corner.

A soft white puff of snowflakes drifted through the door, adding to the shallow drift behind Carl's chair. Now Theo heard movement on the landing. His senses snapped into overdrive and he steadied the revolver. The pristine paintwork of Newton Wimer's door showed against the bare concrete of the landing walls. Theo had stood outside there waiting to deliver his weekly shopping countless times but that seemed like a million years ago. The door swayed slightly in the breeze, the movement sending little electric shocks to his brain. He sighted along the barrel.

He knew. Something was wrong. Suddenly Theo felt his chest tighten and his mouth go dry. The apartment door swayed again. *Breeze, what breeze*? He said to himself. *I shut the balcony door*! His eyes were glued to the front door and he dare not look round. His mind told him it couldn't be true because the balcony doors don't open from the outside. But he knew himself that wasn't true didn't he?

He still didn't want to turn. The gun in his hand trembled. Another gust of wind, stronger this time, slammed the apartment door shut and the spell was broken. He spun towards the balcony but couldn't see it for the kitchen door jam. From the Major's bedroom he would have had a clear view of all the doors, but from this side he could only see Carl's chair, the bedroom and front doors.

He pulled the kitchen door open and stepped into the living room. As he cleared the wall, his breath slammed out of him. The balcony was open; the curtains billowing like a vampire's cape. Standing in the doorway amidst the drift of snow was Charlie Brewer. Only this wasn't the diminutive boxer who had been storing Benson and Hedges because he couldn't bring himself to stop buying them. This was an altogether different being. The infusion of dark energy had stretched the skin and bulged the eyes. He stood taller by a good six inches, and his fingernails had sprouted into talons. The accelerated growth was phenomenal.

Even before It moved, Theo knew he was too late. He had been the sucker, punched and caught napping. Brewer was through the door in a flash and everything happened at once.

Theo fired twice in quick succession, the heavy explosions almost simultaneous. Wood blasted from the door frame sending splinters into the night air. Carl whipped his head round at the sound just in time to see the demon fall upon him. Talons flashed across his throat and he was dead before the head came off, muscle and bone severed in an instant. His head bounced on the floor and rolled towards Theo.

He fired again, this time hitting his target. A bloody gout opened on Brewer's left shoulder and he was knocked back against the wall, screaming in agony. One bullet left. Theo's mind raced. If he killed it now how far could it leap to get to him? Snow swirled through the door. It was all going wrong. He cursed the simple plan; the plan of a child. Had he really expected everything to go as smoothly as those Famous Five books he'd read as a boy? This was a prime example of, "The best laid schemes of mice and men..." When it came to the question of whether he was a man or a mouse, he'd come up short. Very short. But what to do now?

Charlie Brewer pulled himself upright, blood smeared across the wall behind him. The wound had slowed him down but that was all. Now he was coming for Theo. The shrunken head banged against his chest under the coat. Without thinking he whipped it out, yanking the string over his head. Brewer's eyes glinted redly and a bestial snarl hissed from his lips. He moved forward slowly, aware now of being so close to what he sought.

The head dangled from the string, dead black eyes staring out of the wizened flesh. Theo backed towards the front door, the pistol raised against any sudden rush. He was working on pure instinct now, not thinking at all. Brewer kept pace with him, step for step. Theo was aware of how fast it had moved when it went for Carl and he didn't want to be caught by a sudden lunge for the head. Kuta Lametka was his trump card, and if he wanted to get out of here alive he would have to play it carefully.

Another thought played across his mind. *Did he really want to get out of here alive?* He'd come up here to put an end to this, fully expecting to die in the process. He was dying slowly anyway, why not go quickly instead? But he dismissed the thought out of hand. He might be dying, but he couldn't die before stopping the monster that had decimated the population of Darkwater Towers. If he did, it would kill again as it strove to return to its home in the South Pacific.

Theo fetched up against the wall, and panic climbed into his throat. A hint of a smile played across Brewer's lips, splitting them and spilling blood down his chin. The wind blew another snow flurry from the balcony, and Theo felt behind him for the apartment door. It wasn't there. His eyes were locked with Charlie's, afraid to leave them in case he lunged for the head. His hands searched the wall behind him and finally found the door jam, then the handle. He turned it, opened the door, and backed out onto the landing. Brewer took a step forward, then Theo slammed the door shut and ran.

He had never been so afraid in all his life. In that moment he was as close to being clinically insane as you could get while staying out of the nut house. Everything was turned upside down. His friends were his enemies, his home a battleground and his imminent death a lover to be cherished. His breath came in shallow gasps and his head felt like it would explode. A thousand scenarios flashed through his mind and indecision froze his joints. It was like running through treacle or one of those dreams where you're trying to run away but don't seem to be moving. He was conscious of the apartment door, certain it would open in an instant and the beast be upon him.

The main stairs were on his right, snow blustering impotently against the windows, and the elevator was straight ahead. The floor indicator above the doors showed the lift was still on this floor. Without thinking he pressed the call button. Seconds dragged into hours and the lift doors refused to open. Behind him the flat door remained shut, but any second now...

Somewhere in the syrup of time the bell dinged, and the elevator doors crawled open. Newton Wimer's door blasted open and the icy breath of winter chased him along the landing. No time left. Lyrics he had heard in a past life rang in his head. *Should I stay or should I go?* Without another thought he decided with a flick of the wrist. The shrunken head of Kuta Lametka flew into the confined space of the elevator car, bounced off the dull grey metal of the back wall and dropped to the floor. Theo reached in, pressed the ground floor button then dashed round the corner.

Scurrying footsteps hurtled along the landing and Theo held his breath, expecting flashing talons to come swiping round the corner. The simple plan his brain had hatched on the spur of the moment would prove as ill-fated as the one in The Major's flat. Sending the head down in the lift would not fool Brewer into following it any more than playing Bing Crosby had fooled him into walking into Theo's trap.

The footsteps stopped at the lift doors and a blood-curdling roar echoed through the Towers. Overgrown fingernails scraped across the doors, screeching like chalk on a blackboard, then the footsteps were flying down the stairs after the elevator. Theo felt the strength leave his body and he sagged against the wall. His knees buckled and he slid to the floor, watching his hands shake. He curled up, hugging his knees, and closed his eyes.

After a few minutes his heart slowed and his breath began to smooth out into long steady sighs. The wind howled through the upper floors, cold air rifled his ankles and pricked the goose flesh on the back of his neck. They were one part cold and three parts fear but it wasn't fear of the monster that now inhabited Charlie Brewer, or his personal monster, the cancer that coursed through his veins. It was the knowledge of where he had to go next. The wind sent a whispering message as it buffeted the empty apartments upstairs, reminding him that there was still a secret to be discovered and that secret was on the tenth floor.

With the demon heading for the lobby after the head of Kuta Lametka, Theo turned his attention in the opposite direction. He forced himself back to his feet and cautiously peered round the corner, half expecting the clattering footsteps on the stairs to be a feint and the claws to grab his throat as he stuck his head out.

The landing was empty.

Newton Wimer's door flapped in the breeze, sending cold air wafting across the concrete and pointing a wavering finger at the main staircase. Theo followed its suggestion and began to climb the stairs, keeping against the wall so as not to be seen from below.

PART FOUR

TRIPLE SIGHT

Ay, on the shores of darkness there is light,
And precipices show untrodden green;
There is a budding morrow in midnight;
There is a triple sight in blindness keen.

- John Keats

Pandaemonium, the high Capitol
Of Satan and his Peers.

- John Milton

CHAPTER 1

The tenth floor landing was, if anything, even colder than the seventh. It mirrored the drab grey corridor outside Newton Wimer's apartment and the corridors of every other floor in Darkwater towers. But there was something different about it. Theo couldn't quite put his finger on the change. It wasn't the air of dereliction on a floor that hadn't been occupied for almost five years, because that had been apparent on each storey after the seventh, but something else.

The floor was dotted with flakes of plaster and dried paint, the metallic blood-in-the-mouth taste and sharp mouldy smell making Theo feel uncomfortable. The place had that 'damp sheets on a cold night' feel and he shivered at the touch of the chill night air. Then it struck him, that strange quality which made this floor different from the rest.

Ahead and to the left there was a gaping hole instead of a door. Theo glanced to his right and saw that the apartment at the far end didn't have a door either and with the unrestricted way the wind was flowing through the corridor he doubted if any of the others had doors either.

Now that he was here, Theo wasn't sure where to start. Wasn't even sure what he was looking for. Carl had intimated that the others might be kept up here but, now he thought about it, he didn't have the foggiest idea what that meant. He decided to go with the devil he knew and entered the apartment directly above The Major's.

The moon, over in the western sky away from the snow-bearing clouds, lifted the gloom of the empty flat, dusting the walls and floor with its chill blue glare. The balcony doors were closed but curtain-less, and the moon's cold stare was filtered through a swirl of dancing snowflakes, throwing crazy shadow butterflies across the bare concrete floor. There was no furniture, no curtains, not even any wallpaper. That had stripped itself over the years, dampness peeling it off in great rolling strips of flesh that lay unevenly along the skirting boards.

Looking round the apartment was like turning back time. The icy blue light, the rubble-strewn floor and the blank countenance of the balcony doors, all took him back to Theo's flight from McCracken, it seemed a century ago. The splintering wood of the pigeon loft sounded clearly in his ears but like the landing outside there was a subtle difference. Like outside, it was the absence of doors.

Theo knew McCracken had stripped the empty apartments of most of their useful parts - he had been able to hide in the airing cupboard because the boiler had been removed - but he had excelled himself up here. The curtains, railings and pelmets were all gone, as were the light fittings, electric sockets and ceiling roses. All the internal doors had gone, and looking through the gap into the bathroom Theo could see the bath, sink, toilet and taps had been taken as well. If the apartment downstairs was a ghost town, this was a ghost town that had been exorcised.

Theo felt for the revolver tucked in the back of his trousers and its presence reassured him. He felt uneasy, not only by the starkness of the surroundings but also by the noises that filtered through his brain. Soft whisperings that had started the moment he'd walked into the flat, which he was only now beginning to hear.

A quick tour of the apartment showed that whatever he was looking for wasn't here. Both he and Carl had agreed that the others might be being kept for later, but his old friend had been vague about what that meant. With the number of journeys McCracken had made to the tenth floor, it seemed logical this was the place to look. *But if they were being kept up here then where the hell were they?* He asked himself the question. A pain stabbed his chest, and he suddenly realised just how much hope that possibility had given him. Melinda would be in his heart forever but rescuing Delia had always been at the back of his mind. Destroying the virus that had infected The Towers was his prime motive but back there amid his grey cells was the hope he'd be able to save Delia. Now he was up here, in the land of the door-less flats, that seemed even more remote.

He went out of the apartment and along the corridor to the next. Again there was no door, so he walked straight in. Gentle murmurings fluttered around his ears like falling feathers, tickling his inner ear and nudging his balance. His head felt light and airy and he swayed unsteadily on his feet. He listened ... *what on earth was that noise? The wind? The snow? What?*

This apartment was even worse than the last. Not only had it been stripped bare like a leg joint in a piranha pool but two of the walls were missing as well. Whether they were removed to knock two apartments into one Theo didn't know, but the wall to the right of the door was just a wooden skeleton, all the skin and plaster gone. The sidewall of the kitchen had also gone, revealing half stripped wall units like denuded teeth in a face stripped of flesh. Theo could see right through to the far wall of the adjoining flat with its balcony doors under siege by the attacking snow. That meant the entire west side had been covered without anything being found. Theo's heart sank.

The whispering sighs grew louder, more urgent. Theo flapped at his ear as if a moth had fluttered past. If the rest of the flats on this floor were as decimated as these three, then there was nowhere to hide. The possibility of finding Delia and the rest stored in a corner of the tenth floor was fading and Theo was beginning to think this was another foolish plan hatched by a silly old man. His age weighed him down like a diver's belt and not for the first time he longed for the end.

WE WILL NOT DIE,
UNLESS WE ARE FORGOTTEN...

Theo touched the photograph through the fabric of his jacket. No, not forgotten. Never forgotten. He thought of Melinda and yearned to be with her now, wanted this nightmare to end, and to die right here. Electricity jumped from the photo frame, sparking off his fingers. "Don't you damn well give up," Melinda's voice bellowed in his ear. Theo knew that if he looked at her photograph she would have that disapproving look he knew so well. The look she'd given him after he'd read the letter two weeks ago. Test results or no test results, five months to live or no five months to live, that look was as steely as General Patton urging his troops on. "I want you to rip out the enemy's living guts and use them to grease the treads of our tanks..."

There was no messing with Melinda Wolff.

The fluttering sighs suddenly gave an extra burst and for a second they sounded like voices. The Cottingley Fairies at the bottom of the garden or the soft whisperings of a lover in the heat of the night. Short words and long sentences, urgent pleas and calm entreaties. Unintelligible words spoken to him in a dozen different tones and with a myriad different accents and he couldn't make out a single one.

Moon dust sparkled across the gutted apartment floor and the wind spun it up into tiny twisters, conjuring images of forgotten ghosts. The ghostly figures became faces in Theo's fevered imagination, ghosts of Christmas past and present. Souls of the dear departed. Alistair Sim peeked over the top of his sheets, Uriah Lovelycolors knitted quietly and the rattling chains of Jacob Marley - Theo had never been able to get that name right, mixing it with Bob Marley, the dead musician - sounded with a tinkle and a ding.

The whisperers swirled around Theo's head, and the faces tilted their eyes heavenwards in exasperation. The sounds were like snowflakes storming before his eyes, dancing and twirling until he felt dizzy. The words, disjointed and muffled, were just on the other side of coherent. Then the words became clearer and the faces grew louder and larger. The eyes bulged and the skin stretched and blood seeped from spectral cuts. The words buffeted his ears until he thought they'd pop. The eyes stared resolutely at the ceiling and suddenly one word sprang out of all the ghostly mouths. The joint effort entwined the whispers, like strands of cotton forming a rope. Spoke clearly for the first time.

"UPSTAIRS..."

The severity of the communal voice shook him, then the dancing motes of spectral dust formed a montage of faces from the past. Not television faces or Christmas Carol faces but faces he knew or had known. There was Mick McCracken, the cruel caretaker, Newton Wimer in his crisp business suit and... Delia Circelli in her neatly ironed pinafore. Theo felt his breath grow shallow and his heart missed a beat, then the dancing faces spun into one final image. Theo strangled a cry.

Melinda's face, as beautiful as the day he met her, hovered before him in the moonlight, the eyes sad and heavy and full of meaning. He stepped back, he couldn't help it. Whatever was going on he didn't understand it. Had he lost his mind? Had the strain of recent events finally unhinged him? Was he seeing these faces at all or had his imagination conjured them up from the swirling dust of the tenth floor apartment?

Melinda's eyes turned up, unable to believe how stupid Theo was being. He half expected her to tut disapprovingly like a teacher over a particularly dense pupil. Then the word blasted into his ears again.

"UPSTAIRS..."

He turned his owns eyes heavenwards and the voices dissolved into a snowstorm of swirling whispers again. The faces became twists of dust on an empty stage. He agonised. *Upstairs? There was no upstairs, this was the top floor.* Theo's mind struggled with the problem. A top hat might be a top hat but it still had a top. The top floor might be the top floor but it still had a top. The roof.

No, surely not. It was too open out there, and it was snowing like hell.

Theo tried to talk himself out of it, but he knew it was futile. One way or another he had to check the roof, snow or no snow. Finally he turned back towards the landing, trying to think where the access stairs would be, and the soft whisperings sounded more content.

The stairs were at the end of the corridor on the west wing and Theo felt a sense of déjà vu as he entered the stairwell. A single red bulb in a wire cage lighted the dull square of landing and apart from the rubble-strewn steps leading up, bare concrete risers led all the way down as well. This was the service stairwell he had spent so much time hoofing up and down on this dark and deadly Christmas Eve. He looked over the edge, noting the piano keyboard of light and dark spaces as the landings stretched away into the gloom, every second or third floor missing a bulb.

Then he turned his attention to the last flight of stairs leading to the roof. The risers were covered in thick dust and chunks of masonry, which had crumbled from the walls. There were no signs of disturbance. Nobody had walked these steps for many a year. He shook his head in resignation, realising his mind had run away with itself, probably due to the stress of the past two weeks.

But he was here, so he might as well check it out. With a heavy heart and no real expectations, he climbed the stairs. His feet crunched with each step, and the wind buffeted the narrow walls. When he reached the top he paused, looking at the rusted metal handle with no great relish. He remembered the key in his pocket and wondered if it would fit this door as well but it didn't matter, the door was unlocked. With a quick turn of the handle it was open, and Theo stepped out into the storm.

The rooftop was empty, only the dull smear of light from the landing showing across the snowfield. An angry flash of red caught his eye and he noticed the black finger of the air navigation light pointing skywards. On top were a weather vein and a large domed lamp. It flashed a livid red, warning low flying aircraft to keep away.

But that was all. The snow-covered expanse of the flat roof stretched to infinity, cloaked by a swirling curtain of white demons and picked out alternately by the dying rays of the moon and the angry red flare of the navigation light. A gust of wind almost knocked him over and the cold tightened the skin on his face. He hooded his eyes against the snow, peering out of slit lids, and saw nothing. The roof was six inches deep in virgin snow with no sign of footprints old or new. Even allowing for fresh snow filling them there would have been some ridge detail under the topcoat, something other than the constant smooth expanse of white.

Theo let out a sigh that Melinda would have hated. A sigh of resignation. Defeat. He'd given up, she would have said, and she wouldn't have liked that one little bit. He was about to turn back to the door when something caught his eye. Through the blizzard a dull pink line flashed across the night sky, then was gone. Seconds later it flashed again, and Theo realised there was something on the roof after all. He walked two paces towards the line in the sky and saw it was the edge of a snow-covered roof, flashing pink with the navigation light. Two more paces and he could pick out the solid square bulk of the building. It was about fifteen feet square and ten feet high, with a flat roof that was six inches deep in snow. Long icicles hung from the leeward side like huge teeth but, as far as he could tell, there were no doors.

Another gust almost tumbled him into the snow, and he struggled into the lee of the bunker. His mind raced, trying to think what this squat bunker could be on the roof of a ten-storey block of flats, then it came to him. The block was roughly central and about twenty yards from the entrance to the service stairs. That would place it over the main stairwell or, more precisely, right above the lift shaft. This was the elevator motor housing area.

Even in the lee of the building the wind howled around his ears, disguising the spectral whispers that had now started up again. Gentle and urging they guided him round the corner without him realising it. Half way along the wall on the far side from the stairs he found the door, a metal plated affair with non-return screws. This time he knew the door wouldn't be locked, so he opened it and stepped inside.

The storm was cut off as the door slammed shut behind him, and he found himself staring blankly into darkness. It was like being struck blind and deaf at the same time.

"In the Land of the Blind the One-Eyed man is King..."

Carl's cryptic missive popped into Theo's head, but it seemed wholly inappropriate now. He could see damn all. Could hear damn all either. Slowly his hearing began to pick up the sounds of the storm outside. Wind buffeted the door, rattling it in its frame, and howled through the gaps in the structure. The sounds reassured him, giving a sense of reality. They placed him firmly in the 'Here and Now,' and whisked him away from The Twilight Zone.

As he waited in the dark, a dull red light pulsed intermittently into the room. He looked up and noticed three large squares of pink light flash on and off. The wired glass of the skylights were masked under the covering of snow, but the navigation light forced its way through, giving a muted glow briefly before plunging him into darkness.

Theo waited, his breath pluming in front of his face. The room was taking shape, like a mosaic, one piece at a time when the light was on. He looked around to get his bearings, all the time conscious of something else in the room. The air was charged with static, a heavy atmosphere that he could almost taste. His tongue furred in his mouth and he found it difficult to swallow. As the wind continued to howl, another sound filtered into his mind. The soft, sensual whisperings of a thousand lost souls. They murmured into his ears and fluttered round his head, making it hard to think. He concentrated on mapping the room.

Everything was dark and even, with the intermittent glow of red, the things he saw were simply dark shapes in the greater dark of the background. Along the sidewalls were racks of heavy-duty tools, spanners the size of his forearm and bars and levers the length of his leg. At the far end he could just make out the squat shapes of several oil drums, paint tins and plastic methylated spirit containers. Half a dozen stained paintbrushes stood in a cut down plastic tray on top of the drums.

In the centre of the room, directly in front of him, was the imposing bulk of the twin drive wheels, eight feet tall. Greasy twists of cable ran over the top of the huge semi-circles and down into slits in the floor. The navigation light painted the wheels with licks of pink and the drums winked at him redly.

Whispering butterflies fluttered around his head and he had the strangest feeling of being carried on their wings. A dozen voices blew in his ears and unseen hands carried him forward. He walked gingerly around the walkway, aware of the enormous bulk of the wheels. He followed the path round to the other side, smelling the rich oily tang of the drums and the sharp sweet scent of the paint thinners. The taste of it lined his tongue and he wanted to spit but his mouth was too dry. The walkway was slippery with spilled oil and grease and he almost slid into the right hand wheel. He stuck his hand out to steady himself and grabbed the cable. It felt like the scaly skin of a serpent and he whipped the hand back in disgust, wiping it on his trouser leg. Now that he was round the other side, Theo saw something else. A black square in the walkway. As he looked at it he could just make out the rungs of a ladder in the dull yellow light from below.

The whispering butterflies urged him on and once again he was sure he heard Melinda's voice among the crowd. The spectre of her face in the swirling dust slammed back into his head and he paused on the edge of the hole. There was something down there, something dark and mysterious and terrifying. It slithered and moved like the undulating swell of a not quite calm sea. He felt that if he dipped his toes into the black square he would send ripples across a deadly pool.

A heavy thud sounded from above followed by a soft swoosh outside. A large slab of snow slid off the roof and down the wall, flooding the room with evil red light. Then the light was gone, waiting for the reflector's cycle to flick it back on. Once again the red eye shone down, throwing distorted shadows across the floor. Theo watched the cable wheels change into sleeping serpents and the drums march forward like the armies of darkness. The yellow glow from the ladder was the only escape. As his mind screamed to be set free, he turned round and backed down the first rung. One by one his footsteps echoed in a bottomless void and he disappeared into the black lagoon.

Christmas Eve finally crept forward into Christmas Day, the snow battering The Towers with all the venom of a biblical plague. Across the snow-covered wasteland no lights showed in the night, except for the red and green Gents Hairdressers sign and the candy-striped barber's pole. As Theo touched down at the bottom of the metal ladder even that went out, the fuse box blown by a mountainous drift which breached the back door of the little barbershop.

At that moment Theo's mind snapped. Whatever he'd thought he might find, it was nothing compared to this. With a scream that only sounded in his own head he clung on for dear life as he almost tumbled down the lift shaft and into insanity.

CHAPTER 2

Apart from the discovery of Tim Ransom hanging from his cell door, Theo had only known real terror twice in his life. He didn't suppose Tim counted because that wasn't so much terror as shock and that was a completely different thing.

One had been when he was thirteen and just getting into the cigarette experimenting stage. Two miles down from Moor Grange County Secondary school there was an old farm. It wasn't a working farm, not by then. He couldn't remember if it ever had been. When the Moor Grange 'Smokers' Society' discovered its benefits, it was borderline derelict with most of the out buildings demolished or falling into ruin.

The farmhouse itself though had fared better. Theo and three friends, Phil Bambrook, Chris Pratt and Lee Turner, had gone there one night after youth club. The living room was boarded up and the doors were missing. Part of one wall had crumbled into the fireplace but there was still enough room in the hearth to start a healthy fire. They sat around the dancing flames, working their way through a five pack of Woodbines, feeling very grown up, worldly wise and fearless.

The noise in the doorway behind them changed all that. The gigantic shadow flitting against the wall did even more. Even Phil Bambrook cried out. He was the toughest kid at school and it was with some relief they realised they had been caught by the local policeman. They had been taken home and Theo got a spanking the likes of which he never forgot but the night terror they thought had caught them was much worse.

The other occasion was actually earlier than that but he had been far more terrified. He had been nine and two of the same friends were involved, Phil Bambrook and Lee Turner. Chris had joined the gang at school the following year but Phil and Lee lived in the same cul-de-sac, which bordered Clayton Woods.

Clayton Woods were something of an anomaly, since they incorporated a fifty-yard band of woodland with a beck running down the western border - a stream they regularly damned until it burst its banks - and the constantly growing bulk of Clayton Ponds Stone Quarry. Between the two was a nightmare section of twisted trees and dry-stone walls known as The Dead Woods. What a perfect place to test your nerves!

It had been Theo's turn one autumn night, and as dusk faded down towards full dark, the sky glowing an angry red, the three had crossed the band of fertile trees to the wall, which signalled the start of The Dead Woods. Phil and Lee had undergone their rites of passage in the winter when the ground was hard and the woods devoid of wildlife. Tonight the shadowy expanse seemed to be alive.

Somewhere in the trees around them an owl hooted. In the distance a gaggle of starlings squawked noisily as they fought for their perches. Amongst the long grass near the stream, crickets chirruped and Theo reckoned he heard a snake hiss but that might have been his imagination.

One thing wasn't his imagination though. The deepening shadows in front of him, broken only by the shocking witches' fingers of dead trees, were completely silent. Not even the local wildlife ventured in there.

Theo sucked on his sherbet liquorice - he wouldn't progress to the tarry taste of Woodbines for two years - oblivious to the blackening tongue and mouth his mother disliked. The others watched and waited.

"Nearly dark," Phil said.

"Uh huh," Lee added, almost too scared to speak. Even though it wasn't his turn, the ordeal ahead of Theo had him worried.

Theo nodded, but kept sucking the liquorice. The yellow paper tube had been empty of sherbet for almost twenty minutes but he couldn't bring himself to chew the black stick down. That would signal the end to the preamble and the beginning of the initiation and he wanted to put that off as long as possible.

"Scaredy cat," Phil intoned. Careful not to arouse the demons they all knew lurked in the twisted trees.

"Uh, huh," Lee said.

"Not as scared as you were, bogey brains," Theo said to Lee, trying to distract them from the fact that he was scared shitless.

"Never mind him," Phil said. "It's your turn now."

With that there was no putting it off any longer. He swallowed the last of the liquorice, not liking the taste at all any more and pushed away from the wall he was leaning on. He stared into the still night air, picking out wicked monsters just waiting for him among the twisted branches of the dead trees, then clambered over the wall.

Each footstep brought the snap of a twig or the dry sinister rustle of grass no longer of this earth. Theo's breath sounded loud in his ears and his heart pounded like a trip hammer in his little, under-developed chest. He tried to concentrate on one step at a time, ignoring the seventy-five yards or so to the boundary fence of the quarry with its 'Danger - Keep Out' signs fastened to the wire. During the day that journey was not to be sneezed at, but after dark it took on heroic proportions. The Dead Woods weren't dangerous so much as downright terrifying. The blackened stumps of fallen trees combined with the grasping fingers of long dead branches to tear his mind apart.

Keep strong, he told himself. *Halfway there.*

Theo allowed himself a look ahead. He was indeed halfway across the wasteland. Suddenly this enterprise seemed completely stupid. His mind told him and he considered the question. *What did it prove anyway, walking across a few yards of blackened scrubland dotted with trees killed by the unlikely accident caused by lightning setting the undergrowth ablaze?* He contemplated turning back, telling Phil and Lee how silly it was.

But he couldn't. If he did that he'd never be able to look them in the eye again. He'd be branded a scaredy cat for all to see. He gritted his teeth, put his head down, and soldiered on.

Thirty yards to go...

Theo thought about the sherbet he'd eaten earlier, trying to recreate the sweet taste in his mouth.

Twenty yards...

The taste wouldn't come. All that materialised was the sharp tang of the liquorice. He wondered how he'd ever liked that earthy taste.

Ten yards...

He vowed never to touch liquorice again, a decision he would stick to and one his mother would praise even if she were puzzled by it.

The fence loomed out of the dark and Theo felt a surge of relief. Almost there, he sighed inwardly, then the bat swooped through the night and brushed his hair.

That was it. To hell with the fence, and to hell with Phil and Lee. He screamed his lungs out, turned tail and bolted. He covered the distance back like an Olympic sprinter, ignoring the branches snatching at his clothes and arms, only conscious of the vampire bat swooping round his ears. In that headlong dash he felt as mad as a nine year old could be. When he fell into the arms of his friends he was as terrified as he'd been in his entire life.

Until now. Now his mind dashed over the edge again, and his eyes tried to force away the terrible sight before him. His feet grounded on the service platform, which ran round the lift shaft and he backed into the wall.

They were all here. Every last resident of Darkwater Towers, the ones who hadn't died already, only it was hard to tell who was who. Theo's mind shut it out and for a good five minutes he was completely insane. He squeezed his eyes tight shut and only when he had calmed down did he allow himself a second look.

The metal platform was a shadowy walkway, perhaps four feet wide, which ran around the lift shaft. When the elevator was on the tenth floor the platform would allow access to the side panels and when it was on the ninth, engineers could work on the roof pulleys and lift gear. With the elevator car on the ground floor, the only thing that showed in its place was a ten-storey chasm all the way down. Dim yellow service lamps picked out the doors on each floor, and the wire-caged bulb of the tenth floor threw an insipid light across the chasm. Theo could barely see by it.

Along the opposite arm of the walkway, huddled shapes leaned against the wall like sandbags in a grain store. Several more were spread out towards him against the back wall. The shadows were motionless, not even a flutter of movement. The twist of cable twanged up the shaft, echoing like an acoustic guitar in a steel chamber. Wind howled outside sending wisps of snow, which breached the engine room above, drifting down the ladder. Oil from the leaking drums seeped down the near wall - slimy black blood in the devil's pantry.

Theo took a step forward, nerves screaming, his legs bogged down as if in thick black treacle. They didn't want to move and it took an effort of will to force them forward another step. The chaotic whispers were all around him again. It was like walking into a wasps' nest, listening to them buzz round your head, while trying to avoid their vicious stings. Voices sounded amidst the throng. Disconnected words, which made no sense. He edged along the walkway towards the angle of the back wall, and the nearest shapes began to look hauntingly familiar.

During their courtship, Melinda had gone through a phase of embracing the arts. Sculptures and paintings had been her forte, abstract art her favourite. Theo had a simple philosophy when it came to art, "I don't know about art, but I know what I like." That hadn't included anything where people had two heads or poppy fields looked like so much paint slapped on in three colours. One of Melinda's favourites had been the Salvador Dali painting with the melting clocks. Theo supposed it was deep and meaningful but to him it was just a collection of floppy clock faces, draped over the branches of a tree or melting into the angles of the stairs.

The shapes on the walkway reminded him of that painting, only now they weren't simply shapes, they were people. Dali would have loved it. Theo felt sick. The first body was someone Theo knew by sight but didn't know his name. He lived on the second floor. The old man looked like an empty skin discarded on the floor, his face flat as a pancake and his chest and shoulders draped over the edge of the walkway like one of Dali's clocks. It was as if he'd been run over by a steamroller. *Which ward is he in? Wards two three and four.* Theo thought. The old joke surfaced to break the tension but it didn't work. Theo was wound tighter than the cable round the elevator drive wheels.

The next one was old Mrs Korda, along the corridor from Delia's. Her freshly permed hair plumed up around a head flatter than her ironing board. One hand was thrust against the wall and because it was so thin it folded like a sheet of A4 paper, pointing upwards. Theo stepped between the bodies, looking at the bundled corpses against the far wall. They were so tightly packed they had bunched up, giving the impression of sacks when he'd first seen them. They were as thin as the rest, only scrunched up. He could make out their faces, eyes, noses and ears printed on full colour paper, then screwed up.

A powerful gust of wind forced fresh snow into the engine room, rattling the tools in their racks. A handful of flakes tumbled down the ladder. Theo felt his stomach churn over lazily and bile came up into his throat. This was beyond belief. The thought that these people were being kept as spare bodies seemed preposterous. They were dead and flat and useless.

A cough from behind him sent sparks through his body. His skin crawled with gooseflesh and his hair stood on end. Theo whipped round to see who was there but the platform was empty. The cable twanged, and the soft whispers fluttered impatiently round his ears. *What had made the noise?* He stared into the shadows near the ladder but there was no one there.

The cough again. Theo felt a scream building inside him. Every muscle was as taut as the lift cable itself. He glanced down at the old man from the second floor, and his eyes suddenly opened.

"Fucking shitty death." Theo jerked back and almost stepped off the platform into nothingness. The absence of railings to allow workmen access to the elevator car nearly claimed their first victim but he managed to maintain his balance and step to one side, arms flailing at the air. The eyes watched him with a heavy sadness and then the mouth whispered something.

This was disgusting. Theo knew if he didn't get out of here soon he would go stark raving mad. The mouth whispered again but it simply joined the myriad butterflies whispering in his ears. He looked over his shoulder and saw the old lady's eyes open. Then the body next to hers. And the one after that, followed by the scrunched up corpses against the far wall. They all watched him and their voices whispered unintelligibly. *I'm going mad*, Theo thought. *I can't stand this. I'm going mad.*

The one thing that kept him sane was as deep-seated as Melinda's love of the abstract. It was allied to his Good Samaritan streak and if he was honest it was the real reason he'd come up here in the first place.

Where is Delia?

He forced himself to look at the hideously deformed faces of his neighbours. He searched the faces for any sign of the familiar blue rinse and prim features. The whispers grew stronger. He looked at face after face, avoiding their pleading eyes and beseeching mouths. He didn't need to hear what they were saying; the tilt of their mouths was the same as the look in their eyes. Begging for release.

A feeling of grim inevitability settled over Theo's heart. No matter how much he looked he knew he wasn't going to find her here. The spirit, which had infected The Towers as completely as the cancer had infected his body, had other plans for her. It wanted him, needed him, to get away from here. Taking any of these pathetic creatures wouldn't be good enough, wouldn't be strong enough to make the journey home. Delia was the jam in the killing jar and this time it was Theo who was the wasp.

He backed away from the grotesque faces; their eyes boring into him like a thousand tiny drills. The whispers began to form words but the words evaded him, or his mind blanked them out. These tormented souls were just shrink-wrapped bodies ready for when the host needed them and it was their souls that were speaking to Theo now. He flapped at his ears again, fending off the swooping bat from his childhood and was about to turn and run. Run like the wind as he had across the Dead Woods to his friends.

The whispers entwined to form a rope and the rope strengthened until it buffeted his ears. The threads took on a communal voice but the words they spoke came straight from his past.

"Kill me, for God's sake kill me..."

Theo covered his ears but the words weren't touching his eardrums they were touching his soul. His dead wife's final plea twisted in the vortex of time, forming a new twist on an old theme.

"Kill us, for God's sake kill us..."

He was shaken to the core. Three years ago Melinda had begged him to end her suffering and he couldn't do it. It was to his everlasting shame that he had let her agony go on when he could have stopped it. In Newton Wimer's apartment he had been prepared to kill Carl Stensel in order to capture the spirit that infected The Towers but he had failed then as well. Now he was being asked to do it again, not by his wife or his friend but by every surviving resident of Darkwater Towers.

This wouldn't be as simple as pulling the trigger though. There were perhaps twenty or more tormented souls to put out of their misery and only one chance to do it. Theo remembered the narrow white ridge in the sheets, which had been Melinda, so small and frail towards the end. His palms began to sweat. Slowly a plan of action was forming, his mind ticking off each requirement to its success. He felt in his back pocket for the telephone book, an integral part of plan "A" which had not been used, then glanced over at the engineer's control panel beside the ladder, a soiled replica of the one in the elevator car. Next to the control panel was a grubby telephone.

Theo's mind raced. This would all depend on timing. He tried to think how long the lift had been silent. *Half an hour? More?* Whichever, certainly long enough for Brewer to have reached the ground floor and retrieved the head.

The killing jar. The jam. Theo would be drawn into the trap if he wanted to or not, the chance of rescuing Delia demanded it. The question was, *where was it?* He ran through the possibilities. *McCracken's apartment? The reception office? The...*

Even before the thought fully formed in his mind, Theo pulled out the telephone book and leafed through the handwritten pages. There weren't that many internal numbers to search through and at first he couldn't find the one he was looking for. Doubt fluttered across his mind. *What if there was no phone there?* Then he found it under "B". Boiler room.

He remembered the dull red glow and the oppressive heat and it seemed very appropriate. He went to the telephone, picked up the receiver and dialled. He thought he heard the distant ring of the cellar phone but it was just the dialling tone in his ear. It rang with a single long brrrrppp then silence.

Come on pick up the phone.

It rang again.

Please be there.

And again. After an agonising wait the telephone was connected, harsh breath sounding in Theo's ear. He could hear the roar of the furnaces in the background but no one answered. It didn't matter, the fact that he'd picked up the phone meant he wasn't anywhere near the elevator. Theo reached over to the control panel and pressed the call button. The massive wheels in the ceiling sprung into life, the motor deafening in the enclosed space of the lift shaft. The elevator cable sped through the slits above, blurring the strands into a single greasy rod. Far below, the lift banged in its track and began its last trip to the tenth floor, each floor ticking off on the panel.

Melinda's frail shell wouldn't leave him as he went about the preparations. She was there in the back of his mind all the time, lying so still and quiet in the hospital bed where she had died, riddled with the cancer they hadn't even known about until it was too late. He knew what he had to do, painful as that was and he knuckled down to it as the sound of the elevator rattled closer.

Theo climbed the ladder, his feet clanging on the metal rungs, and pulled himself up out of the dark pool into the red and black gloom of the motor room. Wind buffeted the walls and the navigation lamp blinked redly through the blanket of snow on the roof. He brought the five litre plastic containers of methylated spirits to the edge of the ladder and carefully dropped them down to the platform. Then he went across to the far wall near the door and selected an axe from the tool rack.

Melinda blinked at him from her deathbed, "Kill me, for God's sake kill me," hovering over her lips. The tormented souls below echoed her sentiments, fluttering around his ears in deathly whispers.

He swung the axe with more venom than he intended, burying its head into the nearest oil drum. Black gloop splashed out and he struggled to get the axe free, waggling it back and forth. Eventually it came loose and he swung the black bloodied head with more measured strength, twice into each drum, then clambered back down the ladder.

The elevator swept past the fifth floor and the unseeing eyes of Theo's apartment. Along the corridor Uriah Lovelycolors lay dead in a congealing pool of blood, his beloved knitting scattered across the floor. Theo touched Melinda's photograph for strength and he was sure she spoke to him. "Go for it Theo. That's my boy. That's my love. Be strong for me and for the others." He almost cried at the tenderness in her voice.

He leaned the axe against the wall and then took the meths containers two at a time, spreading them among the shrink-wrapped bodies of his neighbours, trying to avoid their expectant stares. A stronger gust of wind forced snow into the engine room, tiny threads of it drifting down the ladder and the elevator cable sang its wailing lament. It tugged at Theo's heartstrings, screwing his stomach into a knotted ball of muscle. He thought he tasted blood in his mouth but it was only the cloying smell of oil.

Melinda willed him on. Theo prepared to kill twenty people he had lived among for seven years and his dead wife urged him forward. His hands began to shake. Their friends and relatives had deserted these people. Their families had swept them under the carpet like so much dust from the past and here was he, Theobald Wolff, ex-custodian of the dregs of humanity, about to do murder.

I cannot do this, his mind screamed. *This is wrong.*

"You must. You must my love." Melinda's voice was urgent. Still loving, but forceful. "For them. For us. Kill us, for God's sake kill us. Now."

The lift swept past the seventh floor, with Newton Wimer's twisted corpse and his apartment's bloody secret. It flowed up into the petrified forest of the upper floors. The Dead Woods. Theo picked up the axe again and pierced the plastic containers with a gentle stab. The sweet smell of the meths stung his nostrils as it spread across the walkway. The platform began to vibrate with the lift's approach.

Theo had never been a religious person. Always reckoned if there was a God he wasn't such a nice person. Any supreme being who allowed even half the things in this world to happen had to be a sadist. All that aside though, he prayed to Him now. He prayed for forgiveness for what he was about to do. Over the edge of the platform the lift flowed up the shaft. The roof swept out of the darkness like a swell on a black sea, rattling the bolts that held the workstation and vibrating up the handle of the axe. Theo dropped it to the floor with a crash. Thick black oily blood flowed down the walls and dripped through the joints in the ceiling. A thousand eyes watched him. A thousand souls urged him on. He closed his eyes, hoping for strength, wishing he didn't have to do this terrible thing.

The lift slammed to a halt beside him and he opened his eyes. The chasm across the walkway was filled by the dirty black walls of the elevator car, blocking his view of the opposite arm and blanking out the faces of his victims. His prayer was partly answered. At least he wouldn't have to look into their eyes as he lit the blue touch paper. He felt in his jacket pocket for the grenade. *Has it been disarmed? Of course not. That would be like neutering your prize bull.* As he stood beside the elevator now, he hoped The Major had done a good job.

The whispering stopped. Even the wind outside abated, allowing the soft white flakes to drift aimlessly. Theo pulled the pin, keeping his fist closed around the release lever and laid the grenade on the floor between two meths containers. When he released his grip the arm flew off, clinking across the metal platform. He stood up, pressed button nine on the control panel and watched the dark bulk of the lift sink beside him. As the roof cleared the platform he stepped into the chasm with all the grace of an acrobat. His feet grounded on the lift roof, legs bent in readiness for the jolt as it stopped on the ninth floor. Seconds ticked by. His hands scrabbled for the hatch in the roof and yanked it open. The smell of paint thinners and oil scorched his nostrils and made him feel dizzy. Taking his weight on both arms he tried to lower himself into the car but all coordination was gone. He crashed to the floor and for a moment felt it would be lovely to close his eyes and sleep. The weight of expectation from his dead wife and his friends and his neighbours was too much to bear and he wanted to end it now. Just wait here for the explosion.

A sharp pain shot up his right side and the photograph of Melinda spurred him on. The lift doors groaned open and Theo half crawled, half threw himself out onto the landing as the doors slid shut, then the entire top floor exploded in a ball of flame. The lift doors buckled with a whumph and the tenth floor walls blew outwards, dumping the roof and winding gear on top of the ninth. Flames sheared the cable, firing the elevator car down the shaft like a bullet. Roof tiles in the corridor buckled and cracked, dropping around Theo like petrified snow.

Then the aftershock blasted through the tower block like a battering ram, shattering every window in the top three floors. Theo was thrown across the landing, fetching up with a crack against the stair railings. His arm screamed as the wound re-opened and his head blasted pictures of all those he had known in a kaleidoscope of broken images. The faces of all those he had just killed. His ears rang with the sounds of the explosion, and from way down below the lift crashed and burned on the ground floor.

After what seemed like an age the noises stopped and the sounds in his ears settled down to a constant humming. The wind started up again, howling through the shattered frames, sending a storm of dancing snowflakes across the ninth floor. Theo let it fall around him, not bothering to move. His head ached and his arm bled and he wasn't bothered about either. He curled up as if going to sleep and cried for all the souls he had destroyed but mostly he cried for his own.

CHAPTER 3

Night wind whistled through the main stairwell, and snow fell down the core of The Towers. The block of flats was truly dead, and as Theo reached the first floor his heart was dead as well.

It had taken him almost half an hour to regain his strength, but it was taking much longer to strengthen his resolve. By the time he forced himself up against the ninth floor railings his back was covered with snow and as he looked around he thought he'd passed through the wardrobe into Narnia. Gone was the dull grey concrete of the landing, replaced by a fine covering of snow, which turned the piles of debris into snowy hillocks.

The wind had free reign through the glassless windows, and the ceiling above the stairwell was a shattered skylight to the heavens. One of the lift drive wheels had tumbled sideways, knocking a six-foot hole in the roof, and wedging itself in the gap. Snow swirled through the opening, drifting down the stairwell like the glass snowstorm he'd owned as a child. The railings were picked out in white.

"That's it my love. Be strong for me, and the others." Melinda's voice nagged at the back of his mind, but at the moment he felt anything but strong. He felt sick. He had never killed anyone before, even when he was in the Army. He had seen death, but never meted it out. Now he had killed twenty people in one go and it was tearing him apart. Something else was squirming round in his stomach. Something he would never have believed possible. He was beginning to hate Melinda.

Theo gritted his teeth, looking down the core of the stairs. Pain scorched his left arm, blood soaking through his jacket sleeve. He remembered the DF tablets in his pocket but ignored them. He deserved the pain - he had earned it. It was nothing compared to the pain in his heart. For most of his

243

adult life he had lived and loved with Melinda. She had been his tower of strength through many crises in their married life, and the shoulder to lean on after the debacle of Tim Ransom's death. Now he couldn't bear to think of her name. He banished her voice from his mind and forced himself on.

With each flight of stairs the fire grew inside him. The anger. Cancer might have taken her from him,
WE WILL NOT DIE,
UNLESS WE ARE FORGOTTEN
but the disease which had infected The Towers had taken away much more. He touched the photograph in his pocket, and felt nothing. The spark was gone. She had urged him on when he had faltered, begged him to murder his neighbours. He wondered if this was the voice so many mass murderers claimed told them to kill. The voice of God or their mothers or...

Their wives!

Blood ran down his arm, leaving a bloody handprint over the pocket with the photograph in. It seemed appropriate. He now had blood on his hands and it was fitting that he should share it with the woman he had shared so many other things with over the years.

His mind became fevered; hot flushes running round his head. By the time he reached the first floor landing his anger was searching for focus. The fire inside him was looking for a target. That target was down there somewhere, waiting for him. The lobby came into view one step at a time as he came down the final flight. It was dark but there was a flickering glow coming from one side. Red and yellow light licked hungrily at the bottom steps, trying to touch his feet.

Over to the right, the elevator doors were buckled and flames leaked out, crawling across the ceiling. The windows of the reception office were shattered by the impact of the lift, and the broken glass reflected the flames like a mimic copying his favourite entertainer. The front doors were closed, their wired glass cracked.

Theo stood on the bottom step for a moment, taking in the scene. Mick McCracken's apartment stood open just past the elevator. Flames painted the door with a demonic flourish. Further on, in the shadowy corner Theo had grown afraid of, the cellar door beckoned despite the sign.

CELLAR - STAFF ONLY KEEP OUT

Snow drifted down around him, sparkling neon flakes in red and white and yellow. Without any inkling of a plan Theo descended the final step to the ground floor. On the way down here he had considered and discarded several ideas; ringing McCracken's flat from the reception desk to draw the demon out; ringing the boiler room from McCracken's flat to distract him while Theo slipped in unnoticed; or banging on the cellar door then dashing round the corner to the garbage shoot and sliding in the back way. None of those plans were any better than the childish scheme to draw the demon into his killing jar using Carl Stensel as bait.

No. There was only one way to do this, and it was the most foolish idea of all. Walk straight in the front door and do what a man had to do. He felt in the back of his pants for the pistol and then drew himself up to his full height. This bastard had taken everything that was dear to him, his friends, his love, and the memory of his wife. He puffed out his chest in that old military way Melinda loved so much, and found he could still smile at that thought. Perhaps all was not lost.

Then he set off across the lobby one last time.

The gates of Hell itself could not have been any hotter than the boiler room. Sweat prickled Theo's neck the minute he stepped through the door, and he was once again struck by the stark contrast between this room and almost every other room in Darkwater Towers. The rusty browns of the walls and floor, and the fiery red and orange of the furnaces were the total opposite of the cold grey expanse of the hallways and landings above. This was truly Hell incarnate and it was the obvious place for the demon to choose. This killing jar was warm and inviting, and Theo walked into it with his eyes wide open.

He scanned the floor from his vantage point at the top of the steps, not quite knowing what he was looking for. Shadows spread their webs from the corners of the basement, painting the recesses with an unremitting black. Theo's mind went back to Carl's entry into the council chamber with Harold Beauchamp, and the village chief. The chamber had been lit by twin torches, one either side of the drum on the platform, and the boiler room was lit by the twin flames from the furnace windows. Those fiery eyes glinted and winked knowingly. Theo left the door open behind him and started down the rutted stairs.

There was nobody on the work floor, that was the first thing Theo noticed, but somebody <u>was</u> down here, he sensed it. There was no point having a killing jar if there was no jam. Delia was in here somewhere. He came down another two steps, pausing to let his heart settle. It was pounding in his chest but that wasn't the worst, it felt like it was swelling into his throat, choking the breath out of him. He forced himself to breath deeply, to unblock the terror that was building in him.

The council chamber changed into Theo's own personal Hell. The Dead Woods. He once again stood beside the wall, sucking on an empty liquorice dipper - the taste sickly in his mouth - only this time he was alone. No friends. No Phil Bambrook or Lee Turner. This time the dead twisted stumps stretched before him, not towards the wall surrounding the quarry, but his new objective, the hungry black mouth of the coalbunker.

He reached the bottom step without even knowing it, and stopped. He felt he would be safe if he just stayed here, keeping his feet off the cracked concrete of the cellar floor. It was like those games he used to play at home when his parents were out, getting round the living room without touching the floor. He had climbed from the armchair to the settee, and from there to the foot stool. Then the tricky bit, climbing onto the dining table without upending it, and finally onto the radio gram. If he touched the carpet at any point it was certain death, melted by the flowing lava of Mount Front room. He knew if he put his foot down on the tarnished floor of the basement it would be fatal, but there was no getting round it. There was no armchair or settee or dining table here. The only way to the coalbunker was the John Wayne way. Bold as brass and straight across.

But John Wayne never had to cross the Dead Woods. He'd never felt that ball-squeezing fear of the unknown, or the monster in the shadows, or the vampire bat fluttering round his head. 'A man might have to do what a man had to do.' But Theo was suddenly nine years old again and he hated the taste of liquorice. The floor beckoned. It was dirty and grizzled and there was a deep crack running across it opposite the furnaces. Wind howled through the lobby above, and a tiny cloud of dust puffed up out of the crack. The movement startled him, sending electric shocks through his arms and up his neck. The floor was molten lava and it flowed through the Dead Woods but there was no getting round it, he would have to cross them.

Theo put his left foot down on the concrete, then his right. Another gust of wind sounded above and the door slammed shut, blocking out the friendly chill of the entrance hall. He glanced nervously to either side, watching the shadows ebb and flow in the flickering light from the furnaces, then set off across the Dead Woods.

At first his feet didn't want to move and he had to force them through the quicksand that tried to suck him down. Each step was an effort of will, his eyes darting from left to right then straight ahead. In the middle of the floor the crack, which dated back to the destruction of Clearwater Towers and Deepwater Towers, grinned at him. It drew his attention, dragging his eyes from the gaping mouth of the coalbunker. He felt it was important somehow but he didn't know why.

Phil Bambrook and Lee Turner watched him go from the back of his mind, The Dead Woods stretching before him. Twisted black trees tried to snag his sleeves and uprooted stumps threatened to trip him. He didn't remember this fissure in the forest floor though. This was something new. The crack was halfway between the stairs and the bunker and it grew nearer with each step. To the left the furnaces roared their approval, eyes spitting fire through the inspection windows and next to them the giant fuse board with its twin gauges glinted redly.

The crack was nine feet away now. It looked deep and dangerous and angry. Theo felt hypnotised by its stare. The taste of liquorice swam in his mouth.

Six feet...

Theo tried to conjure up his sherbet dip but it wouldn't come.

Three feet...

His mother asked him why he didn't like liquorice any more but he couldn't answer. Try as he might his mouth wouldn't form the words because
It was clogged up with that sickly black sharp taste. It was as if he'd never tasted sherbet before in his life, only liquorice. A rolled out ball of the stuff was on the floor in front of him and he tried to avoid it but his feet kept on truckin'.

I hate the horrid black stuff, his mind screamed; the thought twisted even as he mouthed it. *I hate the horrid black,* became, *I hate the black,* and finally, *I HATE THE DARK.*

The roll of liquorice vanished, replaced by the deep black stare of the crack in the floor. Theo stood over it. *I hate the dark.* He knew that as surely as he knew he loved

Melinda. He had hated it ever since he'd been a child, caught by a shadow policeman in the farmhouse near school and even before that when, as a nine-year-old, he had dared to cross the Dead Woods at night.

The realisation brought things into focus. He loved Melinda. On the journey down the snowy central core of The Towers he had lost that briefly, his love twisting into hate. And he was afraid of the dark. This last surprised him because he had never noticed that before but even more damning was the fact that he was surrounded by the dark now. Every corner of the basement was a shadowy cave full of hidden secrets. The coalbunker was a dark pool. The crack before him was a pit of...

Dust suddenly blasted up from the crack, snapping him back to the present. The toothless mouth in the ground moaned softly, sending a chill breeze swirling around his legs. The cold tentacles flapped his trouser bottoms and he almost screamed at their touch. Then the wind subsided and the hole was just a hole again. His fear drew back and focussed on the door of the coalbunker. He felt the photograph in his pocket
WE WILL NOT DIE,
UNLESS WE ARE FORGOTTEN...
Once again it gave him strength. In all the years they had been together he had never hated Melinda. He had fallen out with her many times, even disliked her for a while but never hated her. That dark and dangerous feeling which had grabbed him on the way down here had shaken him to the core because it was so alien to his nature. He loved his wife. He missed his wife. And he never wanted to feel that soul-destroying way again.

The coalbunker. That was where he was going. He focussed on that and stepped over the crack as if it was just a join in the pavement. He was halfway there. The Dead Woods were still around him but he was nearer the quarry than Clayton Woods. In the back of his mind he began to wonder about the vampire bat. Any time now he expected it to swoop down around his head, brushing his ears and touching his hair.

There was movement in the shadows between the furnace and the fuse board. He shot a glance over there but it was just the flames glinting off the dials. The coalbunker grew larger as he approached and he remembered Mick McCracken stepping into the doorway like the shadow of Tim Ransom. He braced himself for the shock but it didn't come. *Of course it didn't*, he told himself. Tim Ransom is just a bad dream now and Mick McCracken is dead.

That may be the case, but as he approached the doorway something was niggling at the back of his mind. Something more than simply discovering he was afraid of the dark. The jam in the killing jar. Theo remembered placing the jar on the low flat roof of the outhouse in his back garden. It had been a sweltering summer and there were wasps by the squadron, prompting a killing spree among the insect population the likes of which he'd not seen before. Those pesky little critters dived into the jar with gay abandon, meeting their fate with equanimity.

That was in the height of summer. As autumn turned the leaves into golden memories there were fewer wasps but the jam was still in the killing jar. Before long there were no more takers, either he'd got them all or they'd grown wary of the easy pickings in the old Branston Pickle jar. Whichever was the truth, the jam waited patiently. Soon it began to fur with mould and then it simply curled up and died, leaving a shrivelled heap in the bottom of the jar. There was no more life in the jam, just the empty pretence of past times.

The coalbunker was right in front of him now. Theo stopped three feet from the door, feeling the pull of the dark within. Even though he hated the dark there was an attraction there somewhere, like the people who were frightened by those horror books Delia disliked so much but couldn't help reading.

The jam curled in the jar. *What did that mean?* Kuta Lametka came to mind, but Theo didn't know why. *No, not Kuta Lametka but the village elder's son.* Theo remembered Carl's tale, and saw again the slack dead skin, which lay on the council chamber floor when Carl entered. Curled up and empty of life, just like the jam. But that had been because...

The idea was growing in his mind. That unsettling feeling that something was wrong. In the back of his mind he thought he knew what it was but his conscious side wouldn't listen. The slack dead skin was empty of life because what passed for life had jumped into Kuta Lametka, like the life of the jam had drained off into the atmosphere. If you left the jam in too long it was useless, that's why he changed it every two weeks during the height of his killing spree.

"This jam's been left too long," he muttered. A heavy weight began to sink through his chest into his stomach. His mouth went dry, and not even the taste of liquorice remained. He stepped aside from the door, allowing what little light there was to filter across the floor. There was something in there; he could just about make it out in the shadows. It was on the floor and it wasn't moving. The rat? No, bigger than the rat. Theo looked round for the lights but the single bulb above him had blown. There was only the gleam from the furnace windows at this end of the cellar.

Theo knew what to expect even before he stepped closer. The truth didn't descend on him suddenly but rather crept on him slowly. This wasn't the random fluttering of the vampire bat; this was a conscious move to scare him. No, to terrify him. Ever since his talk with Carl Stensel in the fifth floor laundry room he'd known. He'd simply shut it out, hoping against hope that he was wrong. The chance of saving Delia from this monster had balanced the certainty that he wasn't going to beat the monster inside himself. The cancer. Now the awful truth dawned slowly like a winter morning.

The shape on the floor was curled into a foetal position, like a baby sleeping on its side. It was a body. Theo stepped through the doorway into the bunker, moving to his right to let the light in. Darkness surrounded him, full of silent whispers. These weren't the soulless voices from upstairs but the drifting cobwebs of his imagination. This was the tunnel of the ghost train where unseen fingers brushed your hair in passing.

Theo concentrated on the body on the floor. Shadows crowded around it like onlookers at the scene of an accident, creeping from the walls and the piled up coal. The body didn't move. Not even a flicker. It was dead. He felt the breath being sucked out of him and his lungs wouldn't take any air in to replace it. He felt light-headed. He found himself praying that it was Delia, a thought that by turns disgusted him and bolstered his courage. If it was Delia then his quest was over. All he'd have to do was confront the spirit of the South Pacific and, win or lose, it would be over.

But he knew that wasn't the case. With the last of his courage he took a pace towards the body and looked down. The wrinkled features of Charlie Brewer stared blankly at the ceiling and Theo felt like crying. The bag of flesh and bones before him changed into the village elder's son, the image wavering in the dim light from the furnaces. No life there. No life in Charlie Brewer either. The spirit had gone, moved on. This was Kuta Lametka all over again, only the spirit hadn't jumped into Kuta Lametka it had jumped into...

A shadow slid across the doorway behind him then was gone. Sparks ran up Theo's neck, bristling the short hairs into porcupine quills. From inside the coal bunker the boiler room seemed unusually bright and for a second he felt like he'd changed places with Mick McCracken. He half expected to see the hesitant frame of Theobald Wolff approaching the coal bunker, then he would step out, surprising him. "Had to splat me a rat," he would say. The irony washed over him. Here he was in the shadows while whatever awaited him was out there in the light.

He squinted to try and see where the shadow had gone. All he could see were the fierce eyes of the furnaces and the glint of fire on the pressure gauges and fuse boards. No, somewhere between the two was a different shape. It stood motionless in the lee of the boiler. Even before he stepped out of the coalbunker he knew what it was. Had known in the back of his mind for quite a while. They stepped towards each other.

Theo cleared the doorway, moving out of the shadows at the same time as Delia stepped into the glow from the furnace, fire licking the side of her face and shoulders, the shrunken head of Kuta Lametka hanging round her neck.

The shocks, which should have rocked his body, never came. Instead there was only sadness and a sense of inevitability. He was rooted to the spot not because he was petrified but because all his plans had been blown out of the water. In an evening of shifting fortunes Theo had made plans with each change of circumstance and not a one of them had been worth a light. They had truly been the plans of a child and now that child had been brought to book. This wasn't the Dead Woods any more but the taste of liquorice persisted. It seemed appropriate that standing here surrounded by the dark he hated, he should be assailed by the taste he hated, because soon he would have to do something else he hated as well.

Delia stepped away from the pressure gauges, steam hissing from the pipes as the dials crept round the face. A heavy clunk echoed from the boiler and rattled through the maze of pipes overhead. The vivid red triangle on the right hand side of the dial made it look like a cartoon eyeball. Theo watched her move and wondered where the prim old woman who had shared Cadbury's drinking chocolate and a Galaxy bar with him had gone. The Delia before him now had grown, not only taller but also wider and straighter. Gone were the arthritic curl of the hands and the painful gait of her walk. The kindly features were now cruel and heartless and mean.

Is this what happens when our souls depart? Theo wondered. *The thing that makes me, me.* Delia stood in the coal dust of the cellar floor. She wasn't Delia at all. Her eyes had bulged and opened tiny splits around the lids. Pinpricks of blood bloomed against her skin and rending tears had appeared down her cheeks. The skin of her forehead was stretched to breaking point and, as Theo watched, a three-inch rip slowly opened up below the hairline. The infusion of energy was tearing her apart and it sickened Theo to see it.

His mind raced. He dare not think up another plan now, couldn't think of anything useful to do. He would have to act on instinct. At the moment instinct was leaving him dry. The photograph felt hard against his hip and he touched it for reassurance. Warmth spread through his fingers and up his arm. Melinda whispered to him in a quavering voice. His hand crept round the back of his trousers, checking that the pistol was still tucked securely in his belt. He wondered how much of Delia was left inside the shell of her body. It suddenly felt important to find out. Instinct took over.

"Hello Delia," he said, struggling to find the right words to test her.

"Hello, Wolfy."

Theo recoiled at the use of McCracken's hateful phrase. Delia's voice was deeper but it was still her own. Just.

"What are you doing down here?" He tried, half expecting her to say, "come to splat me a rat." Instead her head tilted to one side and he thought he saw a look of sadness in her bulging eyes.

"Theo?" A drop of blood ran down from a split under her left eye, a bright red teardrop. Theo felt his heart go out to her.

"Does it hurt?" He asked.

She nodded, then winced at the effort.

"Not the Christmas we'd planned," he said, taking a step towards her, one hand moving behind his back.

"That's right, come closer." The voice was gruff and businesslike again.

"Why? Want to kiss me under the mistletoe? There isn't any down here." His hand slid into the belt next to the pistol and balled into a fist. Tension twisted his stomach and he squeezed the fist to keep it out of his face. The fingernails dug little half moons of white in his palm.

Melinda's face above the hospital sheet drifted before his eyes. "Kill me. For God's sake kill me," she pleaded.

"I can't," he replied.

Another conversation faded in like a weak radio station. Steam spiralled up from a mug of hot chocolate and the old Delia watched him across the coffee table. "Perhaps you will be stronger next time," she said. Then, "I will do it for you when the time comes."

The needle crept into the red. Another hiss of steam erupted from a bend in the pipes and a deep thud sounded inside the boiler. High above there was a pop and a crack and a low scream began to grow in the distance. Theo's hand felt for the butt of the Enfield. A spark leapt from the wires above the fuse board, followed by a yellow and white shower. The giant fuses hummed. Theo thought she still had some control and it was important to find out just how much. Just how much of Delia Circelli was left in that bloated twisted shell?

"Do you remember what we talked about in the lift?" He asked.

Her head tilted to one side again, deep in thought.

You said, "If we can't find a Minister on Christmas Day it will be a poor show."

He was six feet from her now and the cuts on her face glared red and sore in the firelight. Delia didn't say anything but Theo thought he saw something in her eyes. Recognition? Love? That was promising but it also filled him with sadness for the future they had lost. He moved closer and slid his hand round the revolver. Tears were forming in his eyes but he forced them back.

"Well, it's Christmas Day..."

Her face showed a trace of recognition.

"...but I think it's a bit early for the Minister." His voice was breaking, growing husky with emotion. He was close enough to smell her breath, and there was nothing at all of Delia in that rancid sewer stench.

"Now I think about it," he continued, forcing a steadiness he did not feel into his voice, "you didn't answer my question in the lift." The Enfield came out of his belt with ease and he looked into the Delia thing's eyes. She had grown but he was still taller and had to look down at her upturned face. A flash of red flickered angrily behind her pale blue eyes, then was forced aside and for a brief moment the real Delia was back.

"What question was that?" She whispered.

"Will you marry me?"

Her eyes spilled moisture and her lips trembled. He could see the struggle to control her words and she was winning. Just about. It gave him hope, while at the same time breaking his heart. She mouthed a silent answer, her voice stolen by the thief of hearts. She tried again and spoke as clearly as she could.

"Of course I will."

They closed together, Theo's left arm slipping round her waist and he realised he hadn't kissed anyone but Melinda in thirty years. He pulled Delia to him and bent his head to hers. She closed her eyes, not seeing his other hand come round holding the pistol. Steam hissed from the pipes while the needle strayed all the way into the danger zone and the fuse board blasted showers of sparks into the gloom. The red fiery eyes of the furnace windows looked on, a deep angry rumble sounding in their bowels.

He kissed her, bringing the gun up to the back of her head. Her lips were soft and inviting, then they began to pulse. Theo felt a rush of air force its way into his mouth and he drew his head back. Delia's mouth was twisted open, peeling back from her face. The kiss was barely over when he pressed the barrel into the base of her skull and pulled the trigger.

The explosion was deafening, and at the moment of death there was nothing of Delia in those bloodshot eyes. For that Theo was thankful. Blood splattered his face and he recoiled at the feel of it, hot and wet, then he didn't care any more. With the death of its host a great gush of energy flowed into his mouth, forcing its way deep into his lungs. Theo dropped the gun and his hands came up to his throat. Every instinct in his body told him to rip the badness out, to claw at his throat and cut off its access to his soul but he fought it. Not yet, he told himself. Control, must keep control, and wait.

He forced his arms out straight and tilted his head to the ceiling. His hands shook with uncontrolled energy and he felt his body swell. He looked like a glowing crucifixion, tiny motes of light dancing round his outstretched arms. His hair bristled with ecstatic shocks, tingling his skin and mind. This was exquisite, an all over orgasm of the purest form. *Why had he fought it for so long?* He asked himself. He felt control slipping away, but somewhere in the vacuum of his mind a spark of Theobald Wolff remained. He clung onto it with the last of his will, fanning it with his mind so the flame didn't go out.

Then a kaleidoscope of images shot through his head. Shattered pictures of a past he knew nothing about but was now his own. A native boy approached the white crescent beach, palm trees leaning over the sparkling blue ocean. His fingers scrabbled futilely at his throat, then he stopped and calmly walked toward the rough hewn canoe which was drawn up on the sandy shore.

Now heavy throbbing vibrated through metal sheets. Above him the rusty derricks of a cargo ship stood out against a starry night. The sailor was tanned and sturdy but his eyes bulged and solid fingers clenched and unclenched. Soon this big strong man stopped fighting and simply watched the stars with cold calculating certainty.

The pictures fragmented and fitted together like pieces from a broken mirror, but the images didn't match up. The jigsaw was incomplete, entire sections falling broken to the floor. The story hopped and jumped, running into different scenarios that didn't seem like part of the whole. A vicar in a country town. Another native, this time in the jungle. A woman with bright red hair and breasts the size of melons. She was performing oral sex on a man with whisky breath who turned out to be the sailor.

Theo's eyes rolled to the back of his head, his mind fusing with this sensory overload. The main boiler began to vibrate unheard, the pipes leaking steam and rattling fit to burst. Sparks leapt from the fuse board in a dazzling display.

Back in Theo's mind he saw a tramp sprawled among the fallen masonry of a derelict building. His face had collapsed and the skin hung in shrivelled folds like a dried out prune. Blood congealed around his throat and flesh clung to his fingernails. The viewpoint was low down, hugging the ground but enough of the surroundings were visible to show a familiar scene. Theo's body bolted erect, his fingers sparking out into rigid bars.

FOURTH DERELICT FOUND DEAD

He remembered the headline in Carl Stensel's barbershop and the photograph that accompanied it. The police scene tape and the piles of rubble but mainly the skyline. Mounds of bricks and concrete bulked around the rusting tracks of the railroad yards, twisted girders pointing skywards in jagged crosses, like tank traps on the Normandy beaches. And behind it all, the sightless monolith of Darkwater Towers jutted black and horrible out of the desolation.

The eyes moved across the ground then looked back. Theo saw a short expanse of matted grey fur then a long swirl of fleshy tail. A rat. The rat climbed over a ridge of bricks and...

"Had to splat me a rat." McCracken's voice slammed into Theo's mind, the narrow passage leading to the crack in the cellar floor fading in and out. The picture was breaking up and jumped back and forth. The woman sucked cock again and then it was the towering derricks and the starry night. Now the native boy, then the vicar. Theo couldn't hold any single image but all the time he clung on to that spark of humanity, which was his own part in all this. His own piece of the jigsaw. It didn't slot in with any of the other pieces but the recent history he knew already. He just had to hang on to it.

Then another image threw itself into the fray. A neat apartment that looked vaguely familiar. A well-stocked bookcase stood against the back wall and a coal effect gas fire glowed contentedly in the hearth. A clean but careworn easy chair and matching settee filled the centre of the room next to the radio and an old Phillips colour television, which could only get three channels. Beside that was the grandfather clock he'd rescued from Melinda's parents.

Melinda's parents? Wait a minute. Yes, it was his apartment all right, but there was something different about it. Theo scoured his brain to come up with the difference. The

TV, the clock, the radio. All the same. The furniture, the decorations. Nothing changed there. The unknown eyes swept the living room, moving towards the hallway.

Theo's mind caught something out of the corner of its eye, or rather the lack of something. A single piece of jigsaw fell into place, followed quickly by another. The apartment was neat and tidy and above all clean. There was no dust building in the corners or on the shelves. There were no dirty plates on the kitchen table through the door, and no...

The photograph was gone. Theo sucked in his breath and felt a great loss. Melinda's picture was missing and with it the scrap of cardboard with,
WE WILL NOT DIE,
UNLESS WE ARE FORGOTTEN...
written in his own handwriting. The eyes went down the corridor and now they were turning into the bathroom. Here too the decay, which had set in after Melinda's death, was absent. He couldn't understand it. The place was just too damn tidy. And there were two tooth brushes in the jar by the sink, his blue one and Melinda's pink super reach molar special. Despite the inrush of energy Theo felt cold and small. He did not want to see what came next, the feeling sitting heavy in his stomach and sapping his energy.

The eyes moved passed the sink to the bathroom cabinet Theo had fitted as part of their moving in push. He had prided himself on fitting that thing up, mainly because it weighed so much. The mirrored doors were backed by solid pine and had to be adjusted to make them shut properly but, once they were up, there was plenty of room for all Melinda's cosmetics. The eyes approached the doors now, and Theo held his breath. Two more paces and he looked at himself in the mirror. Only it wasn't himself. The face that stared back at him was

Melinda...

Shock ran through his body like a live charge. The picture broke up and once again the kaleidoscope of images ran the gamut of native boy, sailor, whore and vicar. The skyline of Darkwater Towers blurred with the picture of the rat and the tramp lying among the debris.

Carl Stensel's voice drifted in like a badly played voice-over. "I'm sorry," he said; then backtracked. "I don't think this was its first attempt." *What the hell was that supposed to mean?* *That, my man, means it has been here before,* Theo's inner voice said. He called up the memory of the apartment as it was in his vision. Now that he realised when it was, subtle differences tied it down to a certain time. The pictures on the wall. Melinda changed them like the seasons. The remains of a Christmas tree in the corner. A new cardigan hanging lazily over the back of the chair. Theo remembered getting flack for that.

This was Christmas past. Or more precisely just after Christmas. Another blast of memory flared across his mind. Voices as clear as yesterday.

"Want to build a snow man?" Melinda asked.

"Want to play snow balls?" He countered. Outside the railway sidings were blanketed with fresh snow, only the ugly black scars of the greasy rails showing against the pristine whiteness. Her hand snaked between his legs in a shocking change of character and squeezed his balls. "If you like," she laughed crudely. "But what about your favourite number?"

Twenty-twenty hindsight took over. That was the last Christmas they'd spent together. Three weeks later she fell ill and shortly after discovered she'd contracted...

Cancer... That insidious monster which slowly filled her body. Hindsight be damned, this was twenty-twenty triple sight. The bathroom mirror fragmented before him, splintering into a thousand different visions, a thousand different histories. There were far too many for one entity to have collected. This was a collective vision of a hundred different spirits over a thousand different years, joined through telepathy into one single unit. One single memory. Theo didn't know how he knew this but he was suddenly positive. The spirit that worked inside him now was kin to the spirit that had taken Kuta Lametka and resided inside the shrunken head around Delia's neck. It was kin to the spirit that had tried to locate Kuta Lametka seven years ago and on its journey had infected Melinda. She had been strong and had fought it off but at what cost? The cancer it left behind ravaged her body and forced her to plead for the end. "Kill me. For God's sake kill me." Had she known then what had happened to her? Theo doubted it. And how contagious had it been?

The letter was in his hands, the neatly typed lines floating in a backwater of memory.

CANCER...

The word burned into his brain.

AT THE MOST, FIVE MONTHS...

Had the seed, which was sewn in Melinda so many years ago, been transmitted to him as well? A slow fuse waiting to go off? Whatever the mechanics of it all, Theo knew he was dying from the same disease that had claimed Melinda. Cancer? No, not cancer but something very similar. Intended or accidental it didn't matter, the outcome was the same.

The most important thing in Theo's mind now was control. *How much control did he still have over the ravaged body which wasn't his own any more?* He wondered to himself while the shocking pictures flashed haphazardly through his memory. Then he looked around with fresh eyes. The pressure gauge was all the way off the scale, steam spouting from every seam and joint in the boiler. The pipes were shaking as if they had Saint Vitus's dance and the fuse board was a dazzling display of sparks and flames. A chunk of concrete dropped from the ceiling as the pipes shook free of their brackets and the crack in the floor widened.

Theo's eyes were sore and he knew they bulged like squeezed grapes even though he couldn't see them. He could see everything else though. Far too much. "In the Land of the Blind, the One-Eyed Man is King..." That may well be true but right now Theo wished he were as blind as the rest. The visions before him were simply too painful.

"Don't be a damned fool." Melinda's voice was as clear as if she were standing next to him. "You are the One-Eyed Man. That does make you King. Now damn well act like one." He looked round to make sure she wasn't beside him, and one bloated hand reached down to his pocket. The photograph sparked against his hand and for a second Melinda was right there with him. The spirit had taken her but it had also preserved her and with its infusion into him they were joined once again.

Her presence gave him strength and that strength gave him courage. He squared his shoulders and expanded his chest in that old army way she liked so much. Control. He had it now and there was a flutter inside him. The spirit sensed a change in him. With that it knew fear. Theo smiled at the knowledge.

The boiler popped a seam and one of the furnace doors, untended since Mick McCracken encountered the rat in the coalbunker, blasted open. Fire spewed out like a flamethrower, singeing the coal dust and painting the cellar a bright hellish orange. The pipes shook all the way to the ceiling and more plaster and concrete crumbled away. The floor thrummed with a deep steady vibration that opened more cracks in the already weakened concrete. Sparks showered the fuse board and two wires melted clean off.

Fear wormed inside the spirit's nest and as it notched up the scale Theo grew stronger. He turned to the circuit breakers, watching them pop and flare with electricity.

Enough energy to light the ten-storey block of flats and enough energy to put a stop to all this madness. He glanced down at Delia's rag doll corpse then bent down and plucked the shrunken head from round her neck. The little ink spot eyes flared angry and red but there was more than anger in those eyes, there was fear and that was just what Theo wanted to see.

He stood erect, a towering man in his own right and turned towards the circuit breakers. He gripped the head in his fist, stepped forward and rammed it into the mouth of the left breaker. Red-hot pain flashed up his arm and he felt the flutter inside him squirrel up into his throat.

Control, must keep control.

Theo brought his other hand up but something pulled it away from the electricity. The spirit wrapped around his windpipe and he couldn't breath. His hand was clamped in a vicelike grip and he couldn't move it.

"You ARE the ONE EYED MAN..."

He leaned into it, turning his shoulders to give more leverage.

"...and you WILL be King."

Melinda urged him on. His hand inched forward, sweat breaking out on his brow. He gritted his teeth and pushed. The serpent tightened around his throat but he didn't care.

Cancer be damned. Five months be damned. I'm going to end it right now. A brief moment of sadness rushed over him, then he crammed his hand into the other breaker and completed the circuit.

In a flash his mind was his own again, and the seconds that followed stood out with all the clarity of an acid trip. Pain slammed up his arms, cramping his muscles into knots as the boiler whistled the four-minute warning, counting down to Armageddon. It shook violently and steam hissed from the seams as the metal plating began to strain and buckle.

Theo's mouth was forced open, his head tilting skywards and the spirit of Kuta Lametka and Mick McCracken and Melinda and anyone else it had ever touched spewed out. With his eyes peeled back he saw with a keen understanding he never would have believed. Tiny sparks of light danced about in the air above him like fireflies, swirling and twisting from shape to shape. The formless being contorted and grew brighter, searching for another host to keep it alive.

Theo felt his hands begin to melt but was detached from the pain. It was like being on the ceiling looking down, watching his body gyrate in front of the circuit breakers. He was no longer in his body and saw the glint of red flare among the dancing sparks above him, anger and fear resonating from the cloud. A clean white tunnel of light opened up in the ceiling and his other self, the one not in his body, felt drawn toward it.

All around, cracks appeared in the already weakened structure of The Towers. The explosion and fireball, which had destroyed Deepwater and Clearwater Towers, finally took its toll. A huge slab of concrete fell to the floor, and the other furnace door blew open. Flames sprayed the cellar and the boiler began its final heave to oblivion. As Theo watched, the twinkling cloud of lights dimmed slightly, then they were drawn towards the fuse board by the electricity. As they touched it, they flared up momentarily, like flies zapped by a neon bug trap, then blinked out. One by one they disappeared, forming a delicate display of sparkling light.

A heavy thump sounded through the basement, and the wall next to the stairs began to crumble. The tunnel of light beckoned, but Theo felt his eyes drawn to the body he had inhabited for sixty-nine years. Sixty-nine! It would have tickled Melinda - had it not been so serious - to know that was the age he would reach. The thought, which had first entered his head on the day he received his test results returned. His body sparked and jerked in the grip of the electricity.

Whumph... Whumph... The pressure gauges exploded. Twists of pipe flew across the room like shrapnel. The lighted passage above his outer body began to fade and suddenly he was back inside the shell on the ground. Pain fried his brain, and an urge to pull back filled him. He yanked at the left hand and it came free. The circuit broken, his right hand followed suit and his mind raced. He couldn't understand why he wasn't dead but his body felt too weak to do anything about it.

A blast of hot air got him moving. Flames singed what little hair Carl Stensel had left him and he turned away from the furnaces. The boiler went into its death throws and prepared to blow. Sections of concrete and metal fell all around him and high up in the empty apartments thunder signalled the end. In a reflex as old as time, Theo lunged for the only place of safety he knew.

The metal door into the lift inspection pit was still open and he moved as fast as his aching bones allowed. His hands were a mass of bloodied tissue but that didn't matter. He lunged through the door and yanked it shut behind him. As he fell into the cool darkness he had once feared, the boiler finally blew. The explosion welded the door shut and demolished the foundations. With deafening finality Darkwater Towers came crashing down around his ears, concrete and glass thudding into the hollow of the basement.

CHAPTER 4

The screwed up letter hit the wall and bounced into the waste bin in the corner. Theo looked out of the bungalow window across rolling fells, the afternoon sun glinting off the calm waters of the duck pond and throwing shadows across the orchard. It was a warm and pleasant day. The view should have made him feel better but it didn't. The letter should have too but...

He turned his gaze inward and saw nothing there as beautiful as the view outside. Nothing as calm either. As he sat in front of a new Sony television that received five channels, none of which he watched, the pain in his hands pushed the sunshine away. The ugly wreckage of Darkwater Towers crawled back into his mind.

It had taken the fire brigade two days to put out the fires and a further three before they gave up hope of finding any survivors. Theo was found by accident on the sixth day by a Labrador, which had strayed onto the rubble. Its barks raised the alarm and the rescue services dug him out eight hours later. The Northern Gazette called it a miracle but Theo disagreed.

The block of flats had folded like a pack of cards once the foundations had blown out but the broken track in the elevator shaft saved him. The lift had impacted against it and formed a kind of storm cellar. Once Theo had been sealed in by the blast from the boiler, the tumbling debris from ten storeys of empty apartments had flattened the lift but not breached the shelter below.

Theo broke three ribs and his left leg, and received a gash on the forehead. Those things had healed now though but his hands would never be the same again. The heat from the circuit breakers had burned off two fingers on his right hand and the thumb on his left. The skin was badly scarred but the doctors promised that pioneering skin graft surgery could go a long way to repairing the damage. This surgery would be performed free of charge, which was just as well and would elevate the surgeons to near sainthood. The story of Theo's rescue touched the hearts of the nation. A good deed performed on him would be better than donating their services to a needy third world country. Good PR opportunities should never be missed!

A miracle? Maybe. But the miracles didn't stop there. After six months in a hospital bed and three as an outpatient, the letter arrived on Melinda's birthday. That added more than a touch of irony and didn't help Theo one little bit. One phrase stuck out in his mind as the letter uncurled in the waste bin. COMPLETE REMISSION...the letter read. Not, CANCER... or, AT THE MOST, FIVE MONTHS... but, COMPLETE REMISSION...

The faceless doctors in their crisp white uniforms had picked and poked at him for what seemed like an age, then sent him home. Three months later the letter plopped on the doormat of the council bungalow he'd been given. If the Northern Gazette got hold of this they'd have a field day.

Theo closed his eyes but swirling demons came out of the shadows to taunt him. They came when he slept and they came when he didn't and always they were the same. The twisted corpses of Carl Stensel and Uriah Lovelycolors and Delia Circelli. But the death toll stretched back further than that.

He opened his eyes and looked at the cracked photograph on the television. Melinda stared back blankly. There was no expression on her face anymore, and out of everything that was the worst.
WE WILL NOT DIE,
UNLESS WE ARE FORGOTTEN...

She was gone. He had forgotten the touch of her skin and the smell of her perfume and that cute little look in her eyes but, more importantly, he had forgotten her sense of humanity. The very thing that made him a better person. The connection had been broken, and the way her eyes used to follow him round the room and admonish him was gone. She was just a faded photograph in a cracked frame. It was ironic that the demon, which had taken her, now did the opposite for him. *Complete remission? Bastard, I wish I had died in The Towers.* A tear formed in the corner of his eye and he tried to come to terms with what he had really lost. The memory of a good wife, and the comfort of her presence.

Theo pushed himself out of the chair, feeling stronger than he had a right to feel. Complete remission it might be but there had also been a complete resurgence of his former strength. He felt twenty years younger and that brought its own fears. He had been at death's door a few months ago and on the brink of accepting it. Now he felt he might live forever. And all without the comfort of having Melinda with him.

He went into the living room and sat opposite the TV. It was switched off but it wasn't the television he looked at. Melinda stared back now, not a flicker of emotion on her face.

Quality of life. That is what's important in your closing years. He might have a good view and very pleasant neighbours but without Melinda what was the point? He had relied on her more than he realised, and now she was gone.

The sun shone in through the windows, warming his back. Outside a bird began to sing but Theo only had eyes for Melinda.

THE END

Publisher's Note

If you enjoyed this book look out for Colin Campbell's next book

"BLACKWOOD FALLS" due out soon

ABOUT THE AUTHOR

Colin Campbell is a mystery figure himself, with a recent award for bravery in tackling a man with a twelve inch knife.

He understands the vagaries and horrors of the human mind all too well and takes us through the inner doubts and recriminations we may well ourselves have felt to make his hero a real person; one to be identified with as he endures the terrifying circumstances the book portrays.

Colin plans to write more books with the theme of the fight against the horror within.